WHAT SHE KNEW

MIRANDA RIJKS

INKUBATOR
BOOKS

In memory of Louisa Poláčkova

PROLOGUE

You know when you meet someone – you can tell immediately that you're going to like them. It's as if they have a light shining from within, and you're hopelessly attracted to it. I don't mean attraction in a physical way necessarily; it's just something about their energy. Their vitality. It was like that the second she walked into the room. When we got talking, I realised that her brilliance was her acuity, the way she grasped complicated concepts instantly; the way that she cared for other people, not in a self-serving manner, but from a place of genuine curiosity and empathy. I wasn't the only person who liked her. She was a magnet for girls and boys alike. Everyone wanted a little piece of her.

Afterwards, I realised that she reminded me of myself. The difference between us was her naivety and that earnest desire to do good in the world.

No one wants to snuff out a light like that, especially at such a young age, but sometimes you have no choice. I watched her that day as she flitted around as if she were surrounded by a cloud of heart-shaped bubbles, all happy and smiley and oh-so-very-eager. Until curiosity forced the killing of the cat.

I wondered if she would be hard to kill, whether bright people – in every sense of the word – are harder to snuff out. It appears that in death, we're all the same. She was totally unsuspecting, happy to be back here, totally unaware that she would never leave. What a lovely day, what a delightful evening, and then bed. She lay there, her hair splayed out on the pillow, her cheeks downy and her rosebud lips just slightly open. All it took was another pillow. I chose one that was extra stuffed, not one filled with Hungarian goose feathers, because they are expensive and much too good for her. No, I chose one that was filled with polyester, lumpy particles that I could dispose of at the tip, a pillow that no one would want to recycle because it was grubby and uncomfortable.

I watched her sleep for a few moments, and then I brought the pillow down over her face and put the full weight of my body behind it. She awoke and tried to scream and struggle. And she was strong, surprisingly so for someone so slight. She kicked the duvet off the bed, but the harder she fought, the easier it was for me to stay calm. I was focused. I had a plan. I'd done my research.

I was totally still when life left her body. I watched her for several long minutes, just to be sure that her spirit had gone. And then I did what needed to be done.

If you would ask me whether I have any regrets, the answer is no. If you would ask me whether that first killing gave me a taste for more, the answer is no again. But if you would ask me whether I would do it again if I had to, the answer would be yes. In a heartbeat.

1

'Bea, hurry up!'

I'm standing at the bottom of the stairs, the car keys in one hand and Sam's satchel in the other. Our soon-to-be six-year-old son is playing with the paper airplane he made in school yesterday. He's ready for school. As normal, his older sister isn't.

'Stay here, Sam,' I say as I race up the steep staircase. I've felt so tired the past fortnight, I wonder if there's something wrong with me.

'Bea! What are you doing?' I ask as I fling open her bedroom door. She has the cutest room in the house, under the eaves, with the original cast-iron fireplace set in the wall and decorative coving. The window has fine views over south London's rooftops, but this morning, the pink-and-white dotted curtains are still partially closed.

Beatrice is making a cack-handed attempt at braiding her hair.

'That can wait until you're home this afternoon. We need to go now; otherwise you'll get into trouble with Mrs Donovan yet again.'

Bea sighs melodramatically, but at least she is properly dressed in her grey-and-red school uniform, with only her hair looking somewhat dishevelled. She follows me down the stairs. I hate to think how long it will take Bea to get ready in the mornings when she's sixteen, if it's such a complex process aged eight.

Oliver appears from the kitchen. He's tall and skinny, with luxuriant dark hair that's beginning to grey at the temples, and his piercing blue eyes seem to have a magnetic power over everything he sees.

'I'm going to be late home. I'm doing a viva interview this afternoon, and I want to attend an online auction in New York that starts at six our time. I won't have time to come home in between.'

'But you'll be back for supper?' I ask.

'A late one. Nine-ish. Don't wait for me. Eat with the kids.'

'Okay, love,' I say, standing on tiptoes to give Oliver a kiss on the lips before chivvying the children out of the front door.

'Bye, Daddy!' Sam yells.

OLIVER IS a full professor in the History of Art department. Over the years of our marriage, he has never stopped learning and evaluating and immersing himself in all things art. His shrewd brilliance is edged with a commercial nous that would undoubtedly have made him a successful gallery owner or art curator, but for some reason, he eschews all commerciality. He enjoys academia, the comfortable, predictable life that allows him time to write and indulge in his hobbies. He revels in the adulation of his students, not that he would ever admit to such a thing. And adore him they do. There is always a steady stream of pretty girls and boys eager to hang around after their tutorials or catch him as he strides out of his building on the way to the bus stop or the Tube. Once upon a time, I minded. And, of course, once upon a time, I was one of them.

It's no surprise to me that his courses are always oversubscribed, and that he is the most sought-after supervisor for PhD students. My husband is a credit to the department, and if all goes to plan, he expects to be promoted to head of the department for the start of the new academic year. The only thing that consistently baffles me is the fact that I'm his wife. Getting married at the tender age of twenty-three seems as outrageous now as it did then. Who does that in today's day and age? We've been married for just over eight years, and considering the circumstances that threw us together, they've been predominantly happy times. I think back to how I arrived at university, like a weak and wounded bird, trembling and fearful, yet filled with the self-righteousness and conviction of the young. I think Oliver wanted a partner whom he could mould, someone who would put him on a pedestal and adore him in the same way that his students do. In many ways, he chose well, but I still believe I have a core of steel, and perhaps Oliver has never truly recognised that.

I have a few friends amongst the school mums waving their children off as they file into their respective classrooms. But not many. I'm younger than most of them, and I don't work. That sets me apart and also means that I get lumbered with cake baking and accompanying the kids on school outings and all of those stay-at-home-mum-type things that I loathe. But it is what it is, and I can't complain. Especially as, after all these years, I'm back on track to follow the path that I deviated from. I have an essay to complete for my law conversion course, the first step on my path to qualify as a solicitor, so I hurry back home.

Oliver doesn't know I'm doing it. I have brought up the idea of pursuing my legal training several times over the years, but he always dismisses it. He doesn't want me to work as a solicitor; instead, he wants me to focus on being the mother to his children, perhaps taking a little part-time job on the side to keep myself busy, but that's all. It's such an antiquated concept of family life and so very chauvinistic. But I try to understand. He lost his parents when he was just a young boy, and he's desperately trying to create the family life that he missed out upon. And so I'm studying during the daytime when Oliver isn't home, and the only person who knows is Mum. She insisted on loaning me the money for my course, and come what may, I'll have to qualify, because I want to repay the loan. It was her rainy-day fund, the paltry compensation money she was awarded after Dad died half a lifetime ago. There is no way that I am going to deprive her of the around-the-world trip she has always dreamed of. I am both dreading and exhilarated about the day I eventually pass my exams, not that I have to worry about that for many months to come. Sometimes I feel bad about hiding from Oliver what I'm doing, but all marriages have their secrets, don't they? And it's not as if I'm cheating. If anything, I'm contributing, bettering myself, and then when I start work, the pressure for being the sole provider will be eased from Oliver's shoulders.

After clearing away the breakfast things and making the beds, I collect my study materials from a box at the bottom of my wardrobe and settle down at the kitchen table. I've chosen the part-time course, which I'm meant to complete over two years. It's really tough, and the fact that I completed my undergraduate degree in history of art nearly a decade ago and haven't studied since means I'm struggling. On many an occasion, I wonder why I'm putting myself through this. My brain doesn't work nearly as well as it used to, and I doubt myself frequently. After a few minutes of trying to understand some complicated principles in equity and trusts, I give up. My stomach is gurgling, because although I made sure the kids ate their breakfast, I haven't eaten anything myself. I shove the books to one side and get up to make myself a piece of toast. It tastes of cardboard, and I'm so tired, if I lie down on my bed now, I will fall to sleep instantly. And then it hits me.

The last time toast tasted like this was when I was pregnant with Sam, and the time before when I was carrying Bea. No. Surely not! I scroll back through my phone where I put a little asterisk whenever my period is due. My body is normally as regular as clockwork, so how the hell could I have missed it? I'm two weeks late. Two whole weeks, and I hadn't realised.

I cannot be pregnant.

If I'm pregnant, I'll have to stop studying. It's tough enough getting a training contract. Who the hell is going to offer a position to a woman with three young children, one a newborn? There's no way that Oliver will let me work, not with three children. He's made it perfectly clear that a mother should be at home with her kids, that love and attention are more important than money. And I get that; I get that he's compensating for everything he missed out on. But how the hell will we manage? Money is tight enough as it is, and even if Oliver is made head of department, we'll hardly be rolling in it. And this house is too small. It's delightful and in a great location, but it's certainly not big enough for three children. I doubt we can afford to move somewhere larger.

I lay my head on the table.

Perhaps this is just further proof that I am a bad person, but I do not want to be pregnant. And despite these thoughts, I nod off to sleep right here at the kitchen table ... only to be jerked awake by the phone ringing. It's the landline, and I'm tempted to leave it to go to the answer machine. But then I think of the kids at school. I can't take the risk; I grab it just in time.

'Good morning. Is this Stephanie Siskin, previously Stephanie Lucas?'

'Um, yes,' I say cautiously. It sounds strange to be called by my maiden name.

'My name is David Green. I'm a researcher for a documentary television series. We're putting together a series of true crime documentaries, particularly crimes where the victim was never found and/or the defendant continues to deny responsibility.'

I inhale loudly and lean back against the kitchen cupboards.

'Mrs Siskin?'

'Yes.' My tone is flat.

'We're planning to film a programme on the Alison Miller case. I was hoping I could come and talk to you both, because you were Alison's flatmate, and your husband taught her. I know it will be difficult for you, but we often find we're able to uncover truths that the police might have missed. On several occasions, investigations have been reopened due to evidence that we have uncovered.'

I pause for a long time. 'I don't know. It was all so long ago, and I've got children now. I'm not sure it's helpful raking everything up again.'

'I understand you were very close to Alison, and you were her best friend as well as her flatmate for two years. If we are able to discover the truth, the definitive truth, wouldn't that be better for all parties involved? Her parents have given our research their blessing.'

'They have?' There's a lengthy pause whilst I try to digest what this stranger has said. 'You're going to talk to everyone?'

'Anyone who knew Alison in any capacity. It sounds like she was a lovely young woman with a bright future ahead of her. It's tragic.'

'Yes. Yes, it is. And you want to talk to me *and* Oliver?'

'That would be very helpful. I'm free to come over at the weekend or an evening if that would be more convenient.'

'I'll need to discuss it with my husband.'

'Of course. Can we put 11 am on Saturday morning in the diary, and if for any reason it's not convenient, you can let me know?'

'I suppose so,' I say, fumbling for the calendar hanging on the side of the fridge. 'Saturday morning looks okay, although the kids will be at home. Will you want to interview us for the programme?' I can't think of anything more horrific.

'We're just doing research at this stage. It will be many months before we start putting material together for the programme. I'll come to your house at 11 am on Saturday. I look forward to meeting you both.'

He gives me his mobile phone number, which I jot down, and then he hangs up. I stand stock-still, staring at the phone. It isn't until a few minutes later that I realise I didn't tell him where we live.

I try to settle back into the essay, but it's a futile task. I was exhausted before I started; now I can't even muster the energy to read my notes. My lovely friend Alison. Yes, of course I still think of her, but not every day. Not like I used to, when everything I did was tinged with sorrow that Alison would never have a similar experience. My life is so different now, full of domestic responsibilities and the daily minutiae of having kids. My life trajectory wouldn't have been the one Alison would have chosen. She would never have had a family in her twenties. No, she would be in a war zone, single-handedly stopping militia from tearing down statues, and being the spokesperson for museums that needed vital funding for the preservation of their collections. Alison had a bright future ahead of her.

Except she didn't.

2

THEN

'I can't bloody sleep!' I grit my teeth and pull the pillow over the top of my head. It doesn't work, because it makes me too hot, and I can't breathe properly. I turn over and glance at my alarm clock. 2.04 am.

Last term, I said something to Alison. She and Josh are prolific and noisy in their lovemaking, and it makes me want to scream. I could just about cope if it's before midnight, as I can take myself off to the living room and watch YouTube or soak in a bath underneath the fan extractor, which is so loud it blocks out all noise. But when it's in the middle of the night and I'm awakened by the bashing of her headboard against the paper-thin wall and their loud moans and groans, it infuriates me. I plucked up the courage one Monday evening towards the end of last term, seemingly the only night of the week that Josh wasn't staying over at ours. Alison was mortified.

'You can hear everything?' she asked, her cheeks flaming. 'I'm so sorry, Steph. Why didn't you say something before?'

That's the thing with Alison. She's a genuinely lovely person; I got lucky sharing a flat with her. We had adjacent rooms in our hall of residence, and she took me under her wing during that first week of uni. What I didn't realise back then was Alison is a social magnet. She isn't the queen bee type; instead, she's self-deprecating and always eager to care for the underdog. It was Alison who insisted I join her for those dreadful freshers week activities, telling me that if I couldn't keep up, she'd be there to support me. There was no way that she was going to let me hide away all alone in my room. And she kept her word. When that idiot Harry whatever-his-name-is stole some cartons of beer from a corner shop, and the owner went running after him, the whole crowd legged it. There wasn't a hope in hell that I'd be able to keep up with my dodgy leg. Alison linked her arm into mine, and we walked briskly in the opposite direction.

And it wasn't just me she looked out for. When Bruce passed out from too much drink and drugs, it was Alison who cleared up his puke and took the decision to call for an ambulance.

I was never meant to share with her. She was lined up to live in a seven-bedroom student house in east London, but at the last minute she got cold feet.

'I'm not sure I want to be in such a big house,' she told me over a coffee in the cafeteria.

'You can come and live with me in a grotty two-bed apartment,' I said breezily, never for one moment imagining she'd take me seriously. But she did. And here we are. The flat share was successful for our second year, and when Alison suggested we continue for our third year, I certainly wasn't going to say no. It helped that somehow or another, she managed to find us a two-bedder near the Barbican. It costs the earth, being in this des res part of London, but I'll worry about my obscene student loan when I have to.

Those couple of weeks towards the end of last term were much better. Either she stayed over at Josh's or we were all out late, celebrating the end of term and Christmas. It seemed like everyone had a boyfriend to kiss under the mistletoe. Everyone except me. I had a snog with Karim, but only because I needed to kiss someone. I don't even like him. I'm the perfect flatmate: quiet, tidy, accommodating and boring. With no boyfriend, it's not like I'm going to be disturbing Alison. It doesn't mean I don't have friends. I do, lots of them. It's just that I like to compartmentalise.

Josh hasn't been over as much this term, and I'm glad. It wasn't fair that our two-bedroom apartment was being used by three. It's not as if he offered to pay his share of the bills or the rent.

But tonight they're at it again, and I'm at my wits' end. I've got to finish a midterm essay this week and get my teeth into my dissertation, which I've barely started. If I don't get enough sleep, the nerve pain in my leg sears as if it's being burned by hot pokers, and I can't concentrate. I have to do well in my essays and exams. I'm not like Alison, who barely needs to revise and is still on for getting a first.

I knock on the wall, but they don't hear me.

THE NEXT MORNING, I'm in a stinking mood. I thump around the flat, noisily slamming cupboards in the kitchen and clattering crockery in the sink. I don't like myself for behaving like a furious toddler, but that doesn't stop me. I take a mug of tea and two slices of toast into my bedroom and slam the door. A couple of minutes later, I hear the bathroom door shut, the shower is run briefly, and five minutes later the front door thuds. Then there's a knock on my bedroom door.

'Come in.'

Alison opens the door. 'Are you okay?' She's still wearing her white waffle dressing gown, and her hair is mussed up, but she's glowing and pretty. Perhaps that's what all the sex does to you.

'Sorry, I had a bad night,' I say in a tone that suggests I'm anything but sorry.

'Did we wake you?'

'Yup.' Now I feel guilty for being a prat this morning.

'Oh, Steph, I'm really sorry. We got a bit carried away and, well, I can't stay at Josh's all the time. You know how it is.' And then her face brightens. 'I'm going to find you a boyfriend, and then you can be the ones keeping me awake at night!'

I roll my eyes.

'Rahul, Josh's best friend. You like him, don't you? I've seen how you look at him.'

'He's got a girlfriend.'

'He hasn't!'

I glance up at Alison.

'They split up over Christmas.'

'So he's on the rebound,' I say. 'And way out of my league.'

Gethin, the boy I got together with that first term at university, had been on the rebound. He dumped me two days after we slept together, and the following week, he was back with his previous girlfriend. But Alison knows that; she was the one who wiped away my tears. And she knows all about Leroy, the boy who came before Gethin. The boy who I thought was my forever; the boy I truly loved. As Alison said at the time, perhaps I was on the rebound too.

She cuts through my maudlin memories. 'Firstly, Rahul really is over her, and secondly, you are so not out of his league. You're stunning, Steph, and all the more so for not realising it. We're going to a nightclub in Shoreditch on Wednesday night. Come with us.'

'You're sweet, Alison, but Rahul really is way out of my league. Besides, I've got too much work. I don't think I should go nightclubbing midweek.'

'One night out isn't going to make any difference. You and Rahul. It'll be so cute. We can be a foursome!'

When Alison has gone, I lean back in my chair and daydream. She's right; I do like Rahul. He has beautiful dark eyes and a gentleness about him. The only problem is, I can't see him falling for me. I sigh and gather up my books. I've got to hurry or I'll be late for my tutorial.

BOTH ALISON and I are studying history of art. It's a small department in a large London university, and even if we hadn't been put on that same corridor during our first term, we would have met. The first two years we took the same modules, and although we were in different tutorial groups, we were able to support each other. Or rather, Alison explained the complicated concepts my brain failed to grasp. She helped me understand how all things philosophical, cultural and aesthetic converge. This year, we're taking different modules. Next year, Alison intends to take a master's in conservation because she wants a job like the 'monuments men' in the second world war, protecting the world's finest artefacts during times of conflict or natural disasters. She has very big and specific ambitions, carefully plotted out in her ten-year plan. I'm equally impressed and appalled by her ideas. I see life a bit like a giant game of snakes and ladders. When something unexpected comes along and you fall, if you've set yourself big, specific goals, your descent will seem even greater. I know that for a fact.

When I was at sixth form and trying to work out what to do when I left, I announced I wanted to study law. With everything that happened, my teachers felt I wouldn't achieve the grades, so I went for history of art instead. I was delusional to think it might be an easy option. My fellow students are passionate about their subject, and as I've always prescribed to the idea of 'fake it until you make it', that's exactly what I'm doing, too. Ultimately, I want to be a lawyer and specialise in personal injury. I guess I'm driven by justice. Alison says I'm idealistic, and she might be right, but then, she hasn't got any experience of suffering. Pain – both the physical and emotional type – and loss change you. They make you more patient, more compassionate … but they can also be the fuel in your belly to drive change if you let them.

I plan to do that. To spearhead change. All Alison wants to do is protect the status quo. Not that I'd ever dream of telling her I think that.

I'll never forget my university interview. I was petrified. I was already a year older than everyone else, which when you're eighteen or nineteen really matters, and it was the first in-person interview I had. When Oliver Siskin collected me from a chair in the narrow hallway and led me to a square room, lined with bookcases and a window that faced out onto an internal courtyard, I assumed he was an older student, leading me to the study of a grey-haired professor. But no. Wearing ironed chinos and a shirt with sleeves rolled up to his elbows, he sat on the swivel chair and asked me, 'To what degree is it necessary to be an artist to study history of art?'

All the while I was thinking, *This man is too young and too handsome to be a tutor.* Three years on, and I haven't changed my mind, and I'm not the only one. All the girls are in love with Oliver.

Today's tutorial with Oliver is on the avant-garde, and we're discussing the New York School. There are eight of us students, and I'm hoping that I can get away without contributing too much to the discussion. Fortunately, Sara Llwelynn-Carter is in my tutorial group; she loves the sound of her own voice. I zone out. My leg is throbbing, and it's hard to keep my eyelids open.

'Do you agree, Stephanie?' Oliver asks.

I jolt back into the moment. 'Sorry,' I say, feeling my cheeks burn.

'Do you agree with Sara's view that Lee Krasner was marginalised?'

'Um, yes. No.' Help! I don't remember who Lee Krasner was. I keep my eyes on my lap. 'I'm sorry. I don't know.'

I can feel Oliver's eyes on my face and hear the tuts and sighs from my fellow students, but fortunately, Oliver doesn't linger and poses the same question to Serge, who is sitting next to me. He answers succinctly. I remember now. She was married to Jackson Pollock, and of course she was marginalised, not only because she was known as 'Mrs Pollock', but also, as described by her biographer Gail Levin, because she was caught between two generations of female painters: ignored by the male abstract expressionists and not young or glamorous enough to be part of the next generation of female painters. The rest of the tutorial passes quickly, and soon we're all packing up our bags and hurrying out of the room.

'Stephanie, can you stay behind, please,' Oliver says. I freeze.

Sara looks thoroughly annoyed; I think she hoped she could hang around to have a private confab with her favourite tutor. She lets the door slam on her way out.

'I'm still waiting for your midterm essay.'

'Um, yes. I'm sorry. I'll have it to you first thing next week.' I can't look at him, in case those beautiful blue eyes lock onto mine, and then I'll feel my cheeks blush, and beads of sweat will line my upper lip.

'Sit down again, Stephanie.' He gestures to the chair next to his desk.

I do as I'm told.

'I'm here to help you,' he says as he leans forwards, putting his elbows on his knees and his chin in his hands. I can't not look at him. We're so close; close enough for me to smell the musky scent of his after-shave. 'If you're struggling, I'm here to help,' he says.

'No, it's fine. It's really okay; I just got a bit behind.'

'You look tired.'

'Oh,' I say, startled that this man who I barely know might notice such a thing.

'And I saw that you were limping when you came in.'

'Just the old injury. It plays up from time to time.'

He nods, but his eyes never leave my face. He does something to me, melting my insides, making me feel as if he can read me. And I feel nervous, awkward, as if I need to leave now before I do something really, really stupid. I stand up too quickly, and the chair topples over backwards. Now I'm really flummoxed, and he's laughing at me, standing up, putting his hand on my shoulder, telling me to leave it. If I could run, I would. I hurry out of his office as quickly as I can, muttering that I'll have the essay to him first thing on Monday.

. . .

IT'S SATURDAY MORNING, and Alison is packing an overnight bag. I think she's only stayed in our flat one night this week, so we've barely spoken. She wasn't here on Wednesday, and no mention was made about Wednesday night's visit to a nightclub or the possibility of setting me up with Rahul. I'm not too bothered. When I've got this essay out of the way and I've completed more of my dissertation, I'll take her up on it.

'Are you and Josh going somewhere nice?' I ask, trying to suppress any jealousy.

'Yeah. A special weekend.' She holds up a skimpy black dress with spaghetti straps in her left hand and a very short red dress in her right. 'Which one?'

'The black one. It's more sophisticated. Do you think he's going to ask you to marry him?'

Alison turns her back to me and drops the red dress onto the floor. 'I've met the love of my life,' she says, almost under her breath.

'I'm happy for you,' I say. And I am; I just wish I were in the same situation. No one has ever whisked me away for a weekend of passion. 'Right, I'd better get on. Think of me, in the library, when you're having a wonderful time with Josh.'

'Okay. Have a good weekend,' Alison says.

I HAVE A HARD-WORKING WEEKEND, not a good one. I pull a load of books from the library and spend many hours trying to grapple with complicated concepts and make lots of notes for both my essay and dissertation. I work particularly hard on the avant-garde essay, and I know it's only because I want Oliver to notice me, to think that I'm intelligent and able and worthy of the place here at his prestigious university, the coveted place that he gave me. By six pm on Sunday evening, I'm knackered, and my head is hurting from so much concentration. I'm in our miniscule kitchen, making myself an omelette, when the front door opens.

'You're home early,' I shout, turning the flame off the hob and walking out of the kitchen into the living room. I catch sight of the back of Alison's head as she shuts her bedroom door. I walk towards it and stand outside and knock gently.

'Is everything alright?'

'The weekend didn't go to plan,' Alison says.

I know it's schadenfreude, but I'm kind of relieved. It would have made me feel even more inferior if Alison had returned with an engagement ring on her finger. Although that probably wouldn't have happened. Faaiz and Saadiq got engaged a couple of months ago, but they're both from religious families and don't believe in sex before marriage. I feel guilty for thinking badly of Alison, so I ask her if she'd like a glass of wine.

'No, thanks. I'm tired. I'm going to bed.'

'It's only six!' I say. 'Are you sick? Can I get you anything?'

'No. I'm fine.'

'Can I come in?' This conversation through the door is ridiculous. We're normally totally open with each other.

'If you don't mind, I just want to sleep.'

'What happened, Ali?' I'm worried now. This isn't like my friend.

'Nothing. We just had a late night, and I'm knackered.' But I can tell from the wobbling tone of her voice that she's hiding something.

'Hello, sleepyhead.' Oliver leans over me to place a kiss on my forehead. I realise I have fallen asleep on the sofa. 'A tough day?' He doesn't give me the chance to answer before saying, 'I'm starving. Did you keep me some food?'

'Yes. It's in the fridge. I'll warm it up.'

I rub my eyes and walk into the kitchen, taking the dish out of the fridge and placing it in the microwave. I remove a bowl of salad from the fridge and put it on the table. A couple of minutes later, Oliver is slipping into his normal chair. The microwave pings, and I put the plate of homemade lasagne on the table in front of Oliver. I sit down next to him.

'Sorry I'm late. It's been a busy day, and I needed a chat with William after the auction. How was your day?'

'We had a phone call from a television researcher who wants to talk to us. They're doing a programme on Alison.'

'They're what?' he asks, letting his fork clatter onto his plate.

'It's a true crime series. He's coming on Saturday to talk to us.'

'No, he's bloody well not! Those people are vultures. Haven't we all suffered enough? Especially you and poor Alison's parents. They're scum, trying to monetise other people's misery.'

I stand up and walk to the cupboard where we keep our glasses. I'm about to take a wine glass out for myself when I remember I might be pregnant. I choose a water glass instead and pour Oliver a glass of red wine from an open bottle. I sit back down again, wondering if he'll notice that I'm not drinking wine.

'About Alison,' I say. 'It would be such a relief to know what really happened, even if it's just knowing where her body is. It would give a sense of closure for me and her parents.'

'Of course, but at long last, you've managed to put it all behind you. We're settled; life is good. You haven't had a nightmare in years. No, we're not talking to that researcher. And that's the last I'm going to say about it.'

I don't want to go back to those dark days either, and particularly those maudlin nights when I woke up in the early hours, my heart pounding, sweat soaking the sheets after that recurrent nightmare where I was desperately trying to reach Alison. Desperately.

But I need to know. I grit my teeth. It may be the last thing that Oliver wants to say about it, but I disagree.

IT'S THE NEXT NIGHT, and I'm struggling to get Sam to settle. He's in bed but refusing to shut his eyes.

'I'm not going to sleep until I've said goodnight to Daddy,' Sam says, sticking out his lower lip.

'I'll send him up as soon as he's home,' I say. I'm too tired to have a fight with my feisty son.

'What if I'm asleep, and then I won't know?'

'You will. Your subconscious will know, and you'll have happy dreams.' I stroke Sam's forehead and soft hair. He's struggling to keep his eyes open, despite his protestations. Yet again, Oliver isn't home in time to say goodnight to the children. It happened last night, but then he warned me about it. Tonight is unexpected.

'I love you.' I kiss Sam's forehead and watch as he drifts off to sleep. How the hell will I cope with a third child? I have got through the all-consuming baby stage plus the toddler tantrums, and the chance to get my life back again is within my reach. Now I feel like it's being pulled away. I'm normally so diligent in taking the pill, but perhaps I missed a day or two when I had a sickness bug a few weeks ago. It was one of those unpleasant twenty-four-hour illnesses caught from the kids. I suppose accidents happen.

BACK IN THE KITCHEN, I check the casserole on the stove and ring Naomi. In another life, Naomi and I wouldn't have crossed paths, let alone become almost best friends. She is a home counties girl with a cut-glass accent. I've never established whether her voice is the real deal, a result of her expensive, private school education, or whether it is learned from studying the voices of female British news readers from earlier decades. I suspect it might be the latter, because from time to time, Naomi does impressions of our mutual friends, and it's absolutely hilarious. She has an uncanny ability to mimic their facial expressions and intonation, and I've frequently told her she's missed her vocation.

Naomi is married to William, Oliver's closest friend, and our lives are so closely interwoven, sometimes I forget that we're not part of the same family.

'Hi, Steph.'

Naomi sounds like she's out of breath.

'Am I interrupting?'

'No. Just finished a class on the Peloton and need to have a shower before William gets home.'

'That's why I was calling. Oliver's not back.'

'They'll be out together. Friday night drinks or something. I can't remember what Will said.'

Oliver isn't much of a drinker. Unlike William, he is rarely, if ever, found in the pub knocking back a pint or two.

'Anyway, I'm glad you called,' Naomi continues. 'Are you free to come for Sunday lunch? I've got a couple of pheasants that need eating.'

'Yes, that would be lovely. Thanks.'

'Normal time. See you then.'

I smile as I end the call. From the way Naomi talks, one might assume that William and Naomi live in the highlands of Scotland or on the moors of North Yorkshire, with access to grouse and pheasant on their land that they shoot themselves. Not so. Although William is a member of some shooting syndicate in Scotland, when Naomi says she has a couple of pheasants that need eating, it's most likely they'll have come from the organic butcher in Leatherhead.

Oliver stumbles through the door half an hour later.

'Sorry I'm late,' he says, dropping his bag onto the floor and pulling me towards him.

'You smell of whisky and cigars,' I say, wriggling out of his grasp.

'William insisted.'

I raise my eyebrows but say nothing. Oliver's relationship with William is stronger than a brotherly bond, and Oliver won't have a bad word said about his best friend. Fortunately, I'm fond of William, even though he tempts my husband away from me on outings that include booze and cigars. There's no point in me being critical. I've learned that it's a battle I will never win.

'Naomi has invited us for Sunday lunch.'

'Good. I can do with some country air. Sometimes I wonder if we should move out of London, but I can't bear the thought of the commute.'

'You hardly see the kids as it is. If you had to catch the train home, heaven knows what time you'd be back.'

'True. Or maybe you and the kids could be in the country during the week, and I'd join you at the weekends and during the holidays.'

'Absolutely not.' There is no way that I'm going to let that happen. I have seen too many marriages end in divorce once the relationships become long distance. Besides, I want to be in London to pursue my studies and get a job. Not that I intend to get into that debate with Oliver for at least another year.

After supper, we watch a film, but I can't keep my eyes open, so I head off to bed early. I'm not sure what time my husband comes up.

The next morning, the doorbell rings on the dot of 11 am. I haven't reminded Oliver about the visit from the researcher, because I know he'll be angry that I've failed to cancel it. On the one hand, Oliver is right: It will dredge up horrible memories. But it's too late to put the thought back in a box. I've always had niggling doubts about Josh, but most of all, I want to know the truth. Where is Alison? What really happened to her?

Oliver is in his study, marking papers. The children are installed in Bea's bedroom with my iPad and the promise they can watch *Shrek* for the hundredth time so long as they stay there quietly.

I hurry to the door and open it. David Green is a small man, about my height, probably in his mid-forties. He has a sallow complexion and the hint of dark stubble across his jawline. His hair is black and receding slightly, but when he extends his hand and smiles at me, his eyes crinkle and sparkle, and he emanates warmth.

'Mrs Siskin?'

'Yes, but please call me Steph. Do come in.'

'It's a pleasure to meet you, and I'm sorry that it's under these circumstances.'

'It was a long time ago, but still feels like yesterday,' I say, standing to one side to let him pass.

'You live in a lovely house,' he says, glancing at the paintings in the wall of the downstairs hall.

'Thank you.'

'Have you come far?' I ask as I lead him into the living room.

'Just from Brighton, but I was brought up in London, and a lot of my work is here.'

I gesture for him to sit down. 'Can I get you a tea or coffee?'

'A black coffee would be great, thank you.'

I walk into the kitchen and flick the kettle on. I then poke my head around the door to Oliver's study.

'That researcher is here.'

'What the–! For god's sake, Steph. I told you to cancel him. I don't want to speak to him.'

'Maybe, but I do, and Alison was my friend. I want someone to continue digging, to find out the truth.'

'I'm not talking to him.'

'You can't not. It's rude!'

Oliver pales, and his fingers tighten around his antique fountain pen.

'Just pop in for five minutes.'

Oliver hates arguing, but he knows I've backed him

into a corner. I may pay for it later if he spends the rest of the day sulking in his study, but I'll worry about that then. He sighs, gets up and walks stiffly through the kitchen. I pour boiling water into the cafetiere and pick up the tray with coffee mugs and a plate of biscuits. I follow him through to the living room.

Oliver stands in front of the sofa where David is sitting. 'I'm laden down with work. I'm sorry, but it's really not convenient to talk to you at the moment,' he says to David. I cringe.

'I'm sorry to be disturbing you. Your wife said–'

'Stephanie got it wrong. Another time maybe.' Oliver crosses his arms.

I am shocked. He is normally so polite.

'Yes, no problem. We can talk on campus on Monday if you prefer, but I thought it would be more convenient for you to speak here, as I need to talk to Stephanie too.'

'I can't mix private business with university affairs,' Oliver says.

'Of course, and that's why I checked with the dean's office. They confirmed that Alison was your student and said it would be alright to talk to you.'

Oliver opens and closes his mouth. For such an articulate man, he appears lost for words. He sits down heavily in his favourite armchair, crossing his right leg over his left knee.

'In which case, you'd better fire away,' Oliver says.

I pour the coffees and sit down in the chair next to Oliver. David opens his soft leather bag and takes out a notepad, a biro and a voice recorder, placing the little machine on the glass coffee table. 'Would you mind if I record our conversation? It makes it easier for me when I'm compiling my research.'

'No problem,' I say, without glancing at Oliver.

'How well did you know Alison Miller, Dr Siskin?'

'She was a student of mine for a couple of modules.'

'And did you know Joshua?'

'No. Never met him.'

'So beyond her attending your lectures and a few tutorials, you had no dealings with Alison?'

'If I recall correctly, she was a very able student, but I'm afraid I can't fill you in on any more. I will have to leave that to my wife, who knew her extremely well. Everyone at the university was deeply shocked by what happened. It was a tragedy. And that's why I don't understand why you're here digging it all up. It's taken years for Stephanie to get over it. She suffered from terrible nightmares.'

I lean over to Oliver and pat his knee. 'It's fine, love.'

'But it isn't. All you're doing is digging up dreadful memories and upsetting people who have, at long last, achieved some form of equilibrium.'

'I totally understand your concerns,' David Green says. 'We will be as discreet and sensitive as possible. Our only objective is to uncover the truth. I'm sure as a leading academic, you hate injustice.'

'Indeed, but what proof is there to suggest that an injustice has taken place?'

'We received a letter from Josh setting out all the inconsistencies he believes there are in his case, points that he believes the police have ignored or dismissed. My producers think that some of his claims may be worth further investigation. It could be that our research throws up nothing and that Josh was indeed the killer, but we hope at least to discover where Alison's body is and bring a degree of closure to her family. Only time will tell.'

'Isn't it up to his legal team to appeal his case if there are inconsistencies?' Oliver asks.

'Josh has attempted to appeal, but has been refused permission.'

Oliver stands up abruptly. 'I need to check on the children. Please excuse me.' He nods at David, who quickly gets up too. The men shake hands briefly, and Oliver leaves the room without catching my eye.

'Sorry,' I say as I listen to Oliver's footsteps as he climbs the stairs. At least he really is going to check on the kids.

'It's fine. I realise that our questions are intrusive, and I apologise for that. Please can you tell me everything you can remember about Alison, and particularly her relationship with Josh. Did he spend a lot of time in your flat?'

'Yes, he did. They were besotted with each other, and it was like having a third person living in our flat. It wouldn't have surprised me if they had ended up getting married one day. Josh was as worried about Alison's disappearance as I was.'

'So there was no indication that anything was wrong before she went missing?'

I look away from him. 'She sent me a text message asking to talk to me, but unfortunately I got held up and never managed to speak to her.' A shiver passes through me.

David puts his pen down and leans forwards. 'You mustn't blame yourself.'

I pick up my coffee cup and take a sip, but it's cold. 'That's what Oliver says. Easier said than done.'

He asks me a few more questions about Alison's friends, her ambitions for the future, her daily routine and the like, and then he switches off the voice recorder and snaps shut his notebook.

'You've been very helpful, Mrs Siskin. May I come

back to you if I have any further questions once I've spoken to Alison's family and other friends?'

'Yes, of course,' I say.

He hands me a simple white business card with his name, job title of freelance researcher, a mobile number and email address.

I see him to the door. We shake hands, and I close the door behind him. I lean against the wall in the downstairs hall for a moment and shut my eyes. All the memories come back. The horror of the police rifling through our belongings. The guilt that I somehow let Alison down. The trial that I didn't attend. The memorial held a year to the day of the disappearance. The nightmares.

'Mum, has the man gone?' Bea appears at the top of the stairs, a welcome break to my reverie.

'Yes, sweetie. Do you want to come and help me make lunch?'

'No,' she says, disappearing back along the corridor.

No surprise there. I walk into the kitchen. A few moments later, Oliver appears behind me.

'We need to talk,' he says, pulling out a chair and slumping into it. 'I don't want you involved in that man's research.'

'Why?' I ask, crossing my arms.

'Have you forgotten how I had to soothe you night after night? How those nightmares made you dread going to sleep? How exhausted you were; how your mother had to come and help? How you saw that therapist for months and months? We are not going back there, Stephanie. The past needs to stay in the past. There are plenty of other people that researcher can talk to. Okay?'

I nod. But it's not alright. Oliver doesn't understand. Firstly, I'm older and more mature now, with a better perspective. But more than that, he doesn't get how important it is to have resolution. To know for sure what happened to my friend.

It takes me back to when Mum and Oliver insisted I visit a therapist. Mum suggested Sonya Partridge, or if I didn't want to talk to her, she'd find me someone else. I took the pragmatic view that, as Sonya already knew about some of my neuroses due to losing Dad and Leroy, then she was as well placed as anyone to help me through my new loss.

The problem was Alison couldn't be described as a loss. She'd gone missing; we couldn't grieve for her, as there was always the hope she'd reappear. Sonya explained how the relatives and close friends of missing people are more likely to suffer from the symptoms of prolonged grief disorder, post-traumatic stress, or even major depressive disorder. Mum was annoyed that she talked about the latter, because she thought Sonya might have planted ideas in my head. But fortunately for me, I'm not predisposed to depression.

Nevertheless, I had many of the symptoms of PTSD and PGD for a very long time. Whenever I saw a blonde-haired woman who might, just might be Alison, I would hurry up to them, hope bursting through my veins like a shot, only to be dashed again and again. Fear lurked around like a dark fog, and even now, if I'm out alone on a darkened street, I manically look over my shoulder and my heart pounds in my ears. And I worry so very much about Oliver and the kids and Mum. Cognitive behavioural therapy helped a lot, but the greatest healer was time, along with the gradual accep-tance that my lovely friend is dead. I have come to accept that I will probably never know what happened to her. And I will never know whether my failure to respond to her text could have cost her her life.

At least, that's what I thought until David Green appeared. So just because Oliver thinks the past needs to stay in the past, I fundamentally disagree. This is my life; it is me who has to survive the nightmares and the overwhelming fear that is just a breath away. I need to know the truth about Alison.

If Oliver forces me to talk to David behind his back, then so be it.

4

I'm gutted. And angry. Oliver bloody Siskin gave me a lousy grade for my essay. I spent all weekend on it; I thought I understood it; I reread the damn thing one hundred times, and still my grade was equivalent to a third. How the hell am I meant to get sponsorship for my law conversion course with low marks? I really need to get a scholarship and/or sponsorship from a solicitors' firm if I'm going to make my dreams come true. I suppose Oliver marked me down because I didn't pay attention in the tutorial; perhaps it was payback. I'm sick with worry now. These essays matter. I can't even ask Alison to help because she's not doing this module. He's scrawled at the bottom of the essay, 'Come and see me if you want to discuss.'

To hell with that. I think I'll go out tonight and get pissed. If I'm going to fail, I might as well enjoy life at uni, not sit in the flat and work like I did last weekend. Look where that got me! I glance at my watch. I've got a lecture on architecture in modern buildings this afternoon. I debate skipping it, but I'm too diligent, I suppose.

I'm one of the last into the lecture hall and take a seat near the back. Just as I'm sitting down, my phone pings with an incoming text. It's from Alison.

'Can we meet up for a drink this evening? There's something I want to talk to you about.'

I turn my phone onto silent and glance around the lecture hall. She should be here, but she's not. In fact, I've barely seen her this week. She's been with lover boy, I suppose. I grind my teeth. What's so urgent that it requires us to schedule a time for a chat? And why didn't she say anything this morning when we exchanged a few brief words before she left the flat? And then it hits me. She'll be wanting to get out of our tenancy. I suppose she's hoping she can move in with Josh. Well, she bloody can't. It's not like I'm going to be able to find anyone else to take over the lease midway through our final year. She'll have to sort it herself.

The lecture starts, and I try hard to concentrate, jotting down lots of notes that I hope will make sense when I come to read them.

I'm still in a bad mood as I exit the lecture hall, and I walk slap-bang into someone, dropping my books in the process.

'Sorry,' I say, immediately bending down.

'Steph?'

I look up at the boy's face and blush. It's Rahul. Of all the people I have to walk into.

'Here, let me help you.' He bends down and gathers up my books. We stand and look at each other awkwardly. 'I've been wanting to run into you, but not literally, of course. Not like this!' he says.

We both laugh.

'Are you busy? Would you like to go out for a drink?'

I glance at my watch. It's 5 pm on a Friday, and there's nothing I'd like more than to have a drink with gorgeous Rahul. I wonder if Alison or Josh have said anything to him, because that would be really embarrassing.

'Yes, sure. Thanks,' I say. And then I remember Alison's text. I can talk to her later. I need to grab this opportunity now, perhaps bagging myself a new boyfriend in the process. We walk out of the building side by side and turn onto the Strand.

'Have you been in here?' he asks as we come to a halt in front of a fancy new wine bar.

'No. It's not exactly in my budget.' I peer at the menu, which is stuck to the window. A single glass of wine costs what I budget for a whole night out.

'Me neither, but I'd like to splash out. My grandad gave me some money for my birthday.'

'Are you sure?' I ask, feeling as if my eyes are about to pop out. 'I'm not exactly dressed for it.' I glance down at my torn jeans and baggy sweatshirt.

'It doesn't matter. I think you look gorgeous!'

I glance away, embarrassed.

'Come on!' He grabs my hand and pushes the door open.

The wine bar is all chrome and glass, super trendy with ice-blue velvet chairs and angular glasses cut to look like ice cubes. Unsurprisingly for a Friday afternoon, it's packed full, mainly with braying city types dressed in sharp suits, congratulating each other on deals completed or legal cases won. We look totally out of place.

'I'll just nip to the loos,' I say.

'I'll find us a table.'

I weave my way through the throng of drinkers to

the back of the room and follow the steps down to the toilets. I stand in front of the long mirror and run my fingers through my dark auburn hair and swipe a mascara wand over my lashes, which makes my greenish eyes appear wider. As I pout at myself and apply a quick swipe of pink lipstick, I get a strange look from a woman exiting a cubicle. I hold her gaze defiantly until she looks away.

I return upstairs, and for a few moments I wonder if Rahul has done a runner. I can't spot him. It's only when he stands up and waves at me, I realise that he's found a table for two right in the window, looking out onto the Strand. He passes me the drinks menu.

'Would you like a cocktail?' he asks.

'I'm not sure–'

'I'm buying. It's my treat. Have whatever you'd like.'

And so I choose a Sex on the Beach cocktail and feel my cheeks burn when I say the words out loud.

'You're so cute.' Rahul grabs my hand as the waitress walks away. He stares into my eyes, and it makes me feel both claustrophobic and tingly.

'Not sure that most people would call me cute. Obstinate, shy, hardworking.' I pause for a moment, wondering whether that's the sum of me. 'Loyal, perhaps.'

'Beautiful, funny and, according to Alison, a great friend.'

'It's very kind of her to say that.' I look down at my lap, embarrassed. 'What about you? What's your story?'

'My story? Do you want me to explain why I'm sitting here with you, or my background?'

'Your background.' I think I'll turn beetroot red if he flatters me with any more compliments.

'Okay, then. My grandparents come from India. I'm

the eldest of four, and my parents expected me to be a doctor, a lawyer or an engineer. I chose law, but I hate the degree, and I'd like to be an artist. I'm doing a subsidiary in history of art, which is how I met Alison, although I met her through Josh first. Things are a bit tough at home at the moment because Dad's business went bust eighteen months ago, and he hasn't been able to work since. Mum doesn't work, so finances are really tough. I've had to take on two jobs so I can afford to stay in London. This is my first night out in ages.'

'Oh,' I say, feeling chuffed that he's chosen to spend it with me. 'What jobs have you got?'

'Just in a bar and a cafe. Cleaning tables, serving and stuff.'

'Where do your family live?'

'In Leicester, but I'd like to stay here in London when I graduate if I can.'

'What do you want to do after uni?'

'I might become a teacher. Ordinary, boring.'

'Not boring,' I say. I wish I had his life.

'What about your parents?'

'It's just Mum. Dad died when I was twelve.'

'I'm sorry,' he says gently. 'What happened?'

I'm surprised he has asked the question. Most people gloss over it. It's awkward to ask for details about a premature death.

'He had an accident at work.'

'That's awful.' Rahul stares at me with those big, warm dark eyes and tilts his head to one side.

'He was on one of those platforms that window cleaners use on tall buildings. It fell to the ground.'

'How terrible.'

'It's ironic that you're doing the degree I wanted to do. I want to be a lawyer, personal injury ideally, but not with one of those awful no-win-no-fee firms. I want to help people, not prey on their vulnerability.'

'I admire your passion,' Rahul says. 'I'm just sorry you had to suffer like that. And your limp? Was that anything to do with it?'

I open and close my mouth. Hardly anyone asks me about my limp. Alison wanted to know why I was a year older than everyone else, so I told her, and she noticed that I never ran anywhere, but I thought either no one had noticed, or they couldn't care less.

'I was in a car accident when I was eighteen.'

He reaches across the table again, and my cocktail glass wobbles. He rescues it just in time. We both laugh.

'Does it still hurt?'

'Sometimes, but mostly it's fine.'

'It sure explains why you want to be a lawyer.'

I smile.

When we've finished our drinks, Rahul says coyly, 'I'm afraid my finances don't stretch to more drinks. Are you hungry? We could go back to mine, and I can rustle you up something, or we can get a kebab.'

'Are you a good cook?'

'Mum taught me a few dishes before I left home. I can do a mean vegetable curry.'

'Sounds good to me.'

CONVERSATION FLOWS EASILY on our way back to Rahul's. He lives in a three-bedroom flat in Camden. It's furnished sparsely with knackered furniture, peeling paint on the walls and something that looks suspiciously like mould growing from a corner of the wall in the miniscule kitchen, but the location is great.

'Sorry it's a dump,' he says as he opens the small fridge. 'Would you like wine or beer?'

'Wine, please. Where are your housemates?'

'Out or away for the weekend. I wouldn't have suggested you come back here if they were around.'

I smile awkwardly, wondering if he would have been too embarrassed to be seen with me, or that they would get in the way of whatever he has planned next. He pours me a very large glass of white wine, which I drink too quickly. Following the cocktail and with an empty stomach, it makes my head swim. I lean on the doorframe, watching Rahul cook. He's impressive, cutting vegetables as quickly as a professional chef. And then, when everything is bubbling away on the stove, he turns to me, removes the empty glass from my hand, places it on the counter, and he takes my face between his hands and kisses me.

'I've been wanting to do that all evening,' he says when we eventually come up for air. 'You're gorgeous.'

I smile coyly. He's definitely more gorgeous than I am. He then kisses me again, and before long we're shedding our clothes, and he is tugging me towards his bedroom, and we're on the bed, hands and lips everywhere.

Then there's a deafening noise that interrupts our frenetic lovemaking.

'Shit!' he says, sitting up. 'The smoke alarm!' Naked, he rushes out of the room, returning a few seconds later, wafting the air around with his arms. 'I burned the curry.'

'I don't need any curry.'

'Me neither.' He jumps back onto the bed, and we resume where we left off.

It isn't until much, much later, when I'm lying cramped up against the wall on his narrow, single bed, with my head on Rahul's shoulder, listening to his regular breathing, that I realise I totally forgot to contact

Alison. She won't mind. She'll be thrilled that I'm with Rahul. I just hope this wasn't a one-night stand, and that tomorrow – or even better, the day after – I can return to our flat, sore and happy, and be able to tell Alison that I've got a boyfriend, too.

5

NOW

William and Naomi De Villeneuve live in Oxshott. Officially a village, it is an extremely desirable place to live, probably because the average house price is around two million pounds; not exactly your typical English village. Many of the houses are mansions set within gated, exclusive estates, and are home to affluent celebrities and multimillionaires. What makes the De Villeneuves' mansion, (named by Naomi as DV Manor, of course!) even more special than the vast neighbouring properties is the land that sits around it. I don't know how many acres they have, but it is so large and park-like that I have never fully explored their grounds. Oliver told me that they employ a gardener as a permanent member of staff and have two others that work full-time during the summer months.

The first occasion Oliver took me to DV Manor, I thought he was taking me to stay in a hotel. My heart still skips a beat when we come here; not because I would actually like to live here, but because no one can fail but to be impressed. The exterior is built to look like a stately Georgian home constructed from faded red bricks with perfectly proportioned windows. Although the interior rooms have been built in a typically Georgian style, being symmetrical, with fireplaces positioned on end walls, and high ceilings downstairs, they are decorated in different styles. The living room is like a baronial hall, whereas the kitchen is uber modern, almost commercial with its expanse of stainless steel and banks of ovens. Oliver is a little more damning of the place, calling it pastiche, and telling me how William wanted to live in a genuinely old house, grade one listed ideally, with its original features. Unfortunately for him, Naomi demanded her creature comforts, and you can't dig up the floor of a grade one listed property to lay underfloor heating or put a jacuzzi bath into the top-floor master en-suite. For me, it's all of the antiques and paintings and beautiful things inside that notch it up to spectacular. Every room has paintings from a different era, from the Chagall in the living room to the Ed Ruscha pop prints in the downstairs loo.

One of my favourite paintings is by Albert Marquet, a lovely oil on canvas of a boat on an azure sea moored off a small coastal village in the South of France, that hangs in the hall between the kitchen and the utility room, in a place where most people might hang some family photos. I suppose the hunting paintings in the dining room do the least for me. Although I can admire the skills of the likes of Charles Walter Simpson and Heywood Harvey, I'm uncomfortable with those typically British country pursuits. There's a small but very fine oil painting of a horse that looks distinctly like a George Stubbs. When I asked Oliver if he thought it was an original, he changed the subject. I suppose that means it is.

And it's not just the paintings that seem like they

should belong in a gallery. It's the carved jade lamp with its chinoiserie shade, and the rosewood inlaid furniture and the Czech glass vases, and the Japanese ivory netsuke in an oriental display cabinet, and the intricately engraved silver platters.

I often think that the De Villeneuves' place should be opened up to the public. It seems churlish that only a select few can enjoy it. Not that I've ever dared air my opinion on the matter, because William would laugh and Naomi would be horrified.

Despite it being a Sunday, the roads are clogged up getting out of London, and we're running late by the time Oliver can put his foot down on the accelerator on the A3. We pull up to their grand gates shortly before 1 pm.

'Are Phoebe and Hugo going to be here?' Bea asks, removing her headphones.

'I expect so,' I say. My two, Bea in particular, are in awe of Phoebe and Hugo, who are three years older than her. They are twins and have been raised by a string of live-in nannies and have just started at boarding school. I'm assuming they are home for the weekend.

Oliver parks the car to one side of the grand front entrance steps, and we pile out of it. The huge centrally positioned front door, with large lanterns attached to the wall on either side, swings open, and William steps outside.

'Hello, hello! Who do we have here?' He runs down the steps, flings his arms wide open, and grabs Bea and Sam, pulling them in for a squeeze. He is wearing bright orange corduroys and a cream-and-navy flannel shirt, his typical dress-down wear. For work, William dons a bowtie and a waistcoat. He has a walk-in wardrobe full of waistcoats, all in silk and in crazy patterns and colours. It's his trademark look and makes present-giving easy. Running his own auction house, he's become quite famous of late, often featuring as the auctioneer on those game-show daytime television programmes. We rib him mercilessly about his notoriety, and he takes it in good humour. William is a lovely, crazy bear of a man, whom I've grown increasingly fond of over the years.

'Goodness, Sam! What have you been eating? You've grown about three feet since I last saw you.'

'No he hasn't!' Bea says.

'And you, Miss Beatrice, have become even prettier. In fact, you're so dazzling, I think I'd better get my sunglasses!'

Bea giggles. I cringe at William's old-fashioned stereotyping. His children rib him mercilessly for it, and rightly so, but I tend to forgive William his non-woke views just because he's such a warm and generous man.

William leans over to me and gives me a kiss on the cheek, then shakes hands with Oliver and slaps him on the back. I marvel at their friendship. They're like brothers, and even though they see each other several times a week, their greetings are demonstrative and very un-English. Whilst that is understandable on Oliver's part, as he is Canadian by birth, William is as posh English as they come.

'Enter all,' William says, leading us into the grand entrance hall. It has a marble stone floor with the most stunning staircase that curves upwards to the first floor, sweeping in a dramatic arc with a burnished wood handrail and white spindles. There is a massive marble fireplace on the right in which Naomi keeps a large, rather dated and dusty fake-flower arrangement. I've never understood that, because apparently the chimney is in working order.

Whilst it is functional, I find their kitchen sterile. I suppose Naomi would change it if she actually spent much time in the kitchen, but our friend is a pretend cook. She has a live-in Filipino lady who does the cooking and cleaning during the week, and at weekends and when they have people over for dinner, Naomi uses the services of a local chef who makes food in your own dishes. To this day, she hasn't admitted it, but on more than one occasion, I've seen the carrier bags of *Sshush I'm Not A Chef* hurriedly stuffed into her rubbish bin.

'Hello, darlings!' Naomi says, walking into the hallway and greeting us with air kisses. She's wearing a pale pink, floaty floral dress and peep-toe sandals. With her long blonde hair pinned up on top of her head, she's looking summery and pretty. I feel rather plain in comparison, in my chinos and three-quarter-length sleeve T-shirt from M&S. But then again, shopping is what Naomi does best. Perhaps that's a bit mean of me. She does do lots of things for charities, organising fundraising balls and hustling businesses to donate raffle prizes and the like.

'Run upstairs, you two, and find Phoebe and Hugo,' Naomi says. 'They're probably up to no good.' Bea and Sam are out of the room in a flash.

We follow Naomi into the smaller and more intimate of the two living rooms. It has large patio doors that open up onto the stone veranda and offers splendid views of their mature garden and hills in the background. They have a fully stocked bar on the far side of the room, with a shiny walnut wood counter and shelves packed with liqueurs above it. Naomi bends down to open a fridge and produces a bottle of white wine. She knows me well enough not to have to ask what I want, and starts pouring a glass of Pinot Grigio from the local Denbies vineyard. Both she and William are committed British wine aficionados.

'Actually, probably best if I don't drink,' I say. 'I'm the designated driver and am on antibiotics.'

Naomi throws me a sideways glance. 'Everything alright?'

'Yes, yes. Just a bit of cystitis.'

'Too much sex?' She laughs.

Naomi's crudeness always takes me by surprise, and I quickly change the subject.

William and Oliver have already disappeared, no doubt to talk about the latest piece of art they're chasing. I frequently wonder why Oliver didn't follow William into the world of art, as he seems equally obsessed with collecting and antiquities in general. Although it's probably just as well, as William is blessed with family money and the funds to fulfil his hobby (which has become his livelihood too), whereas Oliver and I have to watch the pennies. One of my roles is to complete our weekly outgoings spreadsheet, listing what I've spent on groceries, household goods, clothes for the kids and suchlike. Although Oliver never makes me feel guilty for spending money, I am all too aware that we're living off his earnings.

'Can I do anything to help?' I ask Naomi as she pours herself a very large glass.

'All under control, I think. But perhaps we'd better go and have a look.' I follow her across the hall and into the kitchen. She opens one of the large ovens and spears a pheasant with a thermometer. It beeps at her. 'Looks like we're ready to eat. We'll have to save the girly gossip until later.'

And then there is a ringing sound. It takes me a couple of moments to realise it's my phone, which is in the handbag I dumped on the bench in the hall, just outside the kitchen.

'I need to answer that, in case it's Mum,' I say.

'No problem.'

I grab the phone just in time, saying, 'Hello,' hurriedly, without looking at the caller's number.

'Mrs Siskin?'

'Yes.'

'I'm sorry to bother you again so soon. It's David Green, the researcher. We met yesterday. I've been in touch with Alison's parents, and they're happy to meet me and show me Alison's photo albums. The only problem is, they can't identify any of the people in them, as they didn't know Alison's university friends. I was wondering whether you would be willing to accompany me to their house so that you can identify the people in the photos?'

'Oh,' I say. I can't even remember what Alison's parents look like. I just remember the horror. The media interviews. My guilt.

'They don't live a million miles from you.' There's a rustle of paper; then he speaks again. 'They're in Croydon. Ideally, I'd like to go there tomorrow or the day after, because I'm going abroad for a few days for work at the end of the week. It would be extremely helpful if you could accompany me.'

'I suppose I could come,' I say in a quiet voice. I walk towards the DV's front door. 'I could manage late morning tomorrow.'

'That would be marvellous. I'll message you their address. Shall we say 11.30 am?'

'Okay.'

I put the phone away in my bag and stand still for a moment. Oliver will be livid. He made it perfectly clear that he didn't want us to have anything further to do with the research, and maybe he's right. I feel a tight-ness in my chest, and my leg throbs just at the thought of it, but I'm not doing this just for me. I'm doing it for Alison. At the very least, she deserves a proper burial.

I'm quiet at lunch. I can't stop thinking about Alison and wondering about the what ifs. The conversation flows all around me, but I'm zoned out.

'Steph!' William says. I jump. William leans towards Sam, who is seated at the far end of the table and shovelling his chicken into his mouth as if he hasn't had a decent meal in weeks. 'Your mother hasn't said a word. Have you zipped up her vocal cords?'

'Sorry,' I say. 'I'm miles away.'

But then the conversation moves away, whilst Hugo explains what it's like being at boarding school, and William tells us about an upcoming auction, and I just concentrate on eating the food, which is delicious as always. It isn't until after the meal when the kids have scarpered and we've moved into the living room for coffee that Naomi turns to me.

'You haven't told us what's new in your life,' she says.

I wonder whether to tell her about David Green and decide there's no reason not to. 'We had a researcher visit us yesterday to talk about what happened to Alison. You remember, my flatmate who went missing.'

There is silence for a moment, and then Naomi touches her forehead as if she's recalling what happened. 'Ah, yes. Such a tragedy. An awful time for you,' she says. 'But why on earth has a researcher got in touch?'

'He's putting together material for a true crime docu-mentary. They're looking for new evidence and hope to find out what really happened to Alison. No doubt it will make the headlines and keep the local gossips busy.'

'How horribly intrusive for you. Have you agreed to take part in the documentary?' William asks.

'No,' Oliver says, taking a swig of coffee. 'I don't want us to have anything to do with him.'

'Too right.' Naomi puts her coffee cup down with surprising force. 'They're like vultures, individuals like that, preying on other people's misery. I don't understand this current obsession with true crime. Those programmes are on all the time these days, yet think of the poor relatives who are trying to get their lives back together, and then it's all dug up again for them. I think it's terrible.'

'I agree,' Oliver says. 'It was such a devastating time for Stephanie. I don't want it to be raked up again.'

'Can't imagine the university will be too pleased, either,' William says. He has unwrapped a Bendicks mint and is smoothing out the metallic wrapping paper with two fingers. 'It doesn't make for good publicity to have one of their students missing, presumed murdered.'

'I know,' Oliver agrees. 'But the powers that be have given their tacit approval for faculty who had anything to do with her to be interviewed by this researcher. You'd have thought they would want to batten down the hatches.'

'But surely everyone wants to know the truth!' I exclaim.

'The police uncovered the truth, didn't they?' Naomi says. 'What's his name? Jack, Jimmy?'

'Josh,' I say curtly.

'He's behind bars,' William says. 'What's the point of dragging it all up again just to satisfy a bloodthirsty audience?'

'My point exactly,' Oliver says. 'Which is why we're going to have nothing to do with the programme. It's unethical, and my only concern is to protect Steph. We don't want you going back to those dark times, darling.'

'It was during those dark times that we fell in love,' I say. The coffee is tasting bitter, and I move my half-drunk cup and saucer to one side. 'And I would like to know the truth.'

'Maybe, Steph,' Naomi says. 'But you've got the children now. You need to look after your own mental health.'

What! What the hell is Naomi implying? That I am fragile? That's nonsense. If they had known Alison, they would understand. I need to know. Alison deserves that. I failed her terribly, and I have no intention of failing her again.

6

I'm woken up by a screeching alarm clock. It takes a moment for me to realise where I am. My left foot has pins and needles, and my arm is totally cramped. Rahul sits up in bed and stretches.

'Hello, gorgeous!' he says, running his fingers through my tousled hair. 'Sorry it's so early, but I've got a train to catch.'

I groan as I pull the duvet tightly around me and try to shake some feeling into my foot and arm. I didn't mean to stay all night, and now I feel ashamed. I'm not the sort of girl who sleeps with a boy on their first date.

'What's the time?'

'Six o'clock.'

'In the morning?' I ask.

'Yes. Don't look so shocked.'

'You're up at six on a Saturday?'

He looks at me sheepishly. 'It's Mum's birthday, and I promised I'd go home for the weekend.'

'This early?' I ask, slumping back on the pillow. Rahul gets out of bed, but I feel too shy to look at him.

'I'm really sorry, but you're going to have to leave, too.'

'Sure,' I say, disappointed that we're not going to be spending the weekend together.

He pulls on a pair of underpants and then walks back towards me, standing awkwardly at the side of the bed. 'I'd like to see you again, Steph.'

'Yeah, I'd like that too.' I let out a silent puff of relief. Maybe this is the start of something.

AN HOUR LATER, I'm back at my flat, relieved that the streets are so quiet this early on a Saturday morning. That's one of the many advantages of living in London. The chances of running into anyone I know when I'm returning home in yesterday's clothes are extremely slender. I walk to the bathroom to take a shower and realise that Alison's bedroom door is ajar. And I totally forgot to contact her last night. I peek my head into her room, but she's not there. Her duvet is pulled up to her pillow, and her room is neat. I suppose she's staying over at Josh's place. No surprise. I go into the bathroom and take a shower. Her washbag is still here, but it often is. She's definitely got a toothbrush and some makeup at Josh's.

When I'm out of the shower, I send her a message.

'Sorry for not getting back to you last night. Got big news to tell you!!!'

Then I make myself a cup of tea and go back to bed.

I wake up around lunchtime to the ringing of the door intercom. It sounds like someone has their finger on the buzzer and isn't letting go. I stagger to the door, assuming it's Alison having lost her keys.

'Hello,' I say, pressing the intercom button.

'It's me, Josh. Is Alison there?'

'I'm not sure. Why?'

'Can I come up?'

'Okay.' I unlock the door. I poke my head around Alison's bedroom door, but she's not there. I then hurry back to my bedroom and pull on an old sweatshirt and some joggers.

'What's up?' I ask as I open the front door to Josh.

'I don't know where Alison is,' he says.

'I assumed she was with you. She didn't sleep here last night, or if she did, she left before 6.30 am.'

Josh pushes past me and walks straight to Alison's room. I follow him.

'Shit,' he says. 'She's not answering her phone. I left messages, and now it's like it's switched off, because it goes straight to voicemail.'

'Was she meant to be with you last night?' I ask.

'We didn't agree on it specifically, but yes. She always stays with me at the weekend. I assumed she'd hung out with you or one of her girlfriends and stayed over. It's not like her to ignore me.'

'I thought things were going really well between you two,' I say, but I remember Alison's strange reaction when she returned home last Sunday from her weekend away.

'Yeah,' he says noncommittally. 'I'm probably worrying about nothing.'

I think about how Alison wanted to talk to me. Perhaps I got it totally wrong. Maybe she wanted to tell me she's met someone else. But that seems so unlikely. Josh and Alison have been an item for over a year, and they're all lovey-dovey together. Nauseatingly so. Besides, Josh is as straight as a die; we always tease him for blushing when he's lying, and I can tell that he's genuinely worried.

'Can you message some of her friends, just to double-check?' he asks.

'Sure. And I'll post on Facebook.'

'I might go to the library,' he says, although we both know that that is the last place Alison is likely to be on a Saturday afternoon.

'If you hold on a few minutes, I'll get dressed and join you.'

I MESSAGE all of our joint friends, and most people reply immediately. No one has seen Alison in the past twenty-four hours. In fact, I was probably the last person to see her at breakfast yesterday morning. She was quiet, as if her mind was on something else, but I don't recall thinking anything was wrong. Josh and I spend the next couple of hours walking around all of Alison's regular haunts, going to the library, visiting her favourite café and our old hall of residence. But it's a bit ridiculous. London is a vast metropolis; she could be anywhere.

'Should we be worried?' I say. 'I mean, police worried?'

Josh shrugs his shoulders. 'Hopefully not.'

I try calling Alison's phone, but it's still switched off, and none of my messages have been read. I have that sinking feeling in the pit of my stomach, as if something catastrophic might be about to happen. Or maybe it already has. Then I tell myself to stop thinking so negatively. I remember how Sonya Partridge, my therapist, said that I had a tendency to both project fear into the future about things that haven't happened, and to focus on things in the past that can't be changed. I felt like screaming at her, saying if you'd been through all the shit that had happened to me, you might do the same.

After my third session with her, I told Mum it was a waste of money and I wasn't going back.

But I am aware that I tend to assume the worst, and that right now, it's not helpful.

Alison's probably gone home. Perhaps one of her grandparents died, or the family cat. We're all adults now. We can do what we want.

Josh and I find ourselves in Covent Garden, weaving between groups of tourists. Even if she is here, the chances of spotting her are slight.

'This is ridiculous,' Josh says, his hands on his hips, articulating what I'm thinking. 'We're never going to just stumble across her. I think she's messing with me. This is her way of saying she's pissed off.'

'Really?' I ask doubtfully. If that was the case, she'd answer my messages. And then we're meandering past the Odeon cinema on Shaftesbury Avenue, and Josh comes to a stop.

'I really want to see *How To Train Your Dragon*,' he says. 'Ali doesn't want to go. She says it's too childish.' He looks at the schedule. 'It's starting soon. Do you want to go?'

'I'm not sure. We're meant to be looking for Alison, aren't we?'

'Yes, but we're never going to find her just by wandering the streets. We might as well take a break. Knowing her, she'll turn up by this evening.'

'Okay,' I say reluctantly, although I do feel a bit bad seeing a film with my best friend's boyfriend without her knowing, when we're actually meant to be out looking for her. It would be much more fun canoodling with Rahul in the back row. But too late. Before I can say another word, Josh has walked inside, and I hurry to join him at the counter, where he is buying two tickets.

'You don't need to buy for me,' I say, taking out my wallet.

'You can get the popcorn.'

I buy a big bucket, and we walk into the cinema, settling into our seats. 'Let's leave our phones on vibrate,' I suggest.

'Yes, good idea.'

BOTH OF OUR phones stay silent throughout the film, though I check mine regularly. Not just to see if Alison has rung, but also in the hope that Rahul might ask to see me again. I don't enjoy the film much because my mind is working overtime; I'm worried about Alison. I wonder if I've got her parents' telephone number some-where back in the flat. I don't want to worry them, but it would be good to know if she was at home. That's the problem with not living in a hall of residence. There's no one official to check if you're alright. And as hectic and vibrant as London is, it's also lonely. No one really cares.

Josh walks back to our Barbican flat with me. I'm exhausted now, after my long night and then walking miles this afternoon, and my leg is killing me. I put my key in the door, hoping that it won't be double locked. But it is. Alison isn't here.

Josh tries calling her mobile again, and I check for the fiftieth time on Facebook. No one knows where Alison is.

'Do you think we should call the police?' I ask Josh.

He pales as his eyes widen. 'Dunno. It's a bit soon, isn't it? Don't the police say you've got to wait twenty-four hours before reporting someone missing?'

'You're right. I suppose we should wait until the end of the weekend. She might have gone away with an old friend, or be back at home. If she hasn't returned by eleven tomorrow night, then I think we should call the police.'

'I agree,' Josh says. He looks tired and shaken. I would like to give him a hug. But I don't. He runs his fingers over the faint stubble on his chin. 'All this worry. It's so thoughtless of her not to say where she was going.'

'She's probably lost her phone,' I say. 'Or had it stolen. I'll call you as soon as I hear from her. Will you do the same?'

'Yes, of course. Whatever the time of day or night.'

I STAY in the flat all day on Sunday, trying to keep myself busy by watching mindless YouTube videos. Every time I hear footsteps outside, I hope that it's Alison. It's not. I look for her parents' telephone number, but I don't have it. I try directory enquiries, but Miller is a popular surname, and I've no idea what her parents' first names are, or even where they live. I do a quick search of Alison's room, but all her numbers must be stored on her phone. It's not like anyone has address books these days. Josh calls me at 7 pm, and I ask him if he's got her parents' phone number, but the answer is no. He doesn't know where they live, either. Apparently, Alison has been to stay at his home, but her parents are old-fashioned, and she wasn't comfortable inviting him back to hers. Perhaps it's just as well he doesn't know how to contact them, as I wouldn't want to worry them unnecessarily.

'What should we do?' Josh asks.

'If she's not back by midnight, I'll call the police.'

'Okay,' Josh says. 'Call me, too.'

On the dot of midnight, I call 999.

I had assumed that the police would, figuratively

speaking, roll their eyes and say, 'Another student missing. She's probably with a new boyfriend. We get calls
like this every week.'

But they don't.

The police take it seriously.

7

NOW

It's Sunday night, and I'm tired after our day spent at the De Villeneuves'. I can't sleep, and Oliver's gentle, regular breathing is annoying me. I consider getting up and reading for a while, but in the end I take some Nytol, which if I remember correctly from my previous pregnancies, is the only medication safe to take when pregnant. I drop off eventually, but I wish I hadn't. For the first time in years, I have the nightmare. The nightmare that plagued me for nearly half a decade, that made me dread sleep and weighed down my days. The nightmare I had for the first time the night after Josh's bail hearing.

I am running manically through London's streets, weaving in between ambling shoppers carrying neon-coloured shopping bags, who spit and curse at me as I pass, their faces blank and featureless. I'm running up Regent's Street towards Oxford Circus, and then I'm in Covent Garden, where the shoppers have transformed into clowns, a whole army of them jeering at me as I pass. My heart is pounding, and terror beats through my veins.

I see fleeting glimpses of Alison up ahead, but every time I think I'm within touching distance, she disappears. I need to go faster, much faster. Next, I'm somewhere that vaguely resembles the Barbican with towering grey high-rise blocks and plants hanging off balconies that keep on tumbling to the ground, forcing me to dodge the shower of dead plants. But it's like I'm in a maze constructed of towering prison-like walls, as I constantly come up against concrete dead-ends and have to double back on myself.

I see Alison again, her hair fanning out behind her, over the shoulders of her puffa jacket. I shout. She turns left, and then I'm running along a cobbled street, a place that looks like a street from the Middle Ages. I must reach Alison. I'm the only person who can save her from a savage and terrifying death. She slows down and turns to walk through an open door. I follow her into a dark corridor with cobwebs hanging from the ceilings and hideous, intricately carved gargoyles emerging from the walls, their eyes following me, their mouths uttering silent profanities. Alison comes to a halt at the far end of the long corridor. She has her back to me, and her puffa jacket has gone, replaced with a flowing white nightdress. I shout at her and run towards her. She smiles broadly as she turns around to look at me, as if she's happy to see me. She opens her mouth as if she's about to talk to me, and I feel a momentary sense of relief that perhaps I'm not too late.

But then Josh appears behind her. He holds a long, sharp knife, and as she turns around to face him, he plunges it deeply into her chest. Blood spurts everywhere. I scream as I race towards her, desperately trying to save my friend, begging her for forgiveness for failing to protect her. But then Josh strides towards me, the blood-soaked knife pointing directly at my heart. 'You'll never escape me!' he says. 'I am like a worm burrowing in your head. You made me do this. You made me kill Ali, and then when she was dying, you stole the very essence of her for yourself. I may be a murderer, but you, Stephanie, are so much worse. You will pay. I am going to follow you the whole of your miserable life.'

'Stephanie, are you okay?'

I wake up, whimpering, hugging a pillow to my chest, drenched in sweat, my heart racing.

'Steph, darling. It's a dream.'

I let Oliver hold me and stroke my back. That scene was so real, I could smell the blood, feel its slipperiness and taste the metallic fear.

'Answer me, sweetheart. Are you okay?'

But I can't answer. David Green's appearance and all the talk about Alison has raked up the old memories. And the fact that I might be pregnant, everything is so familiar. I simply can't go back there.

'I'm fine,' I say eventually as my heart rate settles, and I've wiped the sweat from my face. I pull away from Oliver. 'Go back to sleep.'

He does, but I stay awake until the soft grey light of morning seeps through our curtains, worrying about meeting Alison's parents again after so many years, wondering how the grief and the not knowing has ravaged them. It's only when I hear the birds starting to sing that I relax into a dreamless, all too brief, sleep.

8

There's all that anecdotal stuff about the police not launching a missing person's investigation until twenty-four hours have passed, and even then, only taking it seriously if the person is considered at risk. It isn't the case with Alison. The police are awesome.

It's mid-morning on Monday, and the police are here, in the flat, rifling through Alison's room. And I feel sick with fear. They've made contact with Alison's parents and confirmed that she hasn't been home since the Christmas break.

There are two of them. A woman going through Alison's things whose name I've immediately forgotten, and a woman who introduces herself as Detective Sergeant Suzy Smithers, who is the boss woman. She doesn't act or look like a Suzy. She's middle-aged with a lined face and greying hair that hasn't been touched by a hairdresser in a decade. She has narrow, cat-like eyes, and she's prancing around the flat as if she's the landlady.

She plonks herself down on our small two-seat sofa.

Our other seats are two beanbags, one in red, the other in blue. She gestures to me to sit in one. I choose the red one, but it's as if I'm sitting at her feet.

'Let's just go over it again. What was the last communication you had with Alison?'

'The text message asking if we could meet up on Friday evening.' I show her my phone. Tears spring to my eyes as I think of it. If I had agreed, then Alison might be here right now. I make silent prayers. When Alison returns, I'll be a better person, more reliable as a friend; I'll work harder.

'And was this unusual in any way?'

'Asking me to meet up to discuss something? Yes. We live together. We just chat casually. It's like she had something important to say to me, and needed to make an appointment. That's never happened before.'

'But you ignored this request and spent the night with your boyfriend.'

I hang my head.

'Can I have the name and telephone number of your boyfriend.'

'He's not exactly my boyfriend,' I murmur. She narrows her already slit-like eyes at me.

'He's called Rahul. I don't know his surname.' I read out his mobile phone number, blushing at the memory of what we did.

'And he will confirm that you spent all night with him.'

'Yes.' I hang my head.

'What time did you come home?'

'About 7 am. He was catching a train home for his mum's birthday.'

'Did you come straight back here?'

'Yes.'

'How is the relationship between Alison and her boyfriend, Josh?'

I hesitate for a moment, because I'm not sure. I had thought that their relationship was solid, but I really don't know one way or the other. There was definitely something off when Alison returned last weekend. 'It's good, I think. They're in love.' I hope I'm right.

'Yet it was you who went to the cinema with Josh on Saturday?'

'But that didn't mean anything. Nothing happened. We're just friends. I've already told you, we spent all afternoon looking for Alison.'

'Hardly all afternoon if you had time to go to see a film.' She holds my gaze, but I have to look away. There's silence, which I break.

'You're talking to me as if you think something bad has happened to Alison.'

'Do you think it has?' she asks.

'I don't know. That's why we've called you!' My voice goes up in pitch.

The other policewoman comes out of Alison's room.

'We're ready for you now,' she says.

I ease myself up from the beanbag and go into Alison's room. The flat seems so small with these strangers inside. I feel awkward, as if I'm snooping, which of course I am.

'Have a look through her wardrobe and try to work out what Alison was wearing,' Suzy Smithers says.

But it's not that easy. I've never been much interested in clothes, and it's almost impossible to work out what's missing. They're insistent that I come up with a description, so in the end, we agree that she was probably wearing jeans and her navy puffa jacket. The only things I can be confident that she was wearing are the pretty, teardrop-shaped opal earrings that Josh gave her, and the simple gold cross that she wears around her neck. She puts both of those on every day, and they're not here in her room or in the bathroom.

And then the police go, and I'm all alone. I throw myself on my bed and sob. The tears are a mixture of guilt, dread, exhaustion and self-pity. I know I've been jealous of Alison, but I would never wish any harm to come to her. Never. She's my best friend.

RAHUL CALLS ME, but I don't feel like talking to him, and I let the phone go to voicemail.

I ring Mum and sob down the phone. 'Come home, darling,' she says. 'It's too much for you to be there all alone. And what if you're in danger, too?'

My heart thuds. 'Danger? We don't know that anything bad has happened to her,' I say. 'And the police might think I did something to Alison if I leave London.'

'That's nonsense. Besides, it's only been a couple of days. I'm sure she'll surface soon.'

'I can't afford to come home. The train fare is too high.'

'Don't be silly, love. I'll pay for it.'

'Maybe I'll come home at the weekend,' I say. 'I have too much work to do, and I can't miss lectures.'

But Alison doesn't surface. She officially becomes a missing person. The university puts out a statement; her photograph is shown on television, and her parents are pictured leaving their modest, terraced Croydon house, accompanied by uniformed police. Josh and I print out photos of her and plaster them around the university, in student accommodation blocks, outside lecture halls, on phone boxes and in shop windows. Mutual friends mutter as they pass me, and I feel like it's my fault, and everyone knows it.

I can't concentrate on anything. As each day passes, my worry morphs from concern that something bad has befallen Alison to fear for myself. I know that sounds selfish, but so much bad has already happened that I can't shift the thought that it's going to happen again. If something terrible can happen to Dad and to Leroy and to Alison, all three of whom were good people with kind hearts, then why not me next? Perhaps I'll be saved because I'm not a good person; that's the hope that I cling to. But Mum is a good person, and I don't think I could survive if she is taken, too.

I awake at night from the slightest noise outside, covered in sweat, my heart thumping. When I walk to lectures, I'm glancing over my shoulder, suspicious of footsteps behind me, all the while searching for Alison's face. I have to take many more painkillers than normal, because my leg throbs all day and feels like a dagger is being plunged into it at night. And the police come back to the flat. They take fingerprints and spend lots of time in Alison's room, and I have to sign a piece of paper confirming that they've taken away some of Alison's belongings.

Rahul leaves me loads of messages, which is sweet. Under normal circumstances, I'd be excited and flattered. I make a pact with myself. As soon as Alison turns up, I will resume the relationship with Rahul, but until then, I need to punish myself. I barely eat. I drink cheap wine by myself, and I don't answer the messages sent by friends. If I hadn't spent the night with Rahul, I would have known what was up with Alison, and most likely, she wouldn't be missing.

I try to pretend that life is going along as normal, but it's not.

I have a lecture on art patronage in the Middle Ages, but I can't concentrate and don't take any notes. I just watch Oliver Siskin and doodle his square jawline, almond-shaped eyes and luxuriant hair in my notebook. And then the lecture is over, and I feel so tired, almost too tired to collect my files and shove them in my bag and walk out of the lecture hall. My leg is burning again. Perhaps it's my penance.

'Stephanie.'

I redden as I realise that Oliver Siskin has sprinted up the stairs and is blocking my way. He puts his hand out and briefly touches my arm. A jolt of electricity runs through me, and I hope the shock doesn't show on my face.

'I wanted a quick word.'

A few of the other students turn around and stare at us. I follow Oliver back down the stairs to his desk.

'I understand that Alison Miller is your housemate.'

I nod.

'It must be a really difficult time for you.'

'Yes. She's been missing for six days.'

'I can't imagine how awful that is, but I just wanted to let you know that I'm here to talk if you ever need to. The whole Humanities Department is in shock, and we're all keeping faith that Alison will return to university soon.'

'Thanks,' I say. Oliver isn't the first 'official' person from the university to reach out to me. I've been contacted by some woman who has said I can talk to her any time, but Oliver is the first of my tutors to single me out. He taught Alison last year, and if I remember correctly, he awarded her a first in her end-of-year exam.

'How are you holding up?' He's standing very close to me now, those blue eyes locked on mine. It's as if he's peering into my head, our bodies moving towards each other magnetically.

No. This is ridiculous. I take a step backwards. Oliver is my tutor; he's too old, and I'm imagining things. Just because Rahul found me attractive doesn't mean this man does. He's just being kind. Acting in his official capacity, knowing both Alison and me. He smiles at me. I've never noticed his teeth before. They're perfectly straight and very white. I wonder if he uses that whitening stuff.

'How are you getting on with your dissertation?' he asks.

'Um, alright,' I say. But when he raises his eyebrows and tilts his head to one side, I know he sees straight through that.

'I'm here to help, Stephanie. Whether that's advising on your studies, your plans for when you graduate or simply as a friend with everything that's going on.'

'Is that normal?' I ask.

He winces slightly. 'It's normal for me. I like to help my students. I can't talk for my colleagues.'

'Sorry,' I say.

'Don't be. And I mean it. I have a kettle in my study during the daytime and a bottle of whisky locked in my bottom drawer for after hours. Just don't tell Professor Lewis.' Oliver Siskin winks at me, and I feel as if I'm going to explode with desire. What a ridiculously inappropriate reaction. My cheeks are aflame once again.

'Thanks,' I say and quickly turn around and hobble up the stairs. It feels as if his eyes are on my back, but I don't want to turn around, just in case I'm right. Or for that matter, if I'm wrong. The thought of Oliver Siskin liking me is absurd. He's just being kind. I pick up my books and my bag and hurry out of the lecture hall. I'm walking along the corridor at quite a pace.

'Steph!'

It's Rahul.

'Sorry, not now,' I say. My head is full of Oliver Siskin and Alison.

He hurries alongside me, matching my strides. 'Steph, I need to speak to you.' We walk out of the building and onto the street. He glances around as if worried we're being listened to.

I stop and sigh. 'I really like you, Rahul, but with everything that's going on, it just isn't the right time. I hope you understand.'

'Of course I do. And I'll wait. It was magical with you. But did you hear about Josh?'

'What about him?' I haven't seen Josh at all since I reported Alison's disappearance to the police.

'Looks like they're going to arrest him.'

'What!' I exclaim.

'He was taken in for questioning last night, and they're still holding him.'

It feels as if all the blood has been drained from my head. I feel dizzy, and I grab onto Rahul just to stay upright. He lowers me downwards, and we sit side by side on some steps. It's drizzling, but I don't care. He puts his arm around my shoulders, and I realise I'm shaking.

'The police interviewed Josh's flatmates, and no one is allowed into their house now. There are police cars parked outside. His flatmate Adam has moved in with us for a couple of days.'

'Oh, god!' I mutter and put my face in my hands. 'It must mean they think she's dead.'

Rahul squeezes my shoulders. 'Not necessarily. She could have been kidnapped or anything at all. The police won't say anything until they've formally arrested someone.'

I grab my bag and stand up. 'I need to go.'

'Wait!' Rahul says.

'I'll catch you later,' I say over my shoulder.

I sprint all the way back to our flat, even though there is searing pain in my thigh, and I know the running will make it so much worse. As soon as I slam the door shut behind me, I burst into tears. 'Alison, where are you?' I wail out loud.

I find the business card that DS Suzy Smithers left me. Her phone goes to voicemail, so I leave a message. 'Please, can you let me know what's going on? I heard that you've arrested Josh. Is that right?'

I pace the flat, willing my phone to ring. Willing Alison to walk back through the front door, laughing, embarrassed, perhaps, about all the fuss that has been made. I take out my books and try to jot some notes for my dissertation, but the words swim, and I can't concentrate. Is Alison really dead? Have they found her body? And Josh. I liked Josh. He was my friend; Alison's lover. Could we really be so wrong about him? Was he pretending all weekend? Had I sat through that bloody film with him, and all the while, he was thinking how to wipe the traces of Alison's blood off himself, while I just enjoyed the film? Was skinny, gentle Josh really a brutal murderer? I wonder what happened. Were they playing some sex game that went wrong? I can't see Alison or Josh being the type, but they did make a hell of a lot of noise when they were banging each other like rabbits. Perhaps there was a side of her I didn't know. Or was he beating her up all along, and that's what she wanted to share with me on Friday night? But how did he get rid of her body if he killed her in his flat? Nothing makes sense.

My phone rings. It's a withheld number. I gulp,

knowing that my life is likely to be changed for ever when I answer this call.

'Stephanie, this is Suzy Smithers.'

'What's happened? Is it true?'

'I can confirm that we have charged Josh with suspected murder. He will be held in custody until his bail hearing. We are releasing a statement to the media as we speak.'

'Does that mean you've found Alison?' Or more to the point, that they've found her body? I can't bring myself to ask that question out loud.

'No. But there is sufficient evidence to suspect that, regrettably, an incident took place in his house.'

'An incident!' I exclaim. 'You mean murder! Did you find blood?'

'I'm sorry, but I can't comment any further. We have notified Alison's parents and the university.'

There's a long pause.

'You sound very distressed,' she says. 'Is there anyone who can be with you?'

'Yes, yes,' I say, and end the call.

I pace up and down our small living room, trying but failing to think straight. Josh shares a house with two other boys. Perhaps it was one of them who hurt Alison. I don't know either of them. Or perhaps it was someone else altogether. But the police don't make mistakes like that, do they? There are friends I could call. Or Rahul. He was kind to me, but I can't face him. Or anyone else for that matter.

There's a cheap bottle of wine in the fridge. I pour myself a large glass and drink it in two gulps. And then I pour another. I try to drink myself into oblivion, to blank out the terrible images I have of Alison, blood everywhere, her eyes staring glassily up at the ceiling.

Her face is all over the media. The world is horrified that a young, intelligent student could disappear, presumed murdered. And Josh's face is printed alongside hers, a picture of him taken from Facebook where he's laughing uproariously, and he looks ridiculous. Too ridiculous to be a murderer. It's a parody, putting their photographs next to each other. I hate how the media leeches off human misery, and then I wonder whether it's just human nature to want to be shocked. The more we relish it, the more the media panders to our sickening desires. It's a Catch-22 situation. For a short while, I reflect whether I might be better off becoming a media lawyer rather than specialising in personal injury. Perhaps I would have more influence on human suffering in trying to prevent the media from exploiting people's grief.

The days turn into one week, a fortnight, nearly a month. A stretch of the Thames is searched. CCTV is monitored. But her body doesn't appear. Nor does she.

I try to concentrate, but it's so hard. I'm alone most of the time. Friends invite me out, but I say no, preferring to stay in the flat and drink myself into a stupor, night after night, keeping vigil, just in case Alison comes home. At least, that's what I tell myself. In the end, my friends give up calling. Rahul tries, too. He really tries, but even he stops contacting me.

The truth is, whenever I go out, I'm constantly looking over my shoulder, wondering if someone is following me. In the flat, I keep the door bolted and wedge a chair under the door handle. I keep my mobile phone switched on and powered up in case I need to dial for the emergency services. There's no indication that I or anyone else is in danger, particularly as Josh is locked up in custody, but I'm scared, too. All the time. I feel like death follows me. First Dad died, then there was that awful car accident and I lost Leroy, and now, Alison. Perhaps it's me. Perhaps I have some kind of devil living inside me, and anyone who gets close to me will perish. But that means that Mum is also in danger, and I don't know how to protect her. Maybe I should give myself up, be the proverbial sacrificial lamb in order to protect anyone else that may come into my orbit and face the threat of an early death.

I get a note from Oliver Siskin saying my dissertation is four days overdue, but that, under the circumstances, they are giving me a two-week extension. I know it's bloody due, but I can't do it. I just can't. My brain has frozen, and I stare at the unopened library books that themselves are overdue.

And then I get a telephone call from Mrs Miller, Alison's mum. It's a shock. She asks if I could do them a favour and pack up Alison's belongings because they're coming to collect them at the weekend. She apologises over and over, saying she knows she should do it herself, but it's too hard right now. And anyway, perhaps I'd like someone else to move into Alison's room.

But I wouldn't. I don't want some stranger in Alison's room. I just want my friend to come back. Then I worry about the rent. We signed a joint tenancy, and if the Millers stop paying, might I be liable for Alison's part? I really hope that the Millers have come to some arrangement with the landlord, and that he's compassionate.

I leave it until the day before the Millers are due, because I can't face packing up her things. I can imagine Alison returning when her belongings are here, but if the room is empty … I go down to the local newsagent and get several empty cardboard boxes. I start with her books, many of which are the same as mine. But unlike me, Alison was diligent. Her work is neat and ordered; she got high grades for all her essays. And then I see a stack of neatly printed out pieces of paper, with handwritten annotations on most of the pages. I flick to the title page: *Has Sculpture Been Appropriated for Political Display?* I realise it's her almost-completed dissertation, and I can't believe she's nearly finished. I forget for a moment that she might be dead, and roll my eyes at how unfair it is. Pretty, clever, popular. Presumed dead.

I have a quick read through the first couple of paragraphs. I didn't realise she was doing her dissertation on a subject that has so much crossover with mine. She's approaching it from a different angle, but at the core both our dissertations are about the true value of artefacts. It just goes to show how little we talked about practical things and our studies in particular. And then it hits me. No one is ever going to read this dissertation. It's going to go into a box; perhaps her parents will read it and shake their heads in awe at the intelligence of their presumed-dead daughter. But no one at university will read it.

It's then that I have the idea, and I'm disgusted with myself – but I really could pass off most of this dissertation as my own work.

No, I can't. I put the pile of paper to one side.

I have to drink a whole bottle of wine to get through packing Alison's things. The room still smells of her perfume: Fantasy by Brittney Spears. It seems like such a frivolous choice for someone like Alison, who in many ways is much more mature than me. But perhaps she just likes the scent. *Liked* the scent. Another thing we never talked about.

I'm careless with her clothes, because it just seems wrong for me to be rifling through them. I chuck everything into the two large suitcases she keeps under her bed. I wonder if I should strip her bed, and I'm about to leave it, but then I think how awful for Mrs Miller to have to take the linen off her daughter's bed, so I do it. Quickly, whipping the sheets off and shoving them into a bin liner as the tears run down my cheeks.

When everything is done, that pile of paper is still sitting there on her desk, calling out to me. I know in my heart of hearts that it's wrong for me to take it, but it's wrong that Alison is missing. Could I be accused of cheating? I suppose so, but surely I deserve to pass my degree. There's only so much suffering one person can take. It will be a risk if I take it, because if Alison does reappear in the next few weeks, then she may still submit the dissertation, but it's a risk I reckon I can take. Besides, I'd accept being labelled a cheat if it means Alison is fine. A small price to pay for having my friend walk back through our front door. Using her dissertation will be like my silent tribute to her. No one will know, and I'm sure she wouldn't mind. Knowing

Alison, she'd probably tell me to take it, to get some benefit from her tragic demise.

I look for her laptop, but then remember that the police took it. The chances of them sharing her work with any of our professors is about zero. Even if they award her a posthumous degree, they won't have expected her to complete her dissertation. I pick the pile up as if the pages are about to detonate, and then hurry into my room, slipping the stack to the back of my wardrobe. I feel so conflicted. On the one hand it's wrong and a risk; on the other hand, it means that I have a chance of getting my degree and still pursuing my dreams of becoming a lawyer. Alison would approve of that.

Then I start on another bottle of wine, waking at 3 am on the sofa with a cricked neck and a pounding headache.

The doorbell goes at 11 am. The looks on Alison's parents' faces are the look that was on Mum's face in the months after Dad died. Strained, pale, grey and broken.

Mrs Miller does all the talking. I don't think her husband utters a single word. Silently, he carries everything to their car, lifting up each box and each case as if it were the most precious and breakable antiquity.

'Do you know the boy who they say killed her?' she asks.

I nod. 'He seemed really nice. Ordinary. I think he loved Alison. It's such a shock.'

'They found blood all over his room. What's that stuff they use so it lights up? My poor baby.' She sobs, and I have to look away.

'Luminol,' I say quietly. I lean against the wall to stop myself from keeling over. This is the first I've heard about lots of blood. To date, it has only been in my imagination.

'He swears he's innocent,' she says. 'Refuses to say where my baby's body is. But it'll all come out in the trial, won't it? Alison has so much good in her. She wants to change the world, to remind the great and the good that things of beauty shouldn't just be preserved for their aesthetics, but that they represent history that we can learn from. It took me weeks to understand what she was going on about.' She sniffs and blinks rapidly. 'I don't know where she got her brains from, or her love of art. We never had any money to buy stuff, and we certainly never took her to museums when she was little. But you probably know all of that, don't you?'

I nod.

'She was very fond of you, Stephanie. Talked about you a lot. I hope that your dreams come true.'

10

M onday mornings are always a rush. Oliver has an early departmental meeting and leaves home at 7.30 am. Gone are the days when he tore around London on a bike. He had a near miss with an open-topped London tour bus shortly after we were married. It clipped his back wheel, and he was thrown to the ground, fortunately suffering nothing more than cuts and bruises. Heavily pregnant, I freaked and persuaded him that, however environmentally friendly it was to ride his bike around town, I didn't want him to become a statistic. Most of all, I didn't want him to be like me, a semi-invalid. These days, he walks to the Tube station at Parsons Green and takes the District Line to Temple. It's not a bad journey as far as London commutes go, but I know he'd prefer the freedom of his bike rather than a tightly packed Tube train.

I find it particularly hard to get the children ready on Monday mornings. There's always that lingering, treacly feeling left over from the weekend, when the pace is slow and time is to be enjoyed. Despite laying out the kids' uniforms the night before, having their bags ready and lunches packed, I invariably end up screeching to get them out of the house on time. And today is worse than most, because I have to get to Croydon to see Alison's parents without anyone knowing, and I am feeling weighed down with exhaustion from lack of sleep.

After dropping Bea and Sam at school, I race back home, quickly tidy up and study Google maps. Despite the Millers living less than ten miles away from us, I leave myself an hour to get there. London traffic is dreadful, and my sense of direction is dire. And then there's the unavoidable issue: I hate driving. Oliver says it's perfectly normal for someone who has been in a collision as severe as the one I was in to hate driving and to be fearful, but I don't want that fear to permeate to my children. It's for that reason that I force myself to drive. Not often, but sufficiently so that my muscle memory kicks in.

The problem is, it's not only the muscle memory. The pain in my leg, where they inserted a piece of metal, also remembers. The night before a planned drive, I invariably get severe muscle spasms, and the night after it's just as bad, if not worse. But I'm bloody minded and refuse to give in to my fears and pain.

Being an upstanding city dweller with an eco-conscience, Oliver bought a silver Toyota Prius, smug in the fact that his vehicle doesn't pollute London's streets. Personally, I think it plays straight into the stereotype of a professor: comfortably well off, antiques collector, *Guardian* reading, eager for the world to think he's woke and subscribed to the important issues of the day. I was sad that he sold his Mazda sports car when Sam was born. But just because I think the Prius is characterless and dull doesn't mean I eschew driving it when it benefits me. Today, I need the car. I don't put the Millers' address into the satnav in case Oliver goes onto 'last destinations' and sees that I've been to Croydon. Instead, I plug my phone in and switch on Waze for directions.

I can't stop yawning as I navigate the streets of south London. I think about the pregnancy again and hope that I might be wrong. I haven't thrown up in the mornings, but all my other symptoms suggest I am expecting. I swerve the car slightly, causing a black cab to hoot at me. Is it terrible to hope I'm not pregnant? To hope that I am fighting off some virus or going down with the flu instead? I simply can't have another child. Not now.

The satnav on my phone is speaking to me constantly, so I have to concentrate, and I try to banish the thought. I'll deal with it later. And before long, I'm in the Millers' street, on the lookout for both a parking place and a machine to buy a parking ticket.

Alison's parents live in a beige pebble-dashed flat-fronted terraced house in a street that has become gentrified in recent years. Their house is the one that stands out, with paint peeling on the grey front door and weeds snaking up the large bins in the small front yard. There is a low brick wall that runs along the length of the row of houses, dividing each home from the pavement. Number 17's wall is the only one that hasn't been painted. The grout is tinged with moss, and the bricks are flaking. I sit in the car, staring at the house. It looks sad and unkempt.

A taxi pulls up in front of the house, and David gets out. He's wearing a navy blue woollen coat and looks like he's going to work in the City. He wipes the drizzle from his glasses and peers around, so I get out of the car.

'I'm here,' I say, giving him an awkward wave before

locking the car, checking my parking ticket is clearly on display, and walking towards him.

'Thanks for coming,' he says.

I follow him up the short path to the front door. He presses a doorbell, but there's no sound, so after waiting a couple of moments, he raps on the door with his knuckles. I see the shadow of a person through the opaque window in the front door, and then it opens with a creak.

I'm shocked, but I try not to show it. Alison's mother looks many decades older. She must be the same age as Mum, but there is no similarity. Her hair is white and thinning, with the pale pink of her scalp shining through. Her face is lined with wrinkles. She's clearly made an effort with putting on makeup, but powder has settled in the creases of her face, and coral-coloured lipstick bleeds into the fine lines around her lips.

'Come in,' she says. 'Sorry about the mess. And sorry about my husband,' she whispers. 'He's not himself anymore.'

I glance at David, whose face gives nothing away. We follow Mrs Miller into the dark hallway with its old-fashioned patterned carpet in reds and oranges. It's hot and stuffy with the bitter odour of burned dust, as if an electric heater has been turned up to full and the windows never opened.

'We'll sit in the front room,' she says, pushing open the door on the left. There's a grey-haired man seated on an upright chair with a brown rug over his lap, staring out of the window. He frowns as he turns to look at us.

'Who are you?' he asks. His eyes are watery. Mr Miller looks like an old man, withered somehow. He has tried to shave, but missed tufts at the side of his chin.

'Harold, it's that man from the telly who's looking

for our Alison. And this is her friend. I told you they were coming.'

'No, you didn't,' he says flatly.

She turns to us. 'Sorry about my husband. He doesn't remember things. He's got early-onset dementia.'

'I heard you!' he bellows. 'Stop telling bloody lies about me!'

'There, there,' she says, patting his mottled hand.

'Do you want to have a seat?' she asks, waving at the small brown two-seater sofa. David and I settle into it. It's snug for two people. I try to shift to one side.

'Can I get you a cuppa or something?'

'I'm fine, thanks,' I say.

'Thank you, Mrs Miller, but I don't need anything either,' David says. He tilts his head and smiles at her. He's obviously used to this, intruding on people's grief to extract information. I don't know if his sympathetic manner makes me like him more or resent him.

'In which case, how can I help you?' Mrs Miller sits on the matching chair to her husband's.

'On the phone, you mentioned that I could have a look through Alison's photo albums.'

'Yes. I got them out. We've left our Alison's bedroom exactly as it was, because if she comes home, then we want her to recognise it. It's why we can't move, even though the house is becoming a bit much for me, having to do everything all alone. Just think how awful it would be if she comes back here to find us gone, and some strangers living in her home.'

'Comes back?' David asks.

'I'm not going to believe my little girl is dead until it's proven.' Tears well in her eyes.

'Who's dead?' Mr Miller bellows.

'No one, dear.'

She puts her hand in front of her mouth and whispers, 'Half the time he's forgotten what's happened to Alison, so I just tell him she's at university. He was so proud when she got offered that place. The first member of our family to do a degree.' She swipes at a tear that drips down her cheek.

I remember the dignified man who carried his daughter's belongings so lovingly to the car and feel deeply sad that the past decade has had such a devastating effect on him. 'Is this too much for you both?' I ask Mrs Miller. 'We don't want to dredge up bad memories.'

'It's all I think about. And if you can find out the truth, then that's what you must do. I can't go to my grave without knowing. Without knowing what that monster did with my girl and where she is. You'll find out the truth, won't you?' She leans forward, towards David.

'I'll do everything I can,' he says.

She nods and briefly closes her eyes. Then she stands up and walks to the back of the room. It feels small in here, with its dark furniture and the greying net curtains that keep out the sunlight.

'This is what you wanted,' Mrs Miller says, placing two photograph albums on the wooden coffee table in front of us. 'We didn't have enough money for Alison to have one of those fancy phones, so she used Harold's old camera. And those disposable ones.'

I remember that now, how Alison used an ancient Kodak camera with film, and on nights out, she was never without a disposable camera. I went with her to Boots once when she collected her photos; we laughed at the poor quality pictures she'd taken during a student party.

David picks the top album up. It's made from shiny

black cardboard and has transparent films between each page. He turns to the first page.

Mrs Miller leans towards us. 'There she is on her first day at university. Oh, we were so proud of her. She had her own room in that hall of residence. Very nice, too, it was.'

I remember Mum and I standing in an identical room just a bit further down the corridor. Alison and I met during that first week, and I was so thrilled that a girl as outgoing as Alison chose to be my friend. It seems almost impossible to think she was this couple's offspring.

David flicks through the album quite quickly. 'I'm most interested in Alison's friends during her last year. Are they in the other album?' He puts down the first one and picks up the second.

'Yes, dear. She had lots of friends. She always did. And plenty of suitors, too.'

'What were Alison's interests at uni?' he asks.

'She did all sorts of things, didn't she?' Mrs Miller directs the question to me.

'Yes,' I say. 'She was a member of the photography club, and she did debating and musical theatre, although she didn't take that very seriously.'

'She was forever going to exhibitions in museums, wasn't she?' Mrs Miller says.

'Yes. The History of Art department was small, and there was a whole programme of activities out of teaching hours. We visited exhibitions in museums and galleries, National Trust properties, and we attended auctions from time to time.'

'Did all the students in your year go?' David asks.

'No. Most of the trips weren't obligatory, but Alison and I went on many of them. Visiting museums was a novelty for Alison and me, and it was especially important for her, as she wanted to pursue a career in the antiquities.'

'And these trips, were they led by your tutors?'

'Yes.'

'We never had the sort of money to take her to see art and fancy stuff,' Mrs Miller says. 'But she had a good eye, didn't she?'

I smile sadly at the older woman. She has every right to be proud of her daughter. Alison was an exceptional girl.

'Did she ever tell you the story of how she became interested in antiques?' Mrs Miller asks, gazing out of the window. I shake my head.

'She was a little girl. Nine or ten, I suppose. She used to walk home from school and one day, she found this little opal ring. I told her that she couldn't keep it, and she and I went down to the local police station to hand it in. They said they didn't think it was worth much, but they'd hang on to it for twenty-eight days. If the owner didn't come forwards, then it would be hers. She counted down the days, and on the twenty-ninth day, off we trotted to the police station. They gave it to her. A week later, she'd lost it. She shed so many tears over that damned ring. She started getting interested in old things after that. And then that Josh gave her a fancy pair of opal earrings for her birthday. I told her they were bad luck, but she said that was nonsense. She should have listened to me.' Mrs Miller puts a hand over her mouth and turns away from us. It makes me feel terrible. We shouldn't be putting the woman through this, forcing her to revisit painful memories.

David opens the second album. It's about two-thirds full, and he starts at the back. The first picture is of Josh and Rahul. They have their arms around each other and are each holding pint glasses in their free hands.

'Can't look at that evil boy,' Mrs Miller says, turning her head away.

'That's Josh and Rahul,' I murmur. I have this ridiculous urge to run my fingers over Rahul's photograph. He was such a beautiful boy, with those soulful dark eyes.

'Rahul?' David queries.

'He was Josh's best friend.' It all floods back. I don't tell them that I had a one-night stand with him, and if I hadn't, perhaps Alison would be here today. 'Rahul was studying law, and he took a subsidiary in history of art.' I wonder what he is doing now, whether he succumbed to family pressure and became a lawyer as his parents wished, or if he broke free.

'And Josh, what was he studying?' David asks. Mrs Miller shivers.

'Law, like Rahul. We didn't have any lectures with him. I can't remember how Alison and Josh met. At a party, I think.'

As we flick through the photos, I identify the people I recognise, and David takes photos of the photos with his phone, writing down people's names in a little lined notebook. There is a delightful photo of Alison. She's standing in a park, next to a statue of a man holding an outstretched sword. She's smiling, looking happy with rosy cheeks, wearing those opal earrings and a short but pretty dress that I don't recognise.

'Where was this taken?' David asks.

I shrug. He shows the photo to Mrs Miller.

'I don't know. A lovely photograph, though,' she says wistfully.

'Did the police look through these photo albums?' David asks.

'They went through everything. I can't complain

about the police. They were thorough. It's not their fault they didn't find anything.'

David and I catch each other's eyes. He raises an eyebrow.

I gasp aloud at the next photo and immediately apologise. It's of Alison in a graduation gown, her arms out wide, jumping up into the air.

'What? Why is she in a graduation gown?' I stumble over my words.

'She was that excited about graduating; we rented her gown ahead of time. My mother was in an old people's home, and Alison wanted to visit her in the gown. Mother died a week after Alison went missing.'

'I'm so sorry,' I say, feeling as if I've been punched in the gut.

'Are you still in touch with any of the people in these photos?' David asks me.

I shake my head.

'None?' He frowns.

'It was a hard time for me, and then I got married and had a child. My life took a different direction to those of my friends.'

That's the other thing I try not to remember. By the beginning of the next academic year, when most of my friends had started their first jobs or taken up their places in further education, it became public knowledge that Oliver and I were an item. Oliver was worried about how his colleagues might react, but it seems they were sanguine. He hadn't broken any rules by getting engaged to a student, as I was no longer a student, and our relationship started only once I had graduated. Naively, perhaps, I thought that my friends might be impressed, a little envious even, that I'd settled down so quickly, that I was marrying such a successful, debonair man. Without fail, reactions were the opposite. I was dropped from friendship groups like a hot brick.

David asks a few more questions, and Mrs Miller says how grateful she was that I boxed up Alison's belongings, and that they've kept her bedroom exactly as it was when she last slept here, and that only the police have been through her things. 'Would you like to have a look?' she asks David.

'If that's not too intrusive,' he says.

I glance at Mr Miller, but his eyes are closed, and he is snoring gently with his mouth open.

'You can go too, love,' Mrs Miller says to me as she stands up and pats down her skirt.

'Thank you, but I'll let David go alone.' The thought of standing in Alison's room, rifling through her belongings, really does make me feel nauseous. I lean my head back on the sofa as I listen to their footsteps going up the stairs and the creaking on the landing above. Poor Alison. I had no idea she was looking forward to graduating so much. It makes me wonder how well I really knew my friend.

11

I get a 2:1. It's crazy. I'm sure I don't deserve a 2:1. I scraped by with all my work and crammed as much as I could for the exams. It must have been my dissertation that saved me, or rather, Alison's dissertation. And Oliver Siskin obviously marked me kindly. I had told Mum that I'd probably fail or at best scrape a third, so when I get a 2:1, she insists on coming to London for the ceremony. So I, along with all of my classmates, hire my gown and hat and sit through the long, boring ceremony where our names are read out and we shake hands with the dean. Mum wears her Sunday best and sits proudly in her allocated seat. Afterwards, she poses with me for the obligatory selfies.

It feels all wrong that we are celebrating. Our year group is small, and Alison's disappearance weighs heavily on all of us. Other departments have big celebratory parties. I think various groups of friends get together for pub crawls or nightclub visits, but no one invites me. And I'm glad they don't, because I would have said no. Mum takes me out for dinner to Café Rouge on Tottenham Court Road. It's full of tourists, and I'm happy to let her witter on about her cleaning business and how proud she is of me.

Mum wants me to return to Macclesfield with her, but I'm not ready to go home yet. I lie and tell her I've got a couple of interviews lined up, and I will have. I just haven't gotten around to it yet.

The nightmares start that first week of the summer holidays, the week of Josh's bail hearing. The vast majority of my friends have left London, off back-packing around Europe or the Far East, trying to squeeze in their last few weeks of freedom before starting work or commencing a master's or some other further studies. It's like I've been left behind, which in many ways, I suppose I have.

The bail hearing garners a maelstrom of media coverage. Josh is denied bail. You'd have thought that I would be pleased about that, but I am still struggling to imagine Josh killing Alison. Adam, Josh's flatmate, contacts me, and we meet for a drink. I quiz him, but it seems that he knows little more than me. Apparently, the other flatmate, Nick, returned only to sit his exams, and hasn't been seen around the university since. I don't blame him. Neither Nick or Adam had been in the flat that Friday night and had no desire to return. The problem with not knowing the detail is that your brain fills in the gaps with imaginary scenes and events. And my imagination has always been vivid.

I GO to see Oliver Siskin three days after graduation to say thank you and ask for a reference. His door is shut, and I'm rather hoping that he isn't in and I can get away with leaving him a note. I knock.

'Come in!'

I push the door open. He's sitting behind his desk,

his laptop open, a pile of books to his left. His study is small with a window behind him that has a view onto a courtyard below. He's wearing a short-sleeved shirt, open a button too low, the dark hairs on his chest curling upwards.

'Stephanie! How are you?' He looks genuinely delighted to see me, which throws me. I stand a few steps beyond the doorway, awkwardly.

'I just wanted to thank you for your help. I'm sure I didn't really deserve a 2:1.'

He laughs. 'Most students contest a grade when it's too low. You're not querying it for being too high, are you?'

'No, no,' I say hurriedly. 'I just–' Now I feel stupid. Why did I come and see him? He glances at his watch, and I wonder if he needs to be somewhere. I take a few steps backwards.

'Have you got time for a drink?' he asks.

'Um, yes,' I say, caught totally off guard.

'Good. Then you can share your plans with me. I find it hard when my students disappear into their futures without letting me know what they're hoping to do with their degrees.'

My mouth feels dry as I smile. He stands up, reaches for the cream-coloured linen jacket placed over his chair and walks towards me. I stand to one side as he opens the door.

'After you,' he says.

I control a shiver. His aftershave has both spicy and woody fragrances, combined with something musky, peppery almost. Whatever is in it sets my senses on fire. I could lose myself in his scent.

We walk in silence around the corner to a pub I've walked past a thousand times but have never been inside. 'What would you like to drink?' he asks as we approach the bar.

'A white wine,' I say.

'Do you want to grab a table whilst I order drinks?'

I find a table and sit down on an uncomfortable wooden chair. When Oliver walks over carrying two glasses of wine, I take my wallet out of my handbag.

'Put that away; it's my treat.'

'Thanks,' I say, relieved, as money is so tight.

I think back to the last time someone bought me a drink. Rahul. It seems like a lifetime ago. I was a different person then. I feel bad about him, but the timing just wasn't right. As much as I liked him, I wasn't in a good place for a relationship, and Rahul's constant attempts to try to see me, to talk to me, made me feel stifled and claustrophobic. It's strange how external circumstances can make you change so much. I would have done anything to be his girlfriend before.

'You look worried,' Oliver says as he places a hand gently on my wrist. It feels as if a jolt of electricity has sped up my arm, sending heat to all the wrong places. I sit back, then wonder if he thinks I'm rude. He's looking at me, a flicker of amusement on his lips as if he can read my filthy thoughts.

It's warm in here, and Oliver removes his jacket and places his forearms on the table. On the little finger of his left hand he's wearing a large, intricately carved gold ring with a purple amethyst in the centre, possibly a Russian antique. A beautiful old watch with a black leather strap sits on his slender wrist. He leans forwards and holds my gaze. If I thought Rahul gave me butter-flies, this is something else altogether. It's as if this man can see straight into my head, strip me of my clothes and make my body burn with desire. I take a sip of my wine to cool me down.

'What are your plans?'

'In the short term, or for the rest of my life?'

He smiles. 'Let's start with the short term.'

'I'm going to do a law conversion course, but I haven't got my funding sorted. I left it all too late and didn't fill in the right forms, so I'm having to defer until January. I just hope I can get sponsorship and/or a grant.'

'And between now and then?'

'I suppose I'll have to go home and get work in a bar or something.'

'That seems like an underutilisation of your brain.'

'What else can I do? I'm not actually qualified in anything.'

'And your roommate's murder, assuming that is what it is … how has that affected you?'

I blink hard to stop the tears. 'A lot. I'm having awful nightmares, and I just can't believe that Josh, who was my friend too, is a murderer. I'm looking over my shoulder all the time and find it hard to concentrate. It's pretty crap, actually.'

'I'm so sorry to hear that.' He glances upwards as if he's contemplating something. 'A legal career might be emotionally challenging.'

'You think the law will be too much for me?'

'No, I'm not saying that. But it isn't an easy route. Maybe you need to be gentler to yourself for a while. You've been through so much. I will always remember that first interview I had with you, how impressed I was with your maturity, considering what life had thrown at you.'

I'm surprised he's remembered, but I don't want his pity, so I do what I'm best at and ask him a question. 'What about you? What do you do during your summers?'

He leans back in his chair and stretches his long legs forwards and places his hands behind his neck. 'The glorious summers! Most of the time, I have my head in books and furiously write research papers. I go for long walks and stay with friends in the countryside. Occasionally, I'll go on holiday, but it's not much fun travelling alone.'

'You don't have a partner?' The words slip out before I remember the impropriety of asking my tutor such a question.

He smiles but doesn't reply. I take another slow sip of my wine.

'I've had an idea,' he says, leaning forwards. 'Would you like to do a few weeks of research for me? I can't pay you much, pocket money only, really, but it could be good for your CV. What do you think?'

'Really?' I exclaim. 'You're not just being nice to me?'

He laughs. 'I'm not known for being nice. I assure you, the offer is self-serving. I'm writing a book and could do with as much help as I can get.'

I don't need a second to think this through. 'If you're sure, then the answer is yes. I'd love to!'

THAT FIRST DAY of working for Oliver is the beginning of the rest of my life, and I don't need hindsight to realise it. He has rearranged his office so that my desk is directly opposite his. It's a sensible configuration of the room, other than every time I look up, he is gazing at me, his eyes soft and his lips slightly apart. It is so unsettling. I am reading through research papers to precis them for his research. I ask him to explain the concept of *instituent praxis,* and he gets up and walks around the side of my desk so that he is leaning over me as we peer at the computer screen.

His face is just centimetres from mine, and it feels as if the air has been sucked from my body. We are so close, it's as if we're being drawn nearer and nearer, his breath tickling my cheek.

'*Praxis* is just the practice, as opposed to the theory, and in this case–' And then the phone rings. I'm not sure if I'm relieved or disappointed. Oliver throws me a strange look, stands up and answers the phone.

A few hours later, we are packing away our books.

'Would you like to have a drink?'

'Is it alright for a student to socialise with her tutor?' I ask, tilting my head and flirting slightly. I am wearing a lightweight summer dress that has a deep V-neck that reveals my modest cleavage. I can hear Alison speaking. *Go for it, girl! You've got nothing to lose.*

'Fortunately for me, you're no longer my student, and as two consenting adults, we can do whatever we like.'

'And what *would* you like?' I ask. As soon as I say that, I can't believe those words slipped from my lips, and I blush furiously.

He smiles then and stands up. I do the same, but our eyes are fixed on each other's. And then he is in front of me and pulling me into his arms and lowering his lips on mine, and I think I'm going to combust with desire.

'I'm sorry,' he says tenderly as he strokes my hair away from my face. 'You're so beautiful, I can't help myself.'

'I'm not!'

'Oh, little Stephanie. You have no idea what you do to a man.'

I don't know what to say. And I don't understand how this older, devastatingly handsome man could want me.

'Come on. We're going to go out for a drink.'

But I don't want a drink. I want this man, and as I realise how fleeting life is, and how I could be dead tomorrow, I make the first move. So very uncharacteristic. But this is the new me. The person who knows they need to live in the now and not think about the maybes.

I grab the waistband of his trousers and pull him towards me, standing on tiptoes as I mash my lips onto his. When we make love for the first time, his desk is our bed, yet neither of us notice how uncomfortable it is. All I know is that I want this man so badly, I didn't know the definition of longing before this moment.

'I can't believe we did that,' he says afterwards, leaning against the wall, trying to catch his breath. 'Believe me, I've never done anything like this before.'

'I haven't either,' I say, although of course I did, that one and only time with Rahul.

'Come back to my house. I'll make you supper,' Oliver says.

I don't question it. I don't pause to think that one irresponsible, carefree shag might signal the start of something that will literally change my life. I just go along with it, overjoyed that such a beautiful, erudite older man would choose to be with me.

Oliver lives in Parsons Green, a smart residential part of London between Fulham and Putney, with rows of terraced houses that have been gentrified. My heart is thumping as he opens the small wrought-iron gate and takes three steps up to his shiny black front door. The tiny front garden is well tended, and there's an ornamental tree neatly shaped into a ball.

He unlocks the door and swipes a fob over an alarm panel. 'Come in,' he says, an amused smile edging at his lips as he takes in my wide eyes.

I had assumed that a man in his early thirties living alone in London might have a stark, minimalist apartment, furnished with chrome and silver. Not so. I walk into the hallway, and my jaw opens. There are paintings covering all the walls in the hallway and more going up the stairs that climb up to the right. A modest-sized but intricately painted grandfather clock stands in the corner, ticking slower than my heart.

'The living room is in there,' he says, flinging his hand casually to the left. I glance inside; again there arc paintings hanging on the walls, mainly portraits in oils, many miniatures and small pictures of noblemen and women from centuries past. It's evident that Oliver's preference is eighteenth-century art. I glimpse three beautiful antique clocks on the mantelpiece in the living room and a faceted sparkling red glass vase filled with white flowers on the ottoman-style coffee table. There are books stuffed into the built-in book-cases either side of the period fireplace, many of them antique-looking, with beautiful coloured leather spines and gold embossed writing. This is so very obviously the home of a collector, someone who understands and appreciates beautiful artefacts. It's without doubt the most grown-up place I've ever set foot in.

I follow him into the kitchen, which opens out onto a bijou garden at the back. The kitchen has wooden cupboards, but judging by the shelves full of cookery books and the well-stocked spice rack and the gleaming knives magnetically affixed to the wall, this kitchen is owned by someone who loves cooking.

'Have a seat,' Oliver says, pointing to the small wooden table and chairs. He flings open the door to the small garden outside. 'What do you fancy? Vegetable risotto or pesto linguine?' As I'm not sure what linguine is, I opt for the risotto.

He uncorks a bottle of red wine and takes two

sparkling glasses from a cupboard. I listen as the wine glug-glugs into the glasses.

'You do drink red wine, beautiful Stephanie, don't you?' he asks, handing one to me.

'Yes, thank you.'

He raises his glass. 'To you, your magnificent future, and the hope that I may play a small part in it.'

I don't know how to respond, so I take a large sip of wine. It's smooth and delicious.

'I'm going to make supper, but why don't you have a wander around?'

With my glass in hand, I walk slowly around Oliver's home, the fingers of my right hand trailing across intricately carved sculptures, paintings that become more eclectic in style upstairs, where there are three bedrooms, all with built-in wardrobes, and a bathroom. The master bedroom is the largest room, and there are piles of books on both sides of the neatly made bed and auction catalogues on the floor. I sit down on the bed, on what is obviously Oliver's side, where on his bedside table there is a small travel clock in a brown leather case, a miniature photograph of an elderly woman and some earphones neatly curled up. I lower my head to inhale his scent from the pillow, and I wish he would come upstairs right now.

Back downstairs, I find another small room that he has turned into a study, lining all four walls with books. He has framed his certificates, with his PhD certificate taking centre space. Dr Oliver Lucas Siskin, PhD. I feel like an interloper here, as if I'm a child who has arrived in a strange, adult world.

I jump as his arms encircle me from behind, his lips nuzzling my neck. 'First we eat,' he says huskily.

That first night, I will myself to stay awake all night, knowing that this may well be the best night of my whole life. I feel so alive, so special, so in awe of this extraordinary man who knows exactly how to stimulate both my brain and every single nerve ending of my body.

I assume that day will be a one-off, but it isn't. Oliver just expects me to stay, to be with him day and night, and I'm certainly not going to object. Everything about him impresses me, from his delightful home to the way he turns simple, basic ingredients into a culinary masterpiece, to how he makes my brain frazzle as we discuss philosophical and legal concepts the likes of which I'd never considered before.

And then, of course, there is what he does to my body. Within days, I am utterly smitten, and to my amazement, it seems like it is reciprocated. I ask him about the ring on his little finger that he never takes off, and he just says it was given to him by his grandmother, and then he kisses me, stopping me from asking further questions.

The only thing that ruins my utopia is the nightmares.

On the third night at Oliver's, there is yet another sinister ending to my dream. While Josh is standing in front of me, holding the blood-dripping knife, a faceless male figure appears behind me. 'You're a traitor,' he says. 'You're a traitor.'

'Stephanie, you're dreaming!'

I am sitting up in bed, Oliver's arms around me. He is stroking my back and my forehead and placing gentle kisses on my shoulders.

'You had a nightmare, darling,' he says.

'I'm sorry.' I am trembling, goosebumps covering my damp skin. 'I have these awful nightmares.'

'Tell me about them,' he says, running his fingers along my arm.

'I can't. I don't remember them when I wake up.' But I do. I remember every single little detail, and I'm desperate to shake them out of my head.

'You called out Alison's name.'

'Yes,' I say.

'Are you sure you won't tell me about them?'

'They'll go away,' I say.

But they don't.

The days become regular. I don't have the nightmare every night, but they come often enough that they make me scared of falling asleep. Those first few weeks, I am so tired, yet I try very hard not to share the extent of my exhaustion with Oliver. I want to be young and carefree. Our days fall into a regular pattern. We make love in the mornings, and then Oliver brings me tea in bed. By 10 am we are at the university. Sometimes I go alone to the library to research a list of topics that Oliver gives me; other times we're together in his study. He is always focused on work, and that first abandoned sex on the desk is never repeated. When his colleagues pop their heads around the door or we run into them in the corridors, he just introduces me as his ex-pupil assisting with some research. I daren't push for any more. In the third week of our relationship, Oliver drives me in his little British racing green open-topped Mazda MX5 to an Italian restaurant somewhere in Surrey. It's quiet, being in the middle of the summer holidays. By now, I have learned the Italian cookery terms and am more adventurous in my menu choices. Oliver looks at me approvingly and then reaches across the table for my hands.

'There's no point in you continuing to rent your flat in the Barbican. Why don't you relinquish the lease early, perhaps sublet it for the next few weeks if you can? Move in with me.'

'Are you sure?' I ask him, still finding it hard to

believe that he wants to be with me as much as I want to be with him.

He just raises an eyebrow with that stomach-tingling expression he throws me when I say something a bit stupid. I can't stop grinning. I'm ecstatic.

The last weekend in July, Oliver has to go away to attend an auction with a friend. I take the opportunity to return home to Mum for a few days. I don't tell Mum about Oliver because I know she wouldn't approve of me living with my tutor.

'Are you sure you don't want to stay at home?' Mum says. 'London must be such a scary place for you.'

'It's not, and I want to be there. Besides, I'm enjoying my job.' I look away from her so she can't see my cheeks reddening.

I pine for Oliver, and the nightmares seem even more vivid when I wake up in the middle of the night alone. Mum finds me shivering in the kitchen at 2 am, my face wet with tears.

'You've had so much loss for someone so young,' she says, enveloping me in her arms. 'I'm sorry, darling.' When we peel away from each other, she makes me a hot chocolate. 'I think you should see that therapist again, Sonya Partridge. It's totally normal to be feeling grief and fear. She can help you through it.'

'I'll think about it,' I say.

The reunion with Oliver is passionate, and I know for sure that I've fallen in love. Not that I ever use the L word. I'm not that stupid. Whilst this might be the real deal for me, and perhaps he thinks it is for him too right now, I'm afraid Oliver will cast me aside for a new student when the academic year resumes in October. I am dreading it.

August passes in a similar way, yet despite the routine, it is never boring.

In early September, on the third morning in a row that I've gotten out of bed and promptly thrown up, I assume I've got some weird bug, but it's Oliver who sets me right.

'I think you might be pregnant,' he says, sitting on the end of the bed.

'What!' I exclaim. I am twenty-three years old and jobless. 'No! That's not possible. We've been using condoms.'

Oliver glances away from me and bunches up the duvet between his fingers.

'That first night here, the condom split.'

I explode. 'What? Why the fuck didn't you tell me?'

'Because I didn't want to worry you. Because it was so magical, and I never thought for one moment that you'd get pregnant just like that. Anyway, we're jumping to conclusions here.'

'I can't believe you didn't tell me. I can't have a baby. I just can't!'

He edges up the bed and puts his arms around me. 'Don't stress. Let's get a pregnancy test before jumping to any conclusions.' He kisses me on the forehead and stands up.

I stare at him. He looks happy. Surely he can't *want* this to happen?

'I'll go to the chemist now,' he says. 'Stay here and have some breakfast. I'll be back as soon as I can.' He almost dances out of the room.

I lie in bed and stare at the ceiling, tears spilling down my cheeks. He's a thirty-something-year-old man. Isn't it me who's meant to be the young, carefree irresponsible student? That's why a male pill would be a bloody stupid idea. At least we women take responsibility for our own bodies. I knew I should have gone on the pill, but I had no reason to before. It's not like I had a long-term boyfriend. If I'm pregnant, I'll be one of those young, single mothers clawing my way through life, trying to make up for a stupid mistake.

And why does Oliver seem happy, excited even? I would have thought he'd be horrified. Yes, we've had an amazing, passionate few weeks, but I'm too young to settle down. Much too young.

He's back before I'm dressed. He hands me the pregnancy kit box, and I walk to the bathroom, turning to shut the door, but he has his hand on it.

'What are you doing?'

'I want to know the result at the same time as you.'

And so we sit there together, waiting for the three minutes to be up, and when the two lines show in the little window, I stare at it in dismay. I suppose I'll have to have an abortion, and the very thought of that fills me with horror, but then again, the alternative is equally appalling. My dreams will be out of the window, and I'll be struggling on benefits, stuck at home with a baby, any chance of having relationships dashed because I'll be a downtrodden, good-for-nothing single mother.

'Why the long face?' Oliver asks. He then throws his arms around me and kisses me hard on the mouth.

'I thought you'd be horrified,' I say eventually, realising I don't know this man very well at all.

'I'm over the moon! I've always wanted a family.'

'But with me?' I ask. I catch a glimpse of myself in the mirror. I look dreadful with bed hair, wearing a pale pink T-shirt that barely covers my buttocks. And I look so young.

'Of course with you.'

I want to say, *But you've never even told me that you love me; I know so little about you.* But I just stare at him. His eyes are lit up, his teeth white as he smiles widely. He looks like someone who has just been told they've won the lottery. And then he gets down on one knee and grabs my hand, right there in the bathroom, wedged between the toilet and the sink.

'Stephanie Harriet Lucas, will you do me the honour of being my wife?'

On the way back from Croydon, I stop off at the massive Tesco in New Malden. I head straight to the chemist section and buy a pregnancy testing kit. There's a kernel of dread in my chest that should be a kernel of joy. Carefully concealing the box in my handbag, I slip into the ladies' toilets. I know this is something I should be doing at home; it's almost seedy waiting for the results in a public toilet. But I don't want Oliver to know. Not yet. Just in case he takes the rubbish out and sees the stick. It seems less of a deception if I do the test away from home. I know it's stupid. And I don't know why I want to keep it from him.

Adjacent loos flush three times whilst I wait. And then I force myself to look at it.

I'm pregnant.

I suppose in my heart of hearts, I knew. I drop the stick into the bin and shut my eyes. How the hell am I going to manage with three children? I want to sob, but that seems such a betrayal of this new life growing inside me, and of my husband.

Perhaps I could get rid of it. It's such early days …

but no. I'm not sure I could do that, and besides, Oliver would be utterly horrified. He'll want this child, even if it means we have to scrimp and save even more with another mouth to feed. The real reason I don't want another baby is purely selfish. It means I'll have to put all of my dreams of being a lawyer on hold yet again. I can't possibly finish my studies and start a solicitor training contract with a newborn baby to look after. Even if I felt I could, Oliver wouldn't let me. He's old-fashioned in things like that.

I leave the toilets and grab a trolley. I might as well do a shop now I'm here, but I walk around like an automaton.

'Stephanie!'

I turn around with a start and drop the bag of pasta I was holding. I never come to this supermarket. I don't know anyone who lives around here.

'Sorry! Didn't mean to make you jump.'

It's Nahla Madaki. She's another tutor in the History of Art department, an upcoming, bright light with a razor-sharp mind, according to Oliver. She's also strikingly beautiful.

'How are you? We haven't seen you at any of the department events lately,' she says, beaming at me.

I'm not aware there were any department events to which other halves had been invited. Would Oliver have gone without me?

'Busy, busy,' I say, with forced joviality.

'And how are those gorgeous children of yours?'

'Growing up too quickly. They're both at school now.'

'Leaves you a bit of time to visit museums, hopefully?'

I laugh. 'If only.'

'The only time I get to go is on official university

trips.' She rolls her eyes. 'Although I am hoping to visit a new exhibition at the British Museum. It's hush-hush at the moment, but there's a collection from an archaeological dig of Anglo Saxon artifacts from a top-secret site in Cambridgeshire, and I'm hoping to get a preview. You should see if Oliver can take you.'

I smile noncommittally.

'Talking about digs, it's awful about that poor girl who went missing all those years ago. I gather a TV researcher is digging around.'

I frown. 'Yes. How did you know?'

'He came in to talk to Professor Grimstead, and Oliver told me that he had been to talk to both of you. It must be very distressing. Before my time, of course.'

I'm shocked that Oliver shared this with Nahla. He seemed so shut off to any discussion of Alison. And then I wonder: Are Nahla and Oliver closer than they should be? He works long hours, and a lot of the time, I don't know where he is or whom he is with. It would be possible. And it's not like I provide him with much intellectual discourse these days.

'Are you sure you're okay, Stephanie? You look very pale.'

'Yes, yes. Just a bit under the weather.'

'Well, it's lovely to see you. You must stop by the department or join us on one of our trips. Oliver is so good at securing us private viewings. But knowing Oliver, he'll be too modest to tell you what he gets up to. Actually, why don't we meet up for a coffee sometime? It would be lovely to chat.' She takes out her mobile phone. 'What's your number?'

I give it to her, and she immediately dials my phone. 'Now you've got my number. Excuse me, I must be off. I've got a lecture to give this afternoon. But let's meet up soon!'

And then she's gone, and I'm left standing in the dried goods aisle, wondering how much I know about my husband's life. I can't imagine she's having an affair with Oliver if she's inviting me to drop in on them. In fact, why the hell am I even thinking that way? It's not like Oliver has given me any reason to doubt him. We still make love, and he's a caring husband. I place my hand on my stomach. I suppose all these unsettling thoughts are thanks to the hormones. But it reminds me of how reluctant Oliver has always been to talk about his love life.

I was about seven months pregnant, and Bea was proving to be a hectic baby, hiccupping in the womb. We were lying together on top of the bed, and Oliver had his hand on my belly, trying to feel the baby inside me.

'Tell me about your ex-girlfriends,' I said.

'No.'

'Oh, come on. I want to know about your past.'

'My past is my past. You are my present and my future, and that's all I want to talk about.'

'So when are you going to introduce me to your friends and family? You never talk about your family.'

'I don't have any.'

'Everyone has family. Were you adopted?'

'No.'

'So you had family.'

He sighed. 'My parents died in a car crash when I was three years old. I was brought up by my grandmother.'

It sent a jolt through me, reminding me of the crash that Leroy and I were in. Despite our differences, we have so much in common, Oliver and I. 'I'm sorry,' I murmured.

'Grandma never lost her British accent. She moved to Canada when she married my grandfather and brought up her children as true Canadians. My mother was an actress, not very successful by all accounts. My father was her manager, and my grandparents didn't approve of the union. I don't remember my parents at all.'

'That's awful.'

'When I was twelve, Granddad passed away, and Grandma couldn't cope. You can't blame her, really; she'd lost her daughter and her husband, and there I was, a precocious boy turning into a young adult who considered her an interfering old woman. She took the decision to send me to boarding school in the UK.'

'Were you terribly homesick?' I squeezed his hand, trying to imagine how very alone he must have felt.

'No. I got a new home, here in the UK.'

'What do you mean?'

'William and I shared a dorm, and he was assigned to look after me, the foreign boy who spoke English with a strange accent. We quickly became best friends. His parents agreed to become my guardians in England, and I would go back to their house during exeats, half-terms and some holidays, too. It was expensive sending me to school in England, and although Grandma wanted me to return to Canada more often, she couldn't afford the airfares. I would go back for six weeks every summer. By the time I was in the sixth form, I knew that I wouldn't return to Canada. I felt truly English by then, the Canadian accent discarded. I got a place at Oxford to read history of art, and the rest is history.'

'And your grandmother?'

'She passed away when I was twenty-three. Thanks to her inheritance, I was able to buy this house; I was able to pursue a career in academia and carry on researching the subject I love. I am sad I didn't get to know my family better, but William's parents were much more like parents to me.'

'And you have no siblings or cousins?'

'No siblings. I have some cousins, but I wouldn't recognise them if they crossed the street in front of me. Now you know why family is so important to me, Steph. I didn't have a proper one. My role model was William's family, the way his parents listened to their children, put their welfare before their own, were their greatest confidants and supporters. The boarding school thing felt at odds with their attitude, but they genuinely thought they were giving their three children the best education they could afford. I want to create the family I never had, and I am so grateful that you're going to be the mother to my six children.'

'What!' I exclaimed, sitting bolt upright in bed. 'Six children! No bloody way!'

'Calm down.' Oliver laughed, blowing raspberries on my back. 'Seriously though, I'm thinking three or four if we're really lucky.'

I harrumphed and lay back down on the bed. I needed to get this one out of my body before I could start thinking of any more. And what did my husband see me as? A breeding machine? I wanted a life, too.

And here I am, a decade later, in exactly the same position all over again.

BACK AT HOME, I unpack the groceries and make myself a cup of tea. I feel distracted and uneasy, my mind flitting back to thoughts of Alison. I pull out my books and laptop, but I can't concentrate; besides, it'll soon be time to collect the kids from school. There's the sound of post being shoved through our letterbox, which seems to come later and later these days. I walk to the front door and pick up the pile. It's mainly flyers, something from the bank for Oliver, an auction house catalogue also for him, and then a typed envelope addressed to me. I frown as I put the post on the hall table and open the ordinary white envelope. I take out the single sheet of copier paper. There is a sentence typed out in the middle of the page, all in capital letters.

I KNOW WHAT YOU DID.

What the hell?

What on earth does that mean? I haven't done anything. What's this relating to? I let Alison down and I stole her dissertation, but I didn't kill her. Or perhaps it's not about Alison at all. Just because I met up with David and the Millers earlier doesn't mean everything is about her. Or perhaps it's not meant for me. Maybe this is meant for Oliver. I turn over the envelope to double-check, but it's very clearly addressed to me. Mrs Stephanie Siskin.

What else could I have done? I might have snubbed some mums at school, but I just can't think of anything in the past few months or years. It has to be something from longer ago. There's the dissertation and not being there for Alison. And then I go back to that year before university. The year of the accident.

Leroy was my first boyfriend. He had recently got his first car, a battered ten-year-old Golf, which he drove around like a lunatic. We did everything together, and most of my school friends predicted that we'd marry. Leroy and I talked about it. We tried to imagine what our children would look like. Would they have his dark skin with my auburn hair? He hoped so.

That day, we had given ourselves the afternoon off from A Level revision. We were going out to meet friends, and we were planning our summer holidays, that glorious summer before university. I assumed we'd be going away together, so I was shocked when he announced that he and a couple of his mates were going to Marbella for a fortnight. We had an almighty argument, and neither of us were concentrating on the road; neither of us registered the van that was weaving from side to side as it approached us. They told us it was a miracle that we survived, and I suppose it was. I was in hospital for weeks. He was too, but in a different hospital. And then I discovered that he didn't want anything to do with me, that he blamed me for the accident, blamed me for ruining his life. If I hadn't kicked up such a fuss about that holiday with the lads, he would have sat his A Levels and have gone to Oxford; he would have become a scientist. Instead, he became a paraplegic who refused to have anything to do with me, even though the accident was the fault of the van driver who was three times over the drink-drive limit. I heard via old school friends that Leroy and his family moved back to the Caribbean a couple of years later. The climate was better for him. A mutual friend got me his new address, and I wrote to him, but I never heard back.

So it's no surprise that I prepare myself for the worst, that I have nightmares, that I have spent the last decade trying very hard not to be fearful, and that I married a man who promised to care for me, much like a father figure. What I don't understand is the note. In relation to Alison, I didn't do anything really bad. Could it be about Leroy? But if so, why wait all these years? No, it just doesn't make any sense.

This is too much. My head feels as if it's about to explode, and I need to speak to Mum.

We used to live in Macclesfield. Dad came from Cheshire, and after meeting on a holiday campsite, Mum moved from her family home near Worthing to be with him. Macclesfield is where I grew up, where I still call home. You can just about hear the faint accent, especially when I'm tired.

When Dad died, it was such a shock. He and Mum were everything to each other. They'd tried for kids for years and had given up all hope when I came along. I was their adored only child, and although we lived modest lives, our house was filled with love. Dad was a builder; a good, honest trade, he used to say. I don't know exactly what happened the day he died. Mum never told me, and I didn't want to know the gory detail, but there was a lot of talk about corporate manslaughter. That's what got me interested in the law. And then, when I was seventeen and was in that awful car accident and I had all of that time to think, I became fired up with self-righteousness, deciding that justice needed to be sought for every wrongdoing. I was going to become a lawyer. Mum was so proud of me.

Nowadays Mum lives in Barnes, in a one-bedroom ground-floor apartment with a tiny courtyard garden. She moved to be nearer to us shortly after we got married. After that first visit to us in London, we spoke often on the phone. She made it perfectly clear that she thought I was too young to marry, and there was no need to get married just because I was pregnant. I told her I loved Oliver and it was what I wanted.

It's ironic, really. Most mothers would have wanted their daughter to be with someone like Oliver: older, with a secure job, intelligent, interesting and good looking. But not Mum. She said that just because Dad had died when I was young, and I'd lost Leroy, didn't mean that I needed to marry a father figure. She's never actually said that she doesn't like my Oliver; she's much too polite for that. But I know that, at some level, she doesn't approve. Of course, it's not him per se that she has an issue with. It's the fact that I gave up my dreams in order to be with him. And that's why she's supporting me now, in my little lie.

Oliver wasn't impressed when I told him that Mum was moving to London to be nearer to me. I suppose he had coped for so many years without any close family, he didn't understand. Mum and I only had each other. But it's all worked out fine. Everyone is cordial, and I still have Mum to hand when I need her. And today, I need her.

She has had a hard life. After Dad died, Mum had to reinvent herself. She took every job there was going to make ends meet, and after a couple of years, she set up her own cleaning company. By the time she left Macclesfield to move to London, she had twenty ladies on her books who cleaned for her and a business with a healthy turnover. She sold the company and our house. And she also has what she calls her rainy-day fund, the money she got as a payout after Dad's death. But, of course, your money doesn't go far in London, and particularly somewhere that is lovely, with a village feel, like Barnes. But Mum decided to choose location over space. I'm sure she could have afforded to buy somewhere bigger, but she's modest. And when you've suffered as she has, you squirrel away as much as you can for a rainy day.

These days, she works mornings in a little convenience store, mainly stocking the shelves or helping out on the tills. She enjoys it because she gets to meet people, and there's a sense of comradery. I know she misses her Macclesfield friends and the ladies who used to work with her. For me, it's the ideal setup, as she's often free to collect the kids from school or help make their tea. And now I've taken up my studies again, she's bending over backwards to make life easier for me. She's collecting the kids today and again on Friday. Oliver does Wednesdays whenever he can, as he finishes work early. Today, I'm glad I'll have the chance for a chat with Mum.

They come storming into the house shortly before 4 pm, and I'm so happy to see them, squeezing both Bea and Sam extra tightly. Sam wriggles away, and Bea throws me a strange look and announces she needs to work on her geography project. It seems ridiculous to me that an eight-year-old has to do homework, but then, I'm hardly an expert on primary school education.

Mum takes her coat off and hangs it in the hallway. She walks into the kitchen and puts the kettle on, then she turns around and peers at me. 'What's wrong?'

'What do you mean?' I frown, trying to deflect the question. That's the thing with Mum and me. We see straight through each other's facades.

'Are you sick?' she asks. She walks towards me and places the back of her hand against my temple.

'No, I'm fine.'

Mum puts her hands on her hips and gives me her knowing stare.

'I'm pregnant,' I say, and sit down on a kitchen chair with a thump.

'Oh.' Her reaction is an honest one. 'Not planned, I assume?'

'No. I don't know how I'm going to cope.' I bite my bottom lip.

'What does Oliver think?'

'He doesn't know. I don't want to tell him yet.'

Mum raises an eyebrow. 'Why not?'

I shrug my shoulders.

'So many secrets, Steph. Is everything okay with your marriage? You know I'll support you come what may.'

'Yes,' I snap. 'It's just I won't be able to carry on with my studies, and I'd so wanted to do that.'

'Why don't I come and live with you for a few weeks after the baby is born, and afterwards I'll be your nanny for the first year? Then you won't have to give up your studies.'

'Oh, Mum, I can't ask you to do that. There's barely enough space for the four of us in this house, let alone with you and a new baby. And you need a life. Not to be chained to my kids.'

'That's nonsense. There's nothing I'd love more. Bea and Sam can share, I'll have Sam's room, and the baby will be in your room or mine. Think about it.'

I place a kiss on her cheek.

The next few hours pass by in a typical frenzy of teatime, bath time, bedtime and a tasteless pasta that I eat with Oliver.

'I ran into Nahla Madaki today in Tesco's,' I say. Immediately I regret it. I hope Oliver won't ask which branch. I watch his face for any reaction, but detect nothing other than half-hearted surprise.

'Oh?' He carries on eating.

'She mentioned that she hadn't seen me at any of the department socials. I didn't know you had any.'

'I tend not to go. I'd rather come home and be with you and the kids, or spend time with William. But if you want to attend one, then I'll take you. Trust me, you'll regret it.'

I wonder. Do I want to go to one? Do I want to see Oliver and Nahla together so I can study their body language and evaluate how they look at each other? I tell myself I'm being ridiculous. Just because he has an attractive colleague with whom he shares confidences doesn't mean that he's having an affair. I have no reason to suspect Oliver of anything other than being a good husband and father.

After I have cleaned up from supper, I go upstairs and have an early bath. I'm fast asleep by the time Oliver comes to bed.

I scream and sit bolt upright.

'What's the matter?' Oliver switches the light on.

My heart is pounding so hard, and I'm covered in a layer of sweat. I try to calm myself with some deep breaths and lean forwards, hugging my knees. Oliver rubs my back.

'The nightmare again?' he asks.

I nod. It was the same dream, the same corridor, with blood all over Alison, and Josh coming closer and closer towards me. But then I heard a voice behind me. A male voice repeating over and over, *'I know what you did, I know what you did!'* The voice sounded sometimes like Oliver's, and sometimes like David Green's. I turned and ran towards the faceless voice, and then I woke up. Terrified.

'It's because we let that bloody man into our house. That researcher,' Oliver says.

I look at my bedside clock. It's 3.14 am. I swing my legs out of bed. 'Sorry to have woken you. Go back to sleep. I'm going to make myself a cup of tea and will tiptoe back to bed.'

'Are you sure you're alright?' Oliver asks. 'I can make you feel better.'

'Go to sleep.' Sex is the last thing I feel like. I stand up, grab my dressing gown and walk out of the room.

I hid the anonymous note in a classic French recipe book. I'm not sure why, and now I think it would be better if I just show it to Oliver. He knows that I blame myself for not contacting Alison the night of her disappearance. But I've never told him that I stole much of Alison's dissertation. He will undoubtedly be disappointed, as he values academic excellence above everything else, but I regret it, and it was done during an awful period of my life. And he knows about Leroy and the guilt I feel about the accident. I make up my mind as

I pour myself a glass of water from the kitchen tap. I will have to show Oliver the note, as other than Leroy's accident and Alison's disappearance, I genuinely can't think of anything that I've done to warrant receiving it. So the only thing I haven't shared with anyone, not even my former therapist, is passing off Alison's dissertation as my own work. I can't believe anyone would have found out about it – and why now, all these years later? It just doesn't make sense that a stolen dissertation would warrant that note.

I sleep fitfully, slipping back into those old patterns of dreading sleep, in case the nightmare comes again. When the alarm clock goes, I have a pounding headache; my limbs ache and feel too heavy to move. I have burning nerve pain down my right-hand calf.

'You look rough,' Oliver says. 'Did you get any sleep?'

'Not much.'

'Stay in bed. I'll get the kids ready and take them to school. It doesn't matter if I'm late in this morning.'

'Are you sure?' I rub his bare back. Mum once gave Oliver a pair of pyjamas from Marks and Spencer for Christmas. Oliver is not a pyjama type of man.

'Yes. I'll get Bea to bring you a cup of tea and a piece of toast.'

'Thanks, darling,' I say as I watch him stride to the bathroom. He is such a loving man. Today I feel particularly grateful to have married him, and particularly guilty to be keeping my pregnancy and studies from him. If I'm feeling better tonight, we can have a heart-to-heart, and I'll share everything, including the note.

By midday, I've slept again for a couple of hours and awaken feeling considerably better. I have a shower and then pad downstairs. I switch on my laptop and check my emails. I don't get many; they're largely spam or the occasional email from the children's primary school. But today, I get a notification from Facebook that I have a friend request. A friend request from Rahul. My heart pounds as I click on his picture.

He looks exactly the same, actually more handsome, if anything. He has filled out somewhat, and his hair is shorter. It suits him. But why is he contacting me now?

I hesitate. Am I being disloyal to my lovely husband by accepting his request? No. It's not as if I'm looking to have an affair or to rekindle lost love. What a joke. I'm pregnant with my third child. So I press accept. And within seconds, he sends me a message.

'Hi Steph, How are you? I've been contacted by the researcher David Green. I assume you have too. It's brought back lots of memories.'

I have to admit that I'm a little disappointed that he's only got back in touch because of David Green. It would have bolstered my ego so much more if he had contacted me just because. But that's a sentiment I can never share. Just thinking it makes me feel guilty.

I want to know more about Rahul and his life before responding. I look through his Facebook profile, but he doesn't post much. I can't tell if he's married or in a relationship. I go onto LinkedIn and see that he's head of the art department at a comprehensive school in Leicester. That fits. I bet he's a brilliant teacher. He's using his love of art, and hopefully his family approves of him being in a profession, even if he isn't a doctor or a lawyer. I bet all the sixth formers swoon over him, and I wonder if there are more pupils taking art as a result. Good for him.

I message back, rewriting my words a couple of times. *'I'm well, thanks. Still living in London. Married, two kids. You?'*

'I heard on the grapevine that you married Oliver Siskin,

and I found you on Facebook. Congrats. I'm still single. A teacher now. Have you spoken with that researcher?'

Rahul is modest. He could easily have said *I'm head of the art department at a large school.* I need to focus on my response.

'Yes. He came to see us. And you?'

'Not yet. Guess he wants to pick your legal brains.'

I don't correct him; I don't tell him that I never actually became a lawyer. There's a pause for a moment whilst I think of something else to say. And then another message comes through from him.

'Hope to see you one of these days. Take care. Rx'

And then he's gone, and I feel ridiculously bereft.

I can't stop thinking about him and Josh. I was so successful in pushing Rahul away that I never gave him the chance to truly discuss Josh's conviction. That was wrong, because Rahul knew Josh better than I did. Over the years, I have come to accept that Josh's conviction was solid, but perhaps my suspicions were right in the first place. If Rahul had doubts, and perhaps David Green does too, maybe Josh was wrongly convicted. I think of that young man, so slender, so earnest, now in jail for murder. His life is over. When he's eventually let out, his best years will be long gone.

I wonder if David will be visiting Josh in jail to get his side of the story. I assume he must be, and perhaps he's already been. It's a shame the television cameras won't be allowed to interview Josh for the programme, but it would make a mockery of the justice system if prisoners were given a voice outside of the courts.

When I'm walking to the kids' school, one of those prison transport vans drives past, a white van with two very small windows on the side with bars across. It's not an uncommon sight along these London streets, but for the first time, it prompts an idea. I stop dead on the pavement, and a young man walks straight into me. He curses under his breath.

If David can visit Josh in prison, then why can't I?

Blood rushes to my head. Could I? Is it even possible, and if so, would I have the guts? I carry on walking to school, but the more I think about it, the more I want to look Josh in the eyes and ask him whether on that Saturday afternoon when we were looking for Alison, was he really the concerned boyfriend, or was it all a charade, making him the finest actor I have ever met?

'Mummy, are you listening?' Bea asks, squeezing my hand on our walk home.

'I'm sorry, darling, I was miles away.' I've made my decision, though, so I can concentrate on my children now. To hell with what anyone else thinks. I'm going to go find out which prison Josh is being held in, and I'm going to go and visit.

13

A quick online search brings up all of the articles about Josh's trial and sentence, along with reams of debate as to whether proving guilt beyond all reasonable doubt can ever be satisfied when a body has not been found. Assuming he hasn't been moved to another location, various newspaper articles state that Josh is being held at Wandsworth Prison. A wash of sadness settles over me. He's been incarcerated all of these years just a few miles away from us, whilst we've been living our happy and easy middle-class existence.

The process of booking a visit is much simpler than I had imagined, and just two days later, I am making my way to Wandsworth. No one, except the prison personnel and Josh, knows where I'm going.

I arrive in the reception area. It's busy, and the uniformed woman behind the desk tells me to take a number from a ticketing machine attached to the wall. I sit down on a hard chair, waiting for my number to be called. I glance cautiously at the other people waiting. They represent a microcosm of society: different ethnici-

ties and ages, people from all walks of life. I'm wearing
jeans and an old jumper, minimal make-up, and my hair
is tied back in a loose ponytail. Hopefully, I don't stand
out as a prison-visiting virgin. I don't have to wait too
long for my number to be called. When it is, I jump up. I
hand over my confirmation email, my passport and
driver's licence, and then I'm told to put my belongings
in a locker. There are rows of them on the far wall. I
place my handbag, along with my mobile phone, inside
and lock the locker. It makes me feel vulnerable already.

After going through a security area, much like the
scanners used in airports, I'm then directed into a
waiting room, again similar to at an airport. The only
difference here are the prison wardens patrolling with
sniffer dogs, two beautiful German shepherds. I guess I
wouldn't think they were so gorgeous if I had contra-
band stuffed down my trousers.

The visitors room isn't what I expected. It is more
modern and airy and somehow a little less scary than
the exterior of this massive gothic building might
suggest. The prisoners are already in the room, seated at
low tables. It takes me a few long moments to locate
Josh, and if he wasn't waving at me, I'm not sure I
would recognise him.

The change in his appearance is shocking. The puny
young man, with a softness about him, has vanished. He
has broadened out and hardened. His neck is all sinewy,
his biceps visible through his prison clothing. Both
hands are covered in tattoos, with one snaking up the
side of his neck. I hope the shock doesn't show on my
face.

'It's good to see you,' I say as I sit down. A kernel of
fear cramps my stomach.

'Yeah. Why are you here?'

'I wanted to see you.'

'I've been here for nearly ten years and you come now. Why?'

'I wish I'd visited sooner. I'm sorry, Josh.'

'I suppose you thought I did it, just like everyone else. You didn't want to be tarnished with knowing a convicted murderer.'

I look down at my lap. He's right, of course.

'You're married now?'

He's staring at the rings on my left hand.

'Yes,' I say. 'I'm sorry I didn't visit you before.'

He shrugs his shoulders. 'I didn't do it, Steph.'

'I wish I'd looked you in the eyes back then and asked you whether you did it,' I say.

'You can do it now.' He stares at me, and I shift uncomfortably, wishing he'd look away.

'Did you kill Alison?' I ask eventually. I have to sit on my hands to stop them shaking.

He holds my gaze, but then his eyes well up and his lips quiver, and I see a flash of the old Josh. 'No, I didn't do it, Steph. I loved Ali. I would never hurt her.'

'That weekend when we were looking for her–' I say.

'I was genuinely worried. I was set up, Steph. They always accuse the boyfriend or the husband, don't they? I was the fall guy.' He rubs his eyes with the back of his hand. 'Fuck it. None of the old crowd have bothered to visit me in prison. The only people who come are my mum and my sister. Everyone else dumped me.'

'I'm sorry to hear that.' I'm not surprised, though. 'I had a message from Rahul a few days ago. The first time since we left uni.'

'Mmm,' Josh mutters. 'He doesn't count.'

I don't know what Josh means by that and am about to ask him when he carries on talking. 'It was all lies what they said at the trial. You must have known that.'

'I didn't attend. I'm sorry, I couldn't. It was all too much.'

He nods, his shoulders humped forwards. Of course I had wanted to attend, but the trial was just a week after I gave birth to Bea. I was sleep deprived, haunted by that nightmare, and both Oliver and Mum were adamant that it was out of the question that I could leave my baby and sit in a Crown Court for days. I asked Oliver to go on my behalf, but the trial lasted for over a week and he had to work, so I never really knew what was said. With hindsight, I think I had a lucky escape by not attending. It would have been so harrowing.

'She was going to dump me. Didn't she tell you?'

'What?' I frown. I thought Alison and Josh were in love.

'She'd told me that she wanted to split up, and I was trying to persuade her to change her mind. Something had happened to her, and I just needed to know what had changed. I asked her if she'd met someone else, but she said no. I agreed to give her a bit of time to think things through, but I had every confidence that we'd end up together. We were soulmates, and she knew it as much as I did. I loved Ali, and I would never, ever have hurt her. The prosecution built up this ridiculous case that I killed her in revenge for her finishing with me. Of course I was upset, but I would never have laid a finger on her. I'm not the violent type. At least I wasn't before I got locked up in here.'

'Why didn't you tell me that she wanted to break up when we were looking for her?'

'Because it was a blip. I was trying to change her mind.'

'Did you and Alison have a fight the weekend before she disappeared?' I remember now how she came home after that weekend away, locking herself in her bedroom and refusing to talk to me.

'What?'

'You both went away for a steamy weekend. She had an overnight bag and wore her skimpy black dress.'

'The last time Ali and I went away for a weekend was the previous autumn. Neither of us had money to go away somewhere fancy.'

We're both silent.

'So if she didn't go with you, who was she with?'

Josh shrugs his shoulders. 'She was seeing someone else. Didn't you know? I've had nothing else to think about these past years. Saint Alison clearly wasn't the good girl who everyone, including me, assumed she was.'

We're both silent for a few moments. So that was what Alison wanted to tell me. But why didn't the police investigate that further. Or perhaps they did, but I just wasn't made aware of it.

'I think I saw him once,' Josh says. I stare at him. 'About three or four weeks before she went missing.'

'Where and when?'

'It was near the Barbican. She got out of some little sports car. The man got out, too. They talked for a couple of minutes, and then she turned away and started walking towards your building, going home. I didn't get a particularly good look at him, and I certainly didn't recognise him. To be honest, I was more curious as to why Alison had been in a stranger's car than questioning who she'd been with. We had a massive fight over it. She said she'd met up with a contact of her dad's, some solicitor, but I'm not sure I believed her. All the same, we kissed and made up. To be honest, I forgot all about it until she went missing.'

'What did Alison's father say?'

'He didn't have any contacts in the legal profession. It's only with hindsight that I realise she was acting odd those last few weeks. Then, a few days before she disappeared, she told me she wanted to split up, and I asked her if she'd met someone else. She promised she hadn't, but it was obviously a lie. The police didn't believe me.'

'What did the man in the car look like?' I ask.

'Dark hair, wearing sunglasses. Normal looking. Older than us.'

'Anything else? Did you talk to him?'

'Nah. I was in too much of a hurry to catch up with Ali.'

'What was his car?'

'A dark-coloured convertible, a two-seater.'

I swallow hard and grip the edge of the seat of my chair.

'I walked right past him as he was sitting in the car with the roof down. He was looking at something on his phone, I think. The only thing I remember was he was wearing a fancy ring. He pushed the sunglasses up on his nose, and the ring caught the sunlight. It was flashy, too big for a man to wear, I thought. I told the police that, and my legal team. The bloody police thought I was trying to throw them off the scent. They didn't listen to a word I was saying.'

I feel as if someone has just punched me in the throat. My hand rushes up to my neck, and I can feel the blood draining from my face. I have to get a grip, pretend that I'm coughing.

'Steph, what's the matter?' Josh leans forwards towards me. I catch the eye of a prison guard who is staring at Josh.

'Sorry. Sorry,' I say. 'Do you remember anything else about the ring? Was there a stone in it?'

He stares up at the ceiling. 'I've tried not to think

about it over the past years, but yes. There was a purple stone in it. Might have been pink, but I think it was purple. Why?'

I feel nauseous and dizzy.

Josh raises his voice. 'What's the matter, Steph? Do you know who it was? Who the man was?'

'No. Sorry, I just wondered … No.'

Josh narrows his eyes at me and stares. 'You're not telling me the truth, are you? Did you know what Alison was doing?'

'No, it's not that. I didn't know.'

I try to be still, but it's impossible. My breathing is shallow, and my hands are trembling.

'Do you know who the man is?' He glares at me. 'Spit it out, Stephanie.'

'I don't know. Really, I don't.' I dig my fingernails into the palms of my hands, all the while trying to banish the image of my husband wearing that dreadful ring, driving his little green Mazda sports car.

'If you think you know who she was seeing, you've got to tell me!' Josh leans right across the table. It scares me.

'I'm sorry, Josh, I shouldn't have come.' I stand up.

'No! Talk to me, Steph. Please!'

A guard walks towards our table. I turn and start walking towards the exit.

'If you know something, you need to tell the police, Steph!' he shouts as I leave.

The background hum of voices quietens. I sense lots of eyes on me. My heart feels as if it's going to pound out of my body, but I continue striding towards the door. I would like to look back at Josh, but I don't.

By the time I've collected my belongings and walked back to my car, I am trembling all over, swallowing bile to stop myself from throwing up. I try to get a grip; I really do. First, I am making an assumption that it was Oliver driving that car. Surely he can't have been the only man in London with dark hair owning a signet ring with an amethyst at its centre and driving a dark sports car … but who am I kidding? It probably was him.

Even so, they could have been together for a perfectly legitimate outing. Perhaps they had been to a museum or to a lecture in another university. But it seems very unlikely, especially as Oliver has maintained he didn't really know Alison. But most of all, even if Alison had been with Oliver, it doesn't mean he had anything to do with her disappearance. That is the most ridiculous notion. I take a few sips of water from a bottle stashed in the driver's door. Goodness knows how old it is, because it tastes warm and revolting. Then I start the engine and head towards home. All I want to do is curl up in bed and fall asleep, preferably a dreamless sleep. I deeply regret going to the prison.

Back at home, I haven't got time to go to bed, because I need to prepare tea for the kids. Then, as it's a Thursday and not Mum's pickup day, I have to collect them from school. I open the door to our house and pick up the mail, walking into the kitchen. I make myself a black coffee that tastes bitter and unpleasant and burns the top of my mouth. Then I sink down onto a chair and open the post.

Most of it is junk mail, but the last envelope is identical to the previous one I received. It is neatly typed with my name and address and a first-class stamp, postmarked London. My hands are shaking as I open it. Again, out comes a single sheet of copier paper. It's longer this time, but once more, the sentences are typed out in capital letters.

WHY ARE YOU RAKING UP THE PAST? IF YOU KNOW WHAT IS GOOD FOR YOU, LEAVE THE PAST

ALONE. NO MORE TALKING TO TV RESEARCHERS. DO YOU UNDERSTAND???

I KNOW WHAT YOU DID.

I drop the piece of paper. This is all getting too much. Who is sending these notes, and why? Are these letters real threats? Should I go to the police? And what does this person mean, *I know what you did*? I wonder now if Oliver has known all along about the dissertation. Perhaps he recognised segments of it as Alison's work, but if so, he's never mentioned it. But it's ridiculous to think that he would be sending me notes. I know he doesn't want me to talk to David, but Oliver loves me. He wants to protect me. What else have I done that's bad? At least I now know it's relating to Alison's disappearance and nothing else in my past, but why is this anonymous person so eager to stop me from talking to David Green?

And then I think about Josh. He must have been describing Oliver. I think about that ring. Oliver used to wear it all the time when we were first together, but I haven't seen it in ages. I wonder if he's still got it. Am I even remembering it correctly? He has so many rings in his collection now.

I wonder if I should tell David Green about the notes; after all, they're specifically telling me not to talk to him. But then I dismiss the idea. David calls himself a researcher, but he is fundamentally a journalist, and if he gets a hint that someone has something to hide, it'll make him dig even further. And what will the outcome be for me? My head is in a turmoil.

I pace around our kitchen. I take the vacuum cleaner out and furiously vacuum the floor, even though it doesn't really need doing. Just when I decide I need to show Oliver the notes, the phone rings.

It's Anya, the mother of Lily, Bea's best friend.

'Sorry to dump on you at the last minute, but is there any possibility that you could collect Lily from school and have her at yours until about 6 pm? I've had an emergency at work.'

This isn't Anya's first work emergency, and no doubt won't be her last, but as she is a doctor, when she speaks of an emergency, it really is one.

'Of course, no problem.'

'Thanks, hon. I owe you.'

For the next few hours, I don't have the time to dwell on the note or the prison visit. I have to look after the kids, break up a fight between Bea and Sam and prepare supper for Oliver and me. Oliver arrives home just as Anya turns up. One of the downsides of having such a good-looking husband is that all my friends gaze at Oliver with wide eyes. It used to make me feel insecure, but these days, I just smile and count my blessings that I have a husband whom I still find attractive.

'Lovely to see you,' Anya says, placing a kiss on Oliver's cheek. 'We need to get a date in the diary for you two to come over for supper.'

Anya often says that, but it rarely happens. It's normally me who does the entertaining, although our only regular get-togethers are with William and Naomi. I mustn't be harsh on Anya; she's a GP and a mother.

After the kids are in bed, and we've eaten a mediocre chicken stew, I put my cutlery down and turn to Oliver.

'I've got something I need to tell you.'

He raises his eyebrows. I walk over to the counter where I've hidden the two anonymous letters underneath a pile of weekend newspapers that we haven't got around to reading.

'I've received these in the post.' I hand them to him.

Oliver's eyes widen, and he murmurs under his breath, 'What the hell!'

'Do you know who could have sent them?' I watch his face carefully, and I am positive that he is as shocked as I was.

'Absolutely no idea. Who even knows that you spoke to the researcher?'

'Everyone he's spoken to and all my old friends. It could be anyone. I've even had messages on Facebook from uni friends who I haven't heard from since I left. He's been in touch with them.'

'Someone who doesn't want you digging. And what does it mean, *I know what you did*?'

'I don't know,' I say, turning my back to him so he doesn't see my cheeks redden. 'I didn't do anything except be a lousy friend and not call Alison when she wanted to speak to me.'

'Oh, Stephanie, we've discussed that a million times. It is not your fault. But this is exactly why I don't want you to have anything to do with that journalist. Come here.'

He stands up and opens his arms, and although I don't want my husband anywhere near me, I let him hug me, let him stroke my back and then place a gentle kiss on my forehead. All the while, I wonder what he is hiding from me, whether these same arms once held Alison.

I CAN'T SLEEP. I keep on thinking about Josh and how he's changed, and how very desperate he seemed. If he was guilty, would he really have behaved like that when he saw my reaction to his description of the man with the ring? He was imploring me for help. But what about the blood found in his flat? Surely the police wouldn't have got that wrong. Although he looks thuggish now, I still saw the old Josh, the gentle, quiet, unassuming boy.

The person who remembers an amethyst ring. I want to see the ring. It won't prove anything, whether Oliver still has it or not, but it would at least confirm my memory. I listen to Oliver's regular breathing. He is lying on his back, and every so often the air catches at the back of his throat and he makes a little rasping noise. Carefully, I lift the duvet away and slip my legs out of my side of the bed. I sit for a moment. I don't need to look inside the safe now. I could do it tomorrow or any time that Oliver is out of the house. But I know that I won't sleep unless I can be sure of the answer. Does Oliver still have that ring?

I turn to look at him, the faint orange glow of the streetlight outside casting shadows through the closed curtains in our bedroom. He is good to me, is this man. Surely he wouldn't have been involved with Alison without telling me? Oliver cares for me and the children; we're never wanting for anything. I put my hand over my flat stomach. And I know for sure that he won't feel any dismay about having a third child, or worry about the extra financial pressure it will put on us. He will be thrilled. But that doesn't mean I don't want to know about the ring or that I don't care about the true nature of his relationship with Alison.

I slip my feet into my furry slippers and lift yesterday's sweater off the chair, slipping it on over my nightdress. I use my phone as a torch and tiptoe out of our bedroom, not quite closing the door in case the catch wakes him.

I walk downstairs and into Oliver's study, switching on the desk lamp rather than the overhead lights. He has a built-in bookcase and cupboards along the smaller wall. We had been married a few months before I realised that there was a substantial safe built into the cupboard. I had walked in on him one day when he had the safe door open. He seemed surprised that I didn't know about it, but how could I have done, when he hadn't showed it to me? It's much bigger than a typical home safe, and I suspect it's designed for offices, able to house lots of lever arch files and cash boxes. Oliver keeps his collections inside it.

'It's for insurance purposes,' he told me. 'Makes me feel confident that if, God forbid, the house should burn down, there'd be some hope of saving our valuables.'

I don't know how much they're insured for. I've never asked. But he suggested I keep my passport inside it, and asked if I had anything else I wanted to keep safe. The answer was no. I own nothing of any financial worth except the emerald engagement ring that Oliver gave me, and jewellery he has given me for birthday presents over the years. He had changed the code that day, to the date that we had our first kiss. 050712. I thought it was ridiculously romantic.

I open the outer wooden door that hides the safe. I haven't looked in here for a couple of years, probably when I had to last update my passport. I punch in the code. Nothing happens. I do it again. I can't believe that Oliver has changed it. When did he do that, and why? And why didn't he tell me? My passport is inside and the kids'; what if we needed to get them when he was out of the house and couldn't be reached?

I try for the third time, because it is the middle of the night and I may not be reacting rationally. But no. It stays closed. I lean back against his desk and think. What codes would he use? I try all of our birthdays, our wedding anniversary, the digits he uses on his phone, which apparently belong to an old phone number. Nothing works.

Shit. I should probably just switch the light off and go to bed. I'll have to come up with some reason why I need to get hold of my passport. Here I am, all these years later, just about to reach out for the career I dreamed of. But no, we're having another child. I rub my eyes and yawn. I need to go back to bed.

Then I think about the other people who were important in his life. The parents who died when he was a child. His grandmother. He loved her. I can remember her birthday because it's the same day as my father's, but what was the year? I make a few more attempts, and then, to my relief, the lock clicks back, and I open the door.

Oliver has rearranged the contents. I am shocked that there is so much stuff in here now, boxes piled on top of boxes and a small painting leaning against the back wall. I remove some of the boxes in front of it and gently take the painting out of the safe. It's beautiful, in an ordinary wooden frame; an ethereal oil painting of a woman with dark ringlets wearing clothes from the nineteenth century. No wonder we never have any money. Oliver's been purchasing all of these items at auction. I know he spends a lot of time with William, and they buy things, and from time to time, he shows me the signet rings he's bought to add to his collection. But there are way more things here than he has shown me. It irks that he's spending money on his art, leaving me to scrimp and save on clothes for myself and the children. I've brought it up a couple of times, but he tells me that collecting is like investing in stocks and shares, without the income from dividends. Oliver's rationale – that the more the collection grows, the more money we'll have for a rainy day or to help the children get onto the housing ladder – is hard to disagree with. But it reminds me that it's the amethyst ring I need to look for.

I open up box after box, but I don't recognise half of these rings and assume he's never even worn them.

Perhaps they're too valuable and the insurance only covers them if they're kept securely in the safe. It isn't until I open the very last box, the one shoved away at the back of the cupboard, that I find the gold ring with the amethyst in its centre. I gasp. It's exactly how I remember it, and exactly as Josh described it. I take the ring out of the box and I recall how it caught the light when he stood in that big lecture hall and how I stared at it that first day he kissed me.

I have little doubt now that it was Oliver whom Josh saw with Alison, but what were they doing? Was Oliver her new lover, the man she was leaving Josh for? Was she going to tell me about her affair with our tutor?

I let out a quiet moan. That can't be right. Oliver would have told me. He's consistently said that he knew Alison in a capacity as her tutor and nothing more. I suppose that, strictly speaking, he wasn't allowed to date a student, but why would he have kept the relationship from me after she disappeared? It doesn't make sense. I shut the lid of the box and place it back inside the safe.

My legs are cramping, so I stand up for a moment. Then I sense something behind me.

I turn around.

Oliver is standing in the doorway, naked except for his boxer shorts, his eyes narrowed as he stares at me.

14

'What are you doing?' Oliver asks.

I open and close my mouth, unable to speak. For the first time in our marriage, I feel scared. I can't work out if I'm scared of the answer Oliver is going to give me, or if I'm scared of his reaction. Perhaps a bit of both. He takes a step towards me.

'What are you doing in my study in the safe in the middle of the night?'

'Looking for one of your rings.' Then the words tumble off my tongue. 'Were you dating Alison?'

Oliver's mouth falls open, his eyes darken, and he crosses his arms in front of his chest. 'What the hell? What I want to know is how you got into the safe and why you're doing this at three o'clock in the morning?'

He is trying to deflect my question. His defensive body language emboldens me, and I feel a surge of anger.

'Did you sleep with Alison? You need to tell me!'

'I don't have sex with my students.'

'Not now. But before we were together, were you with Alison?' My voice is raised now, because I can tell he's lying. He is scratching his head, and his eyes avoid mine.

'You'll wake the children up. Keep your voice down!' he says in a furious whisper.

'Then tell me the truth.'

'I wasn't seeing Alison. I wasn't seeing anyone, and you're being absolutely ridiculous. It's the middle of the night, and God knows what's got into your head. Did you have the nightmare again? Is it becoming more real? If so, perhaps we need to get you to the doctor for some help. You could have CBT again.'

'Stop patronising me, Oliver. There's nothing wrong with my head. There never has been. All I'm trying to do is get to the truth.'

'Have you been talking to that researcher again?' he asks.

I've had enough. He's clearly not going to tell me what I want to know, and I don't want to tell him an outright lie.

'I'm going back to bed,' I say, trembling as I wrap my arms around myself and squeeze past him to go out of the door.

I snuggle under the duvet, but I can't get warm, and the shivering takes ages to stop. There's no doubt that Oliver is hiding things from me. Even if he didn't have anything to do with Alison, he still changed the code for the safe without telling me. I wait for him to come back to bed, listening out for his footsteps on the stairs, but he doesn't return. Should I go back downstairs and try to have a calm conversation with him? I think back to the times we've had fights. They're rare. Oliver doesn't like direct confrontation.

And then I think of all of those rings and the painting and wonder how much he's spent on acquiring such loot. He is so careful with money, making me keep spreadsheets on our outgoings, telling me that regrettably, he won't be able to afford to give our children a private education like he had had. I had laughed about that. Attending the local comprehensive hadn't done me any harm; I managed to get into a good university. Our only major disagreements had been around me pursuing my legal qualifications and practising as a solicitor. He was adamant I should put my career on hold until the children have left home and no longer need me. What a ridiculously old-fashioned idea. I want to achieve my dreams and firmly believe I can do both. Or at least I thought I could until I discovered I'm pregnant again. I wonder what he's doing downstairs. I glance at the clock every so often, and the hours tick by. I suppose I fall asleep eventually, because I'm awakened by the sound of the shower running next door. Exhaustion pins down my limbs, and for a moment, I consider asking Oliver to do the morning school run. But then I remember last night, and I force myself out of bed. I have time before I need to get the kids up, so I sit for a while on the edge of the bed, my head in my hands. The sound of running water stops, and I look up as Oliver pads into our bedroom, a towel wrapped around his thin hips, his hair mussed up from the shower.

'We need to talk,' he says, looking sheepish. He looks tired too, with rings under his eyes and a grey tinge to his face where he needs to shave. I stare at him, wondering if my world is about to disintegrate.

'I did have a fling with Alison,' he says.

I gulp. He looks away.

'It was short-lived, and Alison and I agreed never to tell anyone because it would have jeopardised my position in the department. It was a mistake, Steph. A nothing. You know how strict they are about condemning relationships between students and staff. That's why our relationship was fine, because it happened after you graduated.'

'When?' My voice sounds croaky. 'When were you seeing Alison?'

'A few weeks before she went missing.'

He then walks around the bed so he's directly in front of me, and he gets down on his knees and grasps my hands in his. He stares at me with those beautiful eyes and pulls my hands to his damp chest. 'I love you, Stephanie. I should have told you about this years ago, when we first got together, but I didn't. And the longer I didn't tell you, the bigger the lie became until I couldn't tell you. Please, my darling, forgive me. I would never do anything to hurt you. I realise that this will feel like a betrayal.' He releases my hands and lays his right palm over my cheek, his eyes boring into mine, his lips slightly open in a lopsided smile. He knows exactly how to look at me to make my insides melt.

But no. This is too important. I pull back from him. I can't decipher if the expression on my husband's face is anger or contrition. It all happens too quickly.

'You withheld information in a murder investigation!' I say.

He shakes his head as he stands up. 'No, I didn't. I told the police about my fling with Alison, and as I had a solid alibi and wasn't a suspect in any way, it was decided that the information didn't need to become public knowledge. What good would it have done other than destroy my career?'

'Did you know that Alison had a boyfriend?'

'As I told you, darling, it was a one-off. A quick fling that meant nothing. I regretted it straight away. I didn't have any real chemistry with her, not like it is between you and me. It was a flash in the pan, the result of too much alcohol, and immediately forgotten. You've also got to understand that girls were flinging themselves at me all the time. I was young, their tutor, and I liked the attention. I have a strong libido. You know that.' He cups my right breast, and I push his hand away. How can he touch me when he's talking about shagging the girls who came before?

'And do you still sleep with your students on the side?' I sneer.

'I am married. I wear a wedding ring.' He holds out his left hand to display the gold band that he hasn't taken off since our wedding day. 'And I have a beautiful wife who gives me everything I need. I meant it when I said I would never cheat on you, Stephanie. I love you.'

I can't look at him now. This handsome man, my husband. Nothing makes sense – although perhaps it does make perfect sense. Alison was stunning and clever and kind and gregarious. Of course Oliver would have wanted to sleep with her.

'You can see why no one must know, can't you?' Oliver stands straight and tightens the towel around his waist. 'God forbid that researcher chap finds out. It would reflect so badly on me, just at the time when I'm about to be made head of department. The whole world would know that Oliver Siskin took advantage of his students. My career would be destroyed.'

'Is that why you don't want to have anything to do with Daniel Green? In case he discovers that you had a fling with Alison before she died?'

'Of course!' he says, an edge of exasperation to his voice. 'So long as the police know the truth, which they do, it's no one else's business. You get that, don't you, darling?'

I glance at the alarm clock. If I don't get the children up now, we're going to be late for school. I will have to continue this conversation with Oliver later. I stand up and walk towards the wardrobe.

'Steph.' Oliver grabs my hand. I keep my back to him. 'Darling, I'm so sorry I lied to you. It wasn't my intention. You will forgive me, won't you?' He tugs me, and I stumble slightly, and then his arms are around me, and his lips are on mine, his fingers slipping under my nightdress.

'Not now,' I say, pushing him away. 'I need to get the children up.'

Oliver is overly bright at breakfast, jostling with Sam, laughing at Bea. He is trying too hard, and I see right through it. I look at this man and see a stranger. If he could keep such a big thing from me, what else has he lied about? Why did he change the code on the safe, and why is there so much stuff in it? We haven't even touched on that. His revelation has changed everything. Although he says that it was just a fling with Alison, I remember so distinctly her telling me that she was going to spend the weekend with the love of her life. Was that Oliver or Josh? Was Oliver with her that weekend before she died? But if the police have checked Oliver out, then my husband must be above suspicion.

I am screaming inside, because this is ridiculous. It's my husband I'm thinking about. Just because he had a one-night stand with Alison doesn't make him a suspect in her disappearance. If anything, it just confirms that original conviction. Josh found out that Alison had fallen for someone else, and, in a rage, killed the woman he loved.

'Can you chase the plumber?' Oliver asks me as he's putting his coat on to leave the house. 'The tap in the utility room is still dripping.'

I can't believe that he is thinking about a tap when he's just admitted that he was seeing Alison. How is it possible for him to compartmentalise his thoughts so neatly? I don't answer him.

'Love you all!' Oliver says as he leaves the house. He normally wishes us all a good day, but he never uses the word *love*.

After school drop-off, I hurry home. I have another essay to write, but it's almost impossible to concentrate. Mid-morning, Oliver sends me a text message saying, *'I'm sorry and I love you.'* I stare at it for a long time and don't reply. I think it's the first time he has ever written down that he loves me, and I can count on one hand the number of times he has said it out loud. I've learned that I don't need the affirmation, because actions definitely speak louder than words. I don't doubt that he does love me and the kids.

Then there's a ping on my phone, telling me I've received another message. I assume it's from Oliver, so it's a jolt when I realise it's from Rahul.

'I'm coming to London on Wednesday. Any chance we could meet for a coffee or lunch?'

I hesitate. Is it a good idea to meet with Rahul? Lovely Rahul, whom I pushed away. What would my life be like now if I had continued our relationship? I would never have got together with Oliver. I would probably be living with Rahul now in a little country cottage, or perhaps we would be in Leicester itself, a city I have never visited. I would certainly have a career and be helping people fight for justice. But I wouldn't have my beautiful children. I laugh at myself for being so fanciful, feeling a slither of guilt for having these thoughts.

Even so, it doesn't stop me from pulling up Rahul's Facebook profile again. Oliver's eyes are gorgeous, but they're cool and all-seeing. Rahul's dark eyes are soft and kind. If I meet with Rahul, I'll be able to ask him what he knew about Josh and Alison's relationship, and whether Josh changed at all in those last couple of weeks. I could tell him that I saw Josh in jail, and that he's not the same man now. Although I can't dismiss the luminol that showed up the blood in his flat, Josh's desperation was such that I truly believe he has been subjected to a miscarriage of justice. I need to share this with someone; otherwise I'm going to implode. Instinctively, I place my hand over my stomach. All this stress will be bad for the baby … Oliver's baby, that I'm not sure that I want.

I look at Rahul's Facebook photograph. It's in black-and-white, and I run my fingers over his face on my laptop screen. Ridiculous. Just because Oliver might have told me a lie doesn't mean I should be in touch with an ex-lover. But then again, I don't want to speak to Rahul to discuss our past; I want to talk to him about Josh and Alison, and he's the only person I can have a frank discussion with. And the only person I know for sure couldn't be implicated, because he was with me, in his single bed, the night that Alison disappeared.

Before I can change my mind, I write a reply.

'Yes, that's great. I'm free for a coffee. Where and when?'

'I'm going to be near Victoria Station. I'll message you the name of a cafe. 1.30 pm?'

I groan. By meeting Rahul, I know that I'm playing with fire. I'm already burned from my past and have no desire to be scorched again. Perhaps I'm just subconsciously trying to get my own back on Oliver for his lie. I have sufficient insight to realise that both Oliver and I are wounded from loss in our early years, and that's most likely a key factor that brought us together. We understand grief and the fact that there is no answer to the question, *Why did that happen to me?*

Another thing that I now realise is that we are both

good at hiding secrets. Rahul, however, as far as I can tell, is straight-talking and from a loving family. The last thing he needs in his life is me. Just because I said I'll meet him doesn't mean I have to go. I can always say something unexpected has cropped up.

15

Naomi calls me. 'I'm coming up to town tomorrow to view some items in William's next auction. Do you fancy having lunch? My shout.'

I know I'm meant to be studying, and have already agreed to a midday meeting with Rahul this week, but the way that I'm feeling at the moment, lunch with Naomi would be a welcome distraction. Of course, I also have to lie to Naomi and pretend that my days are whiled away cleaning the house and stocking up the fridge and doing my bit for the kids' school. I don't think Naomi has ever worked; with their wealth, she's never needed to. We agree to meet at William's auction house at noon.

Naomi always dresses up when she comes to London. It reminds me of Mum, who used to insist I wear my best clothes on the rare occasion we went to the theatre in Manchester. It's such an antiquated attitude and not something I would expect of Naomi. It's as if she's worried she might be photographed by paparazzi and therefore always has to look her best. I saw her dressing room once, and I've never seen anything like it. The whole space is lined with walnut wood cupboards and drawers, bespoke shoe compartments and sliding drawers that hold her handbags. She wears a lot of designer labels. I don't, and even if we had the money to spare, I wouldn't choose to. Each to their own. Even so, I put on a dress, a necklace and some long boots. If she's taking me somewhere for lunch, it's bound to be smart.

Most people have heard of the big London auction houses, the likes of Sotheby's, Christie's or Bonhams, where masterpieces by Picasso or unique evening dresses worn by Princess Diana are auctioned for many millions. I remember being amazed when Christie's sold Hockney's portrait for £37 million. But there are many, many other auction houses, ranging from the businesses that organise house clearances and sell off lots of items of low value, to the book, wine or jewellery specialist auctions. It's a massive market, and if you're not a collector, you're probably not that familiar with it. As I'm surrounded by collectors, I've picked up a fair bit of knowledge over the years.

De Villeneuve Auction House is based in Fulham, which is handy for Oliver, as it means he can regularly meet up with William. It was set up by William's father in the late '90s, specialising in musical instruments. By all accounts, it never did particularly well, because its major competitors were so well established in the marketplace, and trading valuable Stradivarius violins is a bit of a closed shop. Oliver described William's father's business as a passion project. He was a cellist, his wife a violinist, and William's sisters both sang, but weren't interested in the business. Unfortunately for William, he didn't inherit the musical gene, but business acumen is certainly one of his major strengths. The year William and Oliver went off to university, his parents announced they were going to close the business. William begged them to keep it going so that he could take it over, and they indulged him. Today, it is a highly successful auction house selling furniture, paintings and jewellery. How much of the De Villeneuves' wealth comes from William's success versus family money, I'm not sure, but I assume it's mainly down to William's business prowess. His parents, although they have a lovely house in Sussex with far-reaching views of the South Downs, don't live the life of luxury that William and Naomi do.

I've met them a handful of times, and they're an unassuming couple who spend much of the year travelling around the world. When they're in the UK, their hobby is to reunite items they have found on eBay or in auction houses to surviving relatives or the original owners. They might find a painting of a house and then track down the current owners of that house and give it to them. Or if they find a piece of jewellery engraved with a personal message, they'll try to ferret out the relatives of the original owner and give them the ring or necklace. According to Oliver, they have been doing these philanthropic acts for many decades, and it was what inspired both Oliver and William's love of antiques. Unlike William, who trades his antiquities for big bucks, his parents refuse to accept payment when they reunite items to their original owners, getting their buzz from making other people happy. I reckon the world would be a much kinder place if there were more people like the De Villeneuve seniors. I've often wondered what they think of their son's commercial success.

I walk into the entrance lobby of De Villeneuve

Auction House on the dot of noon, my brown leather crossbody handbag flung over the top of my beige rain-coat. There's a young woman sitting behind the glass reception desk, her blonde hair cascading down her back, her pretty face so caked with foundation that her skin looks plastic.

'Good morning, how can I help you?' she asks brightly.

'I'm here to meet Mrs De Villeneuve. Is she here already?'

'Let me find out for you.'

As she picks up the phone, William strides into the lobby and walks towards me, his arms wide open. He pulls me into a tight embrace, then places a kiss on both my cheeks. 'Stephanie! So lovely to see you. You're here to meet Naomi.' He says it as a statement rather than a question.

'Yes. Are you joining us for lunch?'

'Sadly, no. All I get is a measly ham sandwich. That's right, isn't it, Emily?' He winks at the girl at the reception desk. 'Naomi sent me a text message. There's been some holdup on the train, so she's going to be late. Why don't you come to my office, and we can have a chat whilst you wait? Emily, can you bring us some coffees, please?'

He links his arm through mine, and we walk through various warehouse-sized rooms filled with antiques and then into his office, which is behind a door marked *Private*. Today, William is wearing a purple waistcoat with a paisley pattern and a matching bow tie. His two-tone shoes are as shiny as a mirror and clip-clop as we walk.

'Take a pew,' he says, pulling out an ornately carved wooden chair with a plush ochre velvet seat. He sits on the other side of his old-fashioned wooden desk. He leans back in his chair, his hands behind his head. 'So, what's new in your life?'

All I can think of is Alison. Oliver and Alison. And that amethyst ring. If anyone is going to know what Oliver was up to all those years ago, it will be William.

He lets go of his head and leans forwards. 'You look like you've got the weight of the world on your shoulders, Steph.' I don't think William has ever called me *Steph* before. Perhaps it's that familiarity that makes me confide in him.

'Oliver admitted that he was seeing Alison, my friend who disappeared. Did you know?'

William sits very still for a moment as if he's thinking through his answer, which is surprising for him, as he's normally so quick off the mark.

'Yes, I did know,' he says eventually.

I let out a puff of air, and my shoulders sink with both disappointment and relief. At least Oliver wasn't hiding it at the time, but I feel sullied somehow, that they all knew something this important yet never told me.

'I never met her,' William says, as if he's trying to deflect any further questions.

'Oliver must have loved her very much to risk his position at the university,' I say, fishing for more information.

'I seem to recall that Oliver and I talked about it at the time. It was rather frowned upon for faculty to have affairs with students, and yes, he was worried. But it wasn't serious, Stephanie. The relationship with Alison was just a physical thing. Powerful, but just physical. And short. It was more like a fling than a relationship. It was nothing like what you have with Oliver. He loves you. You're the real deal.'

'Oliver never told me about it. Why would he keep something like that from me?'

William shrugs his shoulders. 'I suppose it never came up in conversation, and then it was just too late to tell you. We all make mistakes. I guess it just got past the point where he felt he could tell you. Has this all come to light because of the TV researcher?'

I nod. I don't need William to know the detail.

'Did the police know about Oliver and Alison?' I ask.

'Yes. It was awful at the time. Oliver realised he had to come clean with the police, so he volunteered the information. He was so worried that the police would tell the university about the affair, but fortunately they didn't. Oliver had a rock-solid alibi, and the police quickly concluded that Oliver had nothing to do with Alison's disappearance. Although we've often speculated that Josh might have found out about Alison and Oliver and that was the reason he got jealous and killed her. Unless Josh admits to it, I suppose we'll never know for sure.'

'It was just such a shock to find out that my husband had a relationship with my assumed-murdered flatmate. It's a big thing to keep from me,' I say.

William leans forwards across his desk, shoving to one side some catalogues and his gavel. 'Stephanie, darling. All Oliver wants to do is take care of you, to protect you from all that nastiness and save you from the mental anguish that will come with these bloody journalists raking it all up again. He loves you and the children so much. He's a good man, your husband. We all made mistakes when we were young, had meaningless dalliances that we came to regret.'

'Has he told you about the notes?'

William tilts his head to the side. 'Notes?'

'I've received two typed anonymous notes telling me to back off and to stop having anything to do with the researcher.'

'Bloody hell. No, I don't know anything about that.' William looks genuinely baffled.

'They said, *I know what you did.*'

'And what did you do?'

'Nothing,' I say.

There's a look of pity and understanding in William's eyes that makes me want to share the burden of guilt I've been carrying all of these years. He is a kind man; he'll know how Oliver will react and will help me. And so I tell him.

'I felt terrible guilt. Alison sent me a message asking to see me, but I didn't get around to following it up, and then she disappeared. And there's another thing that I've never told Oliver about; I plagiarised the bulk of Alison's dissertation and passed it off as my own work. I've never told a soul, but I need to come clean.' I feel my cheeks burning with shame.

I'm taken aback when William laughs. A big guffaw of a laugh. 'If that's all you've done bad in your life, I don't think you need to worry too much.'

'But Oliver will be horrified. Perhaps he has known all along. Would Oliver send me notes like that?'

William's amusement stops immediately. He shakes his head vehemently. 'Absolutely not. Why on earth would he do that? There is no way that Oliver would ever do anything to hurt you. He would never stoop that low, and believe me, he loves you. He will be disappointed when he finds out that you nicked a dead girl's work, but that's all. It won't change a thing.'

I cringe.

'He wants to protect you. You know how important

family is to him. It's all he's ever wanted. These last years with you have been the happiest of Oliver's life.'

'I'm sorry I've put you in an awkward position,' I say. 'You're such a good friend to Oliver and to me.'

William gets up and walks around the desk. He takes my right hand and pulls me into one of his big bear hugs. 'I'm your friend, too. I'll always be here for you, and you need to stop worrying.'

'Well, hello! Do I have a reason to be jealous?' Naomi is standing in the doorway, wearing a cream silk shirt, a brown leather skirt and vertiginous heels. She tips her head to one side, and her lips are slightly apart. I am envious of her amused expression, one of utter confidence that she knows she has nothing to worry about.

William steps away from me and pulls Naomi into an embrace, kissing her deeply on the lips. He is so much more open than my husband, tactile as well. Oliver rarely embraces me or touches me just because. He's a wonderful lover, but easy-going tactility just isn't his thing. I suppose that's another result of his upbringing: a grandmother who had little to do with her grandson despite loving each other, and then there's his formative years being spent at boarding school.

'Stephanie is worried about Oliver,' he says when he releases his wife. 'I told her she's got nothing to worry about.' He turns around and walks to his chair. 'Right, ladies, I've got work to do, so you two should scuttle off and do some shopping or lunch or whatever it is that you've got planned. I'll see you later, gorgeous wife, and you, Stephanie, stop worrying.'

I smile at William as Naomi links arms with me. 'Your husband is lovely,' I say.

'I know. But yours isn't too bad, either.'

We grin at each other.

Naomi takes me to a trendy Italian restaurant on the King's Road. There is an awkward moment when she orders me a glass of wine, and I have to lie and tell her I'm still on antibiotics and can't drink. But otherwise, we have a good meal, chat about the children, and she tells me about a holiday she's booked for her and William to some luxury island in the Maldives. By the time we say our goodbyes, I am feeling much more relaxed. And that feeling continues throughout the rest of the day, to when Oliver gets home.

I am so relieved that what Oliver told me fits with William's recollections. That William confirmed the police knew about Oliver's fling and that it really didn't mean anything. Oliver has returned home from work on time for the last couple of days, and it's obvious that he's making an effort with me.

This evening he brings me a bouquet of delphinium and stocks and summer loveliness in hues of pinks, mauves and blues, which he must have picked up from the flower stall outside the Tube station. I wish we had the money so I could have fresh flowers around the house all the time rather than a vault full of jewellery that never gets worn.

'What's this for?' I ask as he hands them to me.

'Just because. And I know you love them.'

I raise an eyebrow.

'I'm sorry, Steph. I really am sorry.'

'I know you are,' I say, placing a kiss on his cheek.

He nods. 'But I still don't want you to have anything to do with that David Green. You've been getting incredibly upset about it all, and I know you've been having the nightmare again.'

'You're right. I have.'

He puts a finger under my chin and tilts my head up

to look at him. He really is so good-looking, and once again, I wonder if he's had secret flings with other pretty students. 'You promise?' he says, his eyes locked onto mine.

'I won't speak to him,' I say.

But I know I'm lying.

16

I spend too long trying to decide what to wear for my meeting with Rahul, which is ridiculous, because I'm happily married, pregnant, and would never cheat on my husband. Never. But I suppose it's normal to want to make a good impression on a past lover. In the end, I keep it simple. I wear a pair of smart dark jeans, a crisp white shirt and a pale grey batwing jumper. I hurry to the underground station and hop on the District Line train to Victoria and, it being the middle of the day, even manage to bag myself a seat.

I had hoped to be early, but as it turns out, Rahul has beaten me to it. He is sitting at a small table in the window, and it takes me back to that drink that we had all those years ago. He's wearing a white shirt with a tie featuring small bumblebees. I have to swallow hard as he leans in to kiss my cheek. He isn't conventionally handsome in the obvious way that Oliver is, but there is something about his face, his eyes in particular, that makes my insides melt. And it's ridiculous. I swivel my wedding ring around on my finger, as I tend to do when I'm nervous, and hurriedly sit down.

'You haven't changed a bit,' Rahul says, beaming at me.

'Nor have you.'

'Larger, greyer, hopefully wiser,' he says.

'It suits you.' I glance away, hoping my cheeks don't give away my feelings.

'What would you like to drink?'

'A mint tea would be great. Thanks.'

'I'll be two ticks.'

He stands up and strides to the counter to order my tea. I would like to watch him but can't, as I'd have to swivel around. Instead, I try to slow my breathing and remind myself that the past is the past, and it needs to stay there.

He returns quite quickly. 'It was a shock to hear from that David Green,' Rahul says as he places the clear glass mug of tea in front of me. There is a large sprig of fresh mint in the hot water.

'Yes. It's brought it all back.'

'The good thing is that it's brought you back into my life.' He must see the look of dismay on my face, because he says hurriedly, 'Don't worry. I know you're married, but I do think about you, Steph. I've always felt that you were the one who got away.'

'Oh,' I say, looking everywhere except at Rahul, shuffling uncomfortably in my seat.

'Anyway, I was surprised when I learned that you married Oliver Siskin. He was one of your history of art professors, wasn't he?'

'Yes. It was all very unexpected, but we're happy.'

'I'm thrilled for you. I really am,' he says, his eyes crinkling as he leans forwards. That's the thing about Rahul; he was always such a nice person. A bit like Alison, in fact.

'Have you met David Green?' I ask.

'No, not yet. But I have visited Josh in prison. A few times over the years, actually.'

'You have?' I'm surprised by that. Josh implied that no one had visited him, and I don't understand why he didn't mention Rahul to me. 'Do you think he's guilty?'

Rahul sighs and pushes up his sleeves. 'Honestly, I don't know. I would never have thought he had it in him, and he protests his innocence, but I can't believe the justice system would have got it so wrong. He's a broken man.'

For some reason, I hold back from telling Rahul that I also visited Josh in prison. The fewer people who are aware, the better.

'Did you know that Alison was going to dump Josh?' I ask.

Rahul's eyes widen. 'No. Is that what the police say was his motive?'

'Didn't you attend the trial?' I ask.

'No. I was in India helping in a school for six months. I missed it all, and to be honest, I was rather relieved. It affected me deeply, Alison going missing and my best friend being accused as her murderer. And my heart was rather broken, too.' He stares at me meaningfully.

Now I feel really uncomfortable. It's not right that I'm here talking to Rahul.

'Don't worry,' he says, laughing. 'Married women aren't my thing.'

'Of course not,' I say, for the first time eager to use Alison's disappearance as an excuse to change the subject of conversation. 'I didn't attend the trial either. I'd just had our daughter. Reading the reports in the papers was quite sufficient for me.'

'Such difficult times,' Rahul says, gazing off into the distance.

And then my phone rings. I glance at it, just to check it's not the children's school. It isn't. It's Oliver, and I feel ashamed that I'm sitting here clandestinely meeting an ex-lover.

'Do you mind?' I ask, gesturing at the phone.

'Of course not.'

'Hi,' I say, missing out my normal 'darling'.

'I'm going to be late home again. Nahla and I have a meeting with a professor from Columbia University who has flown in from the States, and we have to take him out for supper. Also the plumber messaged me because he said there was no answer on the home phone. He's going to stop by to fix the leaking tap in thirty minutes.'

Oliver doesn't give me the chance to say that it's not convenient, or even ask where I might be. He simply says, 'See you later.' And hangs up.

'Is everything alright?' Rahul asks, tilting his head to one side.

All I can think of is Nahla and that my husband is going out for dinner with her. I wonder if there really is a visiting American professor or it's just a ruse to spend the evening with her. Besides, why the hell should I hurry back home? It's so presumptuous of him to think that I'm stuck at home ready and waiting for a trades-person to turn up. On the one hand, I'm tempted not to go home, but on the other, I'm slightly relieved to have an excuse to leave Rahul. Being here with him just feels wrong. Wrong in a 'I wish I could stay here all afternoon chatting to you' kind of way, and I'm in danger of getting out of my depth.

'I'm sorry, but I'm going to have to leave to hurry back to Parsons Green. We've been waiting for days for the plumber to come to fix a leaking tap, and he's going to be there in thirty minutes.'

'That's a shame. It was so lovely to see you, Steph. Perhaps next time we can do lunch?'

I smile tightly. In my heart of hearts, I know that there mustn't be a next time.

He stands up and pulls my chair back, helping me into my raincoat. We stand there awkwardly for a moment, and then he leans forwards, places a kiss on my cheek and says, 'It really was good to see you.'

'You too,' I mutter as I pick up my bag, throw him one last smile and rush out of the coffee shop.

Oliver's home by 10 pm, and I'm ready for him.

'How was your dinner?' I ask.

'Honestly, it was a bit of a bore. He was very full of himself and was one of those types who just love the sound of their own voice, thinking that his research is far superior to anyone else's. Nahla couldn't leave soon enough.'

'What's his name?' I ask.

Oliver frowns at me. 'Professor Robert Cordroy Junior, why?'

I shrug. 'Just curious.'

'How was your day?'

'Fine.'

'Did the plumber fix the tap?'

'Nope. I didn't get home in time. He shoved a note through the door.'

'What do you mean, you didn't get home in time?'

'I was out, Oliver. I hurried back, but it obviously wasn't soon enough. You can't expect me to be sitting around here all day waiting for your instructions!' It feels like I'm trying to pick an argument, as if I'm testing him somehow.

'You could have told me,' he mutters. 'I suppose we'll get a bloody call-out charge anyway. You might have thought about that! Where were you, anyway?'

'Meeting a friend. Next time, give me the plumber's number, and I'll sort it directly,' I say.

I wait for him to ask me which friend I was meeting, and where I was, but he doesn't. He clenches his jaw and turns to walk out of the room. 'I need to pack,' he mutters.

Oliver and William are going to Vienna for a couple of days. They're attending a conference organised by the European Society of Jewellery Historians, and Oliver has been given dispensation by the department to attend. If it had been the school holidays, I would have asked to join them, as I've never been to Vienna and would love to explore the city. It could have been fun, with the four of us and the kids. I can but dream, and I'm feeling increasingly resentful that Oliver gets to go to fancy dinners and foreign trips whilst I'm stuck at home. I'm surprised Naomi didn't join them though, as her two are at boarding school, so she has the freedom. Then again, she isn't exactly a culture vulture. Her idea of a good time is designer outlet shopping at Bicester Village and an indulgent weekend of spa treatments at a six-star hotel or swanning on the beach in the Maldives.

With Oliver away, it allows me a couple of days to get my head back into my studies, so when David Green calls me, I stare at the incoming call on my phone and press cancel. Not because I'm worried about betraying Oliver's confidence, or because I don't want to talk to David, but because I really want to get as much work done whilst I can.

However, when Naomi calls me shortly afterward, my resolve weakens.

'Hi, Naomi.'

'I'm coming up to London today for a doctor's appointment. Can I pop in and see you later?'

'Of course you can. Is everything alright?'

'Yes, yes. I'll tell you when I see you. Should be at yours around 3.30 pm. Does that muck up the school run?'

'A bit, but I'll see if one of my friends can collect the kids for me.' Annoyingly, it's not Mum's day for picking up the children, and she does so much for me, I don't want to call on her unless it's absolutely necessary.

'Would you like to stay for supper?' I ask Naomi.

'No, that's kind of you. I need to get back. Besides, I've got a driver today, so I don't want to keep him waiting too long. But I couldn't come up to town without saying hello, considering we're practically driving past your front door.'

I can't recall the last time Naomi came to our house. William stops by from time to time, but whenever Naomi and I meet up just the two of us, it's for lunch in a restaurant, and at the weekends we go to their house, accepting their indulgent hospitality. After arranging for the mum of one of Bea's friends to bring my children home, I glance around and realise I need to do a serious job of cleaning and tidying to make this house look vaguely respectable. There are coats piled on top of coats in the hallway, shoes randomly shoved together on the floor. The kitchen is home to piles of papers and general detritus and, as I look around it, I realise it could definitely do with an upgrade. The whole kitchen is looking dated, with its orange-tinted wooden units and a stained butler's sink.

When I first moved into this house, everything was so neat and tidy, but with the children and all of their gear accumulated over the years, it feels as if the place is about to burst at the seams. Oliver has been surprisingly relaxed about it; in a strange way, I think he likes the mess because it represents family. The only room that is immaculate is his study, a room that is strictly out of bounds for the children. Even I am discouraged from going in there to clean. But I'm definitely feeling resentful. He's got all of those antiques piled up in the safe doing nothing, when he could be spending on updating the house or even moving to somewhere bigger. I reckon it's about time that he sold a few of his collectibles and pays for us to have a new kitchen.

As I manically tidy up, shoving things in cupboards, hoovering everywhere, it hits me that I'm being ridiculous. Naomi is my friend. I may not have chosen her as my friend, and if we're both being honest, we have very little in common. For starters, she's nearly a decade older than me, she's widely travelled, had a private education and money is no object, but she's kind to me and spoils our children terribly. She's accepted me as the unlikely wife of her husband's best friend. And she makes me laugh with her wicked impersonations.

By the time I've finished tidying up, I'm utterly exhausted. I don't recall being so tired during my previous pregnancies. Perhaps it's just because I'm older now, with more responsibilities. Once I've reached twelve weeks, I'll go to the doctor. I really need to tell Oliver soon, too. When he's back from Vienna.

I make myself a sandwich and drink a glass of water, then heave myself upstairs. I lie down on my bed, set my alarm for 2.30 pm and fall into a deep sleep. I'm in the middle of the nightmare when the ending changes; there's a horrible siren going off, like a fire alarm, but so loud I think it's going to burst my eardrums. Josh is laughing at me, and then a headless person is coming closer and closer. I gasp as I sit bolt upright in bed. What the hell!

And then I hear the ringing of the doorbell. Damn. Is Naomi here already? It's just before 2.30 pm, so I switch my alarm clock off, run my fingers through my hair and hurry downstairs. I hope I don't look too much of a mess in my crumpled clothes with a damp forehead, the remnants of the nightmare still evident in the sheen of perspiration on my body. I swing open the front door, ready to apologise for how I look.

'Oh,' I say. 'It's you.'

It isn't Naomi standing on my doorstep, but David Green.

'I need to talk to you, and you haven't answered my calls.'

'I don't mean to be rude, but it's a really bad time.' I try to close the front door, but he puts his foot out to stop it from closing.

'Please, Stephanie. I've got a few more questions, and I get the feeling you want to find out the truth as much as I do.'

'The thing is, it's a job for you, but this is my life. I have nightmares about Alison every single night. I'd only just got over them, and now they're back again, thanks to you.'

'I'm sorry to hear that. But surely if you find out the truth about what happened to your friend, your mind will be able to rest, and the nightmares will go. I'm no psychologist, but don't you agree that my thesis makes sense?'

My shoulders drop. He's probably right. It's the not knowing that is so very difficult.

'Okay. You can come in, but just for five minutes, because I'm expecting a visitor at 3 pm.'

'Thank you. Much appreciated.'

As David follows me into the kitchen, I wonder if he has found out that I visited Josh in prison. I pull out a chair and gesture for him to sit down, but I don't offer him a drink.

'I was hoping you could tell me a bit more about the

History of Art department and the outings that students and tutors went on.'

'Why don't you ask Oliver?'

'I couldn't get hold of him.'

'He's in Vienna. And is it really so urgent that it can't wait until he's back?' My voice is laden with sarcasm.

'Your husband isn't very keen on talking to me. Do you know how often they go on trips and where they normally go?'

'No. It's just one of the many things that Oliver does on the side for the university.'

'When you were at university, did you go on lots of trips with your professors?'

'A few. Why are you asking?'

I'm worried now. What is it that David really wants to know? Has he caught wind of the fact that Alison might have been spending more time with Oliver than she should have done? Why is he homing in on Oliver when on the face of it, it was me who spent the most amount of time with Alison?

'I'm just trying to build a bigger picture. Did Alison ever talk about Oliver?'

'No!' I have to keep my voice under control. What is this man getting at? Does he know about their relationship? I think of the appointment of professorship that Oliver is likely to get this year. It's such an honour and an achievement, and it's so very important to him, not just for prestige, but from a financial perspective too. I am kicking myself for letting David into the house. 'Sorry to be rude, but I'm expecting visitors any time now.'

David stands up. 'Is it okay if I use the toilet quickly, just before I leave?'

It's not like I can say no. He follows me out to the

hallway. 'It's the second door on the left,' I say, pointing to it.

'Thanks.'

I walk back into the kitchen and get out my teapot. I pour milk into a matching jug and find a box of biscuits, which I empty out onto a plate. No doubt Naomi won't touch them, but at least I'm being polite. And then, as I stand at the kitchen window looking out onto our postage-stamp-sized garden at the rear, I realise that David is spending a long time on the toilet. I tiptoe out of the kitchen and back into the hall. The loo door is still closed, but I hear a rustle coming from Oliver's study next door. I walk towards the door just as David is walking out.

'What are you doing?' I exclaim, my breath catching.

'Sorry–' And then the doorbell chimes, and we both jump.

'That'll be my friend.' I'm stuck now, wedged between David Green, who is nosying around our house, and Naomi, who is no doubt waiting at our doorstep.

'I wasn't snooping. I just saw the certificates that your husband has framed on the wall, and I wanted to look at them. I'm sorry.'

'It's okay,' I say, even though it absolutely isn't. I can't remember if the door to Oliver's study was open or closed. I squeeze past David, walk to the front door and open it, glancing back over my shoulder to make sure that David isn't doing any further snooping.

'I thought you'd forgotten that I was coming!' Naomi says, leaning in to give me an air kiss.

'Sorry, just had an unexpected visitor,' I say. 'Come in, come in.' I stand back, and she walks past me in a cloud of floral perfume. She's wearing fitted navy trousers that flare out slightly at the ankles, making her thighs look impossibly thin, and a pale pink blouse with lots of chiffon ruffles. Large chandelier earrings in sparkling pink stones dangle from her earlobes, making little tinkling sounds as she moves. She has bags over her left wrist.

'Hello.' She stops still, tilts her head and raises her eyebrows at David.

'David Green. I'm just leaving.'

'David Green, as in the television researcher?'

He nods.

She turns back to face me. 'For God's sake, Stephanie. I thought you weren't going to have anything to do with this man!'

What is it with everyone at the moment? Naomi is treating me like a child, David is trespassing around my house, and Oliver, well, I'm not sure I can trust him. Naomi takes a step forwards. She puts her Birkin bag and a large white paper carrier bag down on the floor in the hallway and wags her diamond-encrusted finger at David.

'I don't know how you can live with yourself, digging up all the miseries that my friend has had to deal with. You true crime people are just capitalising on ordinary people's misfortunes, turning their real lives into entertainment, making money off the back of human suffering.' Naomi swivels and puts her arm around me, pulling me towards her. 'You've no idea what this poor woman went through. And I don't suppose you care, do you?'

David lowers his head. I feel a little bit sorry for him, not sure how he can possibly defend himself in light of Naomi's diatribe. At the same time, it feels good to have someone stand up for me. Naomi is one of those people who has strong opinions on everything and isn't scared of making her views heard. Ironically, I think she'd make a great barrister. She's articulate and persuasive; it's just that she has no desire to work. No need to work. David opens his mouth as if to say something, but in light of Naomi's glower, he closes it again. He nods his head at me and walks out of the front door.

As soon as he's gone and I've closed the door, Naomi turns to me. 'Why did you let him in?'

'I didn't think it would do much harm and—'

But Naomi talks over me. 'I just can't believe people like that. They're like leeches. So insensitive.' She shakes her coiffured blonde hair. She follows me into the kitchen, where I put the kettle on. I lean back against the countertop.

'The thing is,' I say. 'I want to know the truth about Alison. I have these awful nightmares and would love not to see her in my dreams every single night. It's exhausting.'

'Oh, you poor love. Why don't you go and see someone? I know a great counsellor. He does hypnotherapy and is a specialist at treating post-traumatic stress disorder.'

Whilst she's fiddling with her phone, I pour hot water into the teapot. Naomi glances up.

'Oh, goodness, I almost forgot,' she says. 'I bought some patisseries for you and the kids.' She clip-clops back out into the corridor and returns with a large white paper cake bag and places it on the kitchen table. I peer inside.

'You don't need to give us all of those,' I exclaim. There must be a dozen slices of cakes inside, all different types of patisseries, mostly exquisitely formed and looking and smelling divine.

'My treat, and something yummy for the kids. Pass me a couple of plates.'

I take two large plates and put them on the table.

Naomi carefully removes all of the slices from their
white cardboard boxes, and places my plate with shop-
bought biscuits back onto the countertop.

'I thought the cupcakes and gingerbread should be
for the kids, and the rest for us to choose between.' She
winks at me.

We sit in the living room. Naomi removes her navy
high heels and tucks her bare feet underneath herself.
Her toenails are painted black, and I notice that she has
the beginnings of a bunion. I have put the tray with our
drinks and cake on the coffee table.

'I won't have a whole piece,' she says as she cuts off
a sliver of an eclair.

After we've taken a few sips of tea, Naomi leans
back into the sofa. 'William told me that you hadn't
known about Oliver's silly little dalliance with Alison.'

I turn my head away so she can't see the shock on
my face – not about William sharing my conversation
with Naomi, but because of her appalling description. It
may have seemed like a silly little dalliance, but to me,
it's revelational.

'Honestly, darling,' she says, leaning towards me. 'If
it had been of any importance, I would have made sure
you knew about it before marrying Oliver. It was nothing. Please don't think any of us kept this from you
deliberately. It was just of so little importance.'

Is she protesting too much? The fact she says they
didn't keep it from me deliberately makes me wonder
whether perhaps they did. 'Did you know Alison, too?'

'Good heavens, no. I never met her. Oliver only
introduced us to serious girlfriends.'

'He doesn't talk about his women before me.'

'Nor does William.'

'But you and William have been together since you

were nineteen. He can't have had many girlfriends before you.'

'You know, I think it's healthy to leave the past in the past. Oliver and William are good like that. Perhaps it's a male thing, being able to compartmentalise and focus on the here and now. That's why it's so bad for your mental health to have any involvement with that little researcher man.'

I stop myself from flinching at Naomi's description of David. She can be so pompous.

'Won't you tell me about Oliver's girlfriends?'

She sighs. 'It's such a long time ago, Steph. He's only had eyes for you ever since the two of you got together. I'm sure he'd tell you if you pushed him. I can't tell you how relieved William and I were when he introduced you to us. I knew straight away that you'd be good for him, and I've been right, haven't I? All's good in the Siskin household, isn't it?'

'Yes, yes,' I say hurriedly. I know perfectly well that anything I say to Naomi will get straight back to Oliver, so I am always careful.

'It's only that damned little man who has created a blip in the road. Gosh, it makes me angry the way the media leeches off victims. Fair enough that they cause grief for convicted criminals, but the innocent parties, that's just not right.'

'The thing is,' I say, 'I've always wondered whether Josh was capable of murder.' I think of Josh in prison and realise I can't possibly tell Naomi that I visited him. It would get back to Oliver in a nanosecond.

'Do you really think the police would have got it so wrong? And the prosecution service and the courts and the jury? How often is there such a major miscarriage of justice?'

I can think of many instances, but I'm not going to get into a debate over it.

'All of this needs to be put to bed, Steph. Imagine how terrible it would be if it that researcher got wind of the fact that Oliver had a little flingette with Alison. He'd lose his job, and your husband would never forgive you.'

'I suppose you're right. So long as the police knew that Oliver and Alison were briefly together and they discounted it, I guess it's irrelevant.' But rather than seeing my husband in my mind's eye, I see Rahul. I wonder if Rahul knew that Alison had been unfaithful to Josh. I've never asked him the question.

'You're miles away,' Naomi says. 'How about you join me on the board of one of my charity fundraiser dos? It would take your mind off all the miserable things from the past.'

'I'm not sure I'd be any good at that,' I say, thinking that's the last thing I need what with my secret studies and a baby on the way. 'More importantly, you said you went to the doctor. Is everything okay?'

She throws me a half smile. 'When I said "doctor", that was in the loosest sense of the word. I'm just planning a few little tweaks and lifts, nothing too obvious, but just enough to keep me on my A game.' She taps the side of her nose. 'No telling on me, you promise? I don't want William to know.'

'Of course not.'

She leans towards me and places a kiss on my cheek. 'And that's why you make such a good wife to dear Oliver. Everyone can always count on you to do the right thing.'

17

I sleep surprisingly well without Oliver at my side. I have got into this ridiculous pattern of being scared of going to sleep, terrified of that nightmare. I've tried every sleep remedy there is, from herbal pills to melatonin (which is prohibited without a prescription in the UK but easy to get, at expense, from American websites) and even the occasional sleeping pill, although I don't have many of those left. I've tried listening to meditations whilst I'm lying in bed, and I've got a machine that plays the gentle rhythmic sounds of the ocean. I thought Oliver might complain about the sea sounds, but he can sleep through anything, and he's willing to try whatever it takes to give me a peaceful night's sleep.

Oliver is expected back later, and I've survived pretty well in his absence, all things considered. I'm reading through a complicated chapter on estates law when the doorbell rings. Sighing, I put a pen in the text-book to mark my place, shove my books in a drawer and stride to the door. I'm relieved that it's only Mum.

'What are you doing here?' I ask, giving her a kiss on the cheek.

'I brought you some lunch. Reckoned with that husband of yours being abroad, you might not be eating properly, just snacking on whatever you give the kids. And with a new baby on the way, you must take care.'

'Thanks, Mum.' She is right, but nevertheless I feel slightly riled. This is my third pregnancy; I'm no longer a naive young girl. But Mum means well, so I let her follow me into the kitchen. I take my books out of the drawer and settle down at the table again to try to concentrate on my studies.

'Still hiding your books, then?' she asks, with a raised eyebrow, placing a Tesco's carrier bag on the ground.

'I'll tell him when I've passed,' I say. 'Don't stir.'

'I found this on your doorstep.' She puts a small brown parcel about the size of half a shoebox on the table. She removes a quiche from her bag, switches my oven on and pops it inside. She then takes out a plastic bowl filled with salad.

'Are you going to open your parcel?' she asks, motioning towards the small box.

'Probably something from Amazon for Oliver,' I say.

'No, it's addressed to you, and it was on your front doorstep. Didn't the courier ring the doorbell?'

I shake my head. I shove my books to one side and look at it. The parcel is wrapped in brown paper and addressed to me. I use a knife to open it up. Inside, there's another parcel wrapped in bubble plastic, but no note or invoice in the box. I unwrap the bubble plastic and am left holding a small jam jar half filled with dark red viscous liquid.

It takes me a moment to process what it is.

'Oh my God!' I screech, putting it onto the table and recoiling.

'What's the matter?' Mum swivels around to look at me. 'What's that?' She peers at the jam jar, but it's only when she reads what I've already seen that she looks as if she's about to faint. She staggers backwards.

There's a typed label stuck on the glass jar that reads, '*Back off.*'

'Is that blood?' Mum whispers.

I pick the jam jar up and place it back into the box. 'I think so.'

'Why the hell is someone sending you a jam jar filled with blood? What's going on, Steph?'

I sigh and shut my eyes. 'I've been getting these stupid threatening letters telling me not to talk to the researcher who's doing the programme on Alison.'

'Oh, darling, why didn't you tell me about them?'

'I didn't want to worry you. Oliver wasn't too concerned, but this takes it to another level.'

'Show me the letters. Let me have a read of them, and then we'll call the police.'

It's at times like this that I realise how much I need Mum. She's calm in the face of an emergency, and she understands me better than anyone else in the world. Mum nudges the box to the end of the table.

'It's postmarked London,' she says, peering at the front of the box. 'But there's no return address.'

'Do you think it's human blood?' I ask, shivering.

'I very much doubt it, but let's not think about it,' she says. 'Show me the letters that you got.'

I find the two notes. She reads them, sighs, and places them back down on the table. She is silent for a few long moments. 'Someone doesn't want this researcher to carry on digging because they've got something to hide. Who could that be?' Mum asks, getting up from the table and walking to the kitchen counter.

'It's got to be someone David has spoken to. In fact, I think I need to tell David about all of this, because then we can find out if anyone else has received these threats, too.'

'Let's have some lunch, and then you can call the police. It's not an emergency, so you'll have to use that other number.'

'You mean 111?' I ask.

'That's the one.' Mum gets up and takes the quiche out of the oven, placing a portion on each of our plates. She then dollops out some salad and brings both the plates over to the table.

'I'm not hungry, Mum,' I say as I tidy up my study things.

'You've got to eat, for the baby if not for yourself.'

I sigh. 'I'll just take my books upstairs and will be back down again in a second.'

We have just started eating when I hear the sound of a key in the front door. I jump to my feet, adrenaline bursting through my veins, before I take a breath and realise that a burglar wouldn't have a key.

'Anyone home?'

I am relieved to hear Oliver's voice. I wasn't expecting him back until this evening, as his flight was due to arrive at Heathrow first thing, and he was planning on going straight to work. It has always worried me that Oliver might return home unexpectedly during the day and find me poring over my law books, but to date, that has never happened. Nevertheless, it's just as well I tidied them away before lunch.

I hurry out of the kitchen to the front hallway and see that William is with him, too.

'You're early,' I say. He throws his arms around me, and I'm surprised that I feel such relief that he's home.

'Just stopping off here to dump my things before going to the university.'

'Our flight was delayed,' William explains.

'Was it a successful trip?' I ask.

'Yes. I'll tell you all about it later.'

'Are you hungry? Mum's here, and there's enough quiche left over for you each to have a slice.'

'It would be rude to say no to Mrs Lucas's finest quiche Lorraine,' William says with a grin.

I follow the men into the kitchen. After giving Mum a cursory kiss on the cheek, Oliver clears some space at the kitchen table and reaches out towards the box.

'Don't touch that!' Mum says.

'Why?'

'Put on a pair of rubber gloves or pick it up with a paper towel,' Mum says. 'Don't want to leave your fingerprints on it. It's already got Steph's and my prints.'

Oliver pales. 'What's going on?'

Mum hands Oliver a piece of paper towel. 'You'd better have a look for yourself,' she says, nodding her head towards the box.

He looks inside the box and stares at the jar. 'Bloody hell.' His face is white. He shows William the jam jar and then places it back in the box before walking around the table towards me and throwing his arms around me in a very uncharacteristic display of emotion.

'It's only just arrived,' Mum says. 'We were about to call the police.'

Oliver releases me and scratches his head. 'Yes, good idea.'

'Who would send something like that?' William asks.

'Obviously someone who is worried about what that researcher will discover,' Mum says.

'Either Josh is in prison for a murder he didn't commit, or someone is playing sick games with me, or both,' I add.

'I agree,' Oliver says. 'We need to involve the police. They're bound to have procedures in place for this sort of thing. I just want to make damned sure that you and the kids are protected.'

Both men look genuinely distraught. That shocks me. Oliver may not tell me he loves me, but I feel a warmth at his obvious show of concern. Even Mum is looking worried.

'I'll call 111,' I say.

'No. It'll take ages for anything to happen if you do that,' Oliver says. 'The police are so overstretched. I'll go to the local police station and drop off the parcel and show them the letters. I can do it now on my way into work.'

'I can go,' I say.

All three of them talk at the same time. 'No.' 'You shouldn't go.' 'It's not safe.'

'It's best if Oliver or Mrs Lucas reports it,' William says. 'Just in case someone's following you.'

A shiver goes down my spine.

'William is right,' Mum says.

'I want you to stay here, Steph.' Oliver puts a firm hand on my shoulder. 'Keep the doors locked and just hunker down until I've had the chance to get advice from the police.'

'I'll collect the kids from school,' Mum says.

'I think you're all overreacting,' I say, pacing up and down the kitchen.

'Better to be safe than sorry,' William adds.

18

I'm a nervous wreck by the time Oliver returns home from work. The slightest little thing makes me jump, from a car door being slammed outside to the creak of the floorboards as the kids run around upstairs. I can't decide if I'm happy that Oliver has gone to the police or embarrassed that I didn't do it myself. I understand that he's trying to protect me, but even so, I think Mum, Oliver and William were overreacting. Let's face it: The red liquid was probably that fake blood that you can buy at a dressing-up shop. It was designed to scare me, not to physically threaten me. Even so, it's set me on edge, and it's taking me further and further back to those dark days of the past.

Oliver brings me up to date over a late supper.

'I showed the letters to the constable on duty, and he took the package. He's going to forward everything on to the team who investigated Alison's disappearance in the first place. He said it could take a while, but obviously, if there are any further threats, or if you feel scared at any time, you must ring 999. I've bought you a personal alarm.' He hands me what looks like a little fob on a keychain.

I recall how Mum sent me one of those personal alarms shortly after Alison first went missing. It was a device that emitted a high-pitched screech if activated. Fortunately, I never had any reason to use it, but I did carry it around in my pocket for years.

'Will they run fingerprint checks on the package?' I ask.

'He wasn't sure.'

'So he thought we were overreacting?'

'Absolutely not. He said we did exactly the right thing by notifying the police. Someone doesn't want you digging, Steph, and I want my wife to be safe. So, as we agreed, no more contact with David Green. Let's try to put this all behind us. I've also made you an appointment to see the doctor.'

'What! Why?' I frown.

'Because these nightmares aren't doing you any good. You never complain, but you're limping a lot more, and you look pale and exhausted.' He leans across the table and takes my hand. 'I'm worried about you, darling.'

'You don't need to be,' I say, but just the fact that he's concerned ramps up my fear. I wonder if I should tell him about the baby now, but we're interrupted by Sam, who says he's feeling sick, but I think it's merely a ruse for having his dad tuck him back into bed.

After the car accident with Leroy all those years ago, the doctors had to reconstruct my leg. I've got metal in it, and lots of scars, which have mostly faded by now. What hasn't faded is a subconscious link between fear and pain. Whenever I am fearful or stressed, the pain in my leg flares up like a dramatic reminder that *Yes, you do need to be concerned, because something terrible happened before, so it could happen again.* Even though therapists and doctors have reassured me that lightning doesn't strike twice, it does, doesn't it? With hindsight, I'm surprised I didn't have more pain during that year following Alison's disappearance, but I was so consumed with passion for Oliver and my pregnancy, perhaps that dampened it down. But in the years since, I have noticed a direct correlation. If I get stressed or scared, my leg screams. Weirdly, my nightmares don't particularly trigger the pain, it's mainly a correlation between my conscious thoughts and pain. And it's very tiring. As long as the pain isn't too bad, I try to push through it, keeping as active as possible, but the pain has definitely been more intense during the past few weeks.

It's a sunny morning, so after dropping the kids off at school, I walk the long way home, hoping that walking will lubricate my leg somehow and stop the limp. I'm also planning on going into town today to have a browse around Peter Jones in Sloane Square. It's Mum's birthday in a couple of weeks, and I've been saving a little bit of housekeeping money to spend on a present for her, a new bag perhaps. I'm trying very hard to ignore the fact that someone might be following me, and absolutely refuse to give in to terror.

I nip into the newsagent to buy a carton of milk. I glance up, looking at the street out of the shop window, and it's then that I see her. There's a flash of blonde hair, the way she walks, just something else that I can't place my finger on. I dump the milk and race out of the door, almost barging straight into an elderly man as he's entering. I mutter my apologies and then sprint along the pavement in the direction the woman was walking. I can see her up ahead, wearing black trousers and a pale-yellow jumper, striding quickly, a black bag over her shoulder. As I race to catch up with her, I'm panting, breathless, as I place my hand on her arm. 'Alison?'

The woman turns around.

'Oh,' I say, taking a step backwards. 'Sorry. I thought you were someone else. I'm sorry.'

She couldn't be Alison. She's too young; besides, she looks nothing like her. As the woman walks away, shaking her head, I lean against the brick wall and hang my head. I'm regressing by years. This is how I used to be, seeing her in the window of passing buses or on the opposite escalator in the underground or as a silhouette behind a shop changing cubicle.

But it was never her, and that brief moment of hope sank me further and further into sorrow. They say that a baby picks up on her mother's emotions from her pregnancy. But I don't believe that. If so, Bea should be a very confused child, for my emotions during those first couple of years yo-yoed from the joy I felt from being in love with Oliver to the dark guilt and grief of not knowing about Alison. Yet Bea has turned out to be a straightforward little girl, neither emotionally stunted nor advanced. That, at least, brings me solace.

As my breathing steadies, I walk home slowly, conscious that I didn't put the personal alarm that Oliver gave me in my pocket. I'm just putting my key in the door when my phone rings. It startles me, and it's a number I don't recognise. For a moment, I consider not answering. But I'm not going to give in to those fears, so I answer it.

'Steph, it's Rahul.'

I turn around in the doorway and glance both ways on the street. There's no one there. I then turn my face up towards the sun and smile.

'How are you?' he asks.

'There's been a lot going on. I'm sorry I had to leave

in such a hurry the other day.' I wedge the phone between my chin and shoulder, walk into the house and lock the door behind me.

'It was great to see you even if it was too short. Just thought I'd let you know that I had a conversation with David Green.'

'Oh.'

'He told me that he thinks Alison was having a relationship with someone other than Josh. Did you know that?'

I lean back against the wall, my head nudging one of Oliver's paintings.

'Yes, he suggested that to me too.' Of course he didn't; it was Josh who planted that seed in my head.

'Did you know about it back then?'

'No. No, I didn't.'

'Well, let's hope David can unearth who that person was. I think that's the only hope of getting to the truth. Anyway, that wasn't the reason I was calling you. I have to be in London for a conference in a fortnight's time, and I was wondering if you'd be free for lunch. Nothing more, just lunch and a chance for a proper catch-up.'

I'm silent. I simply can't think about meeting up with Rahul, not whilst David Green's investigation seems to be homing in on my husband.

'Stephanie?' Rahul asks.

'Can you message me the dates? I'll let you know,' I say. 'I've got quite a lot on at the moment.'

'Yes, of course. I don't want to put you in an awkward position or anything,' he says, the earlier joviality and confidence gone from his voice.

'It was lovely of you to call,' I say.

I do a couple of hours studying and then get ready to go shopping. It's Wednesday, the day when Oliver picks the kids up from school, so I don't have to hurry home, and I won't have to hide my shopping bags from Mum. I have just got off the bus on the King's Road when Oliver calls me.

'I forgot that I have a dentist's appointment this afternoon at 3 pm, so I won't be able to collect the kids from school. Can you do it?'

I don't recall seeing anything about a dentist appointment in the diary.

'Have you got a toothache?' I ask.

'No, no. Just routine. Hygienist and a check-up. Sorry to dump you in it, but I've got a tutorial now, so I have to go.'

'Okay,' I say. But I stare at my phone and frown. It is very unlike Oliver not to remember that he has an appointment. It's frustrating as well, because it means I don't have nearly as long as I'd hoped for to browse the shops.

I'm thinking about Oliver as I'm taking the escalator up to the first floor in Peter Jones. I can't put a finger on it, but I reckon he's lying about his dental appointment. It's just he's normally so conscientious about his diary, and he cherishes his one day a week collecting the kids from school. On the other hand, he could have said that something has come up at work, and I wouldn't have questioned that. Why would he say he had a dentist's appointment if he didn't?

But something is bugging me. I stop walking and stand in a doorway, taking out my mobile phone and calling Mum.

'Any chance you could collect the kids from school this afternoon? Oliver's got a dentist appointment, and I've come into the centre of town to pick up a few bits and pieces, but haven't managed to get everything done.' I hate lying to Mum, but needs must.

'No problem, love. Are you feeling alright?'

'Yes, yes. All's fine. Just doing a bit of shopping.' I can imagine Mum's raised eyebrows. She knows I don't like shopping. 'Thanks, Mum. Love you.'

Next I telephone Oliver's dentist. He goes to a private dentist on Welbeck Street, the same dentist that William visits, apparently. I went there once when I chipped a tooth and was horrified by the exorbitant prices, although rather enamoured by the luxurious premises that give the feeling that you are in someone's London house rather than visiting a dental clinic. Normally, the kids and I go to a very ordinary practice in Putney.

'Good afternoon,' I say in as posh a voice as I can muster. 'I understand that my husband, Oliver Siskin, has an appointment with you at 3 pm. Could I just double-check with you that it's today and not tomorrow?'

'Certainly, Mrs Siskin.' I hear the receptionist clicking on a keyboard.

'No. I don't see any appointment for Mr Siskin at 3 pm. Would you like me to look for tomorrow?'

'No, no. It's fine,' I say and hang up.

My heart is pumping too quickly. Oliver was lying to me, but why?

Next I call Oliver's departmental secretary, Laura. After some brief small talk, I ask, 'Has Oliver left yet for his dentist's appointment? I didn't want to disturb him, but want to catch him before he goes.'

'No, he's still here. Do you want me to put you through?'

'Don't worry. I'll catch him in twenty minutes or so.'

I hurry back down the escalators and emerge onto Sloane Square. I walk as quickly as I can around the square to Sloane Street Tube station, buy a ticket, hurry down the escalators, and jump onto a circle line train

just before the doors close. It's only five stops to
Temple.

I want to see where my husband is going. I know
this is ridiculous, that I should have no reason for not
trusting him, but the simple fact is, I don't. I have no
idea where he is most of the time. I have no idea what
he spends his money on, and judging from what is in
our safe, he must buy up a lot at auction. And I have no
idea if he's telling me the truth about Alison. All I can
think about is that bloody ring and Josh's story. And the
way Josh was so utterly desperate.

I ask myself the question, do I think my husband is
guilty of a heinous crime? The answer is no. I don't
think he has it in him. But there is a lot I don't know
about my Oliver, and it's about time I find out.

There is a side entrance to the university that Oliver
always uses, one that leads away from the grand
neoclassical building. It leads into an alleyway that, if
you didn't know it was there, you would never find. I
make a promise to myself: I'll wait around for twenty
minutes and not a second longer. If he doesn't come out,
I'll go home.

I hang back inside a doorway, set in shadows, and
when the occasional person passes, I pretend I'm busy
texting on my phone. And then I see him. He's
carrying his messenger bag and is also studying his
mobile phone, striding quickly towards the Strand. I
turn and walk in the opposite direction until he's
passed where I was loitering, and then I double back,
following him. When he's on the main street, he stops,
and I realise he's hailing a cab. I'm going to have to do
the same. Fortunately, there is a stream of black cabs,
all with their lights on. I suppose 2.30 pm on a
Wednesday afternoon isn't a busy time of day for
them.

I feel like laughing hysterically as I say to the driver, 'Can you follow that cab, please?'

He doesn't even raise an eyebrow, so perhaps people do this all the time. I rather assumed that only happened in movies. As Oliver's taxi winds its way up Regent Street, passes busy Oxford Circus and turns left onto Margaret Street, I wonder if I have got it all wrong. Perhaps he is going to Welbeck Street after all, because we're going in exactly the right direction. But no. The taxi is indicating to the left and pulling up outside John Lewis on Cavendish Square. Even if Oliver is going to walk from here, he'd have to sprint to make it to the dentist on Welbeck Street for 3 pm. I wait in the back of my cab until Oliver has paid and watch as he gets out of the taxi and strides into the department store.

'Thanks,' I say to the cab driver, giving him a very healthy tip. I hurry into the same door as Oliver and peer around for him. It's only then that I realise I have no backup plan should Oliver see me. I'd have to tell him the semi-truth, that I was looking for a birthday present for Mum, and she had offered to help out with the kids whilst I stayed in town. And oh, what a coincidence it would be, Oliver and me running into each other like this.

But I don't have to have that conversation, because he's vanished. I glance around the menswear department on the ground floor, and he's not here. At least, I don't think he is. Where else would he go? Other than buying clothes, I suppose he might be meeting someone for a coffee. I rush towards the escalators, then double back on myself. He might see me on an escalator. Better if I take the lifts. I jab the button for the fifth floor and hurry inside, but to my frustration, the lift stops at every floor. I wonder if I look harried, crazy even.

The Place To Eat is big, and pretty much every table

is full. How the hell am I going to spot him without him seeing me? That's even assuming he's here.

But I have a sixth sense with my husband, and my eyes are drawn to the far left-hand side. And there he is, seated at a table for two, facing me. He's smiling at a woman, talking animatedly, as if he's fascinated by what she's saying. She has blonde hair. At least it's not Nahla. I try to get a glimpse of her from another angle, but it's too much of a risk. If Oliver looks up, he'll see me. And if I have such a good homing instinct with him, what's to say he doesn't with me?

'Excuse me.' A woman carrying a tray laden with coffees and slices of cake needs to get past me. She jolts me to my senses. What the hell am I doing here, spying on my husband? He could be meeting a student, a colleague, someone from the art world. Absolutely anyone, in fact. And it's not as if he's going to behave inappropriately in John Lewis' restaurant. The truth of the matter is, I don't suspect Oliver of infidelity. I bite the inside of my mouth and then turn around, hurrying back down the escalators towards home. I think he's lied to me – about Alison, about what he spends his money on, about whom he spends time with – and believe me, there's nothing worse than doubting the person you share a bed with. Yet I have no real reason to suspect him of anything.

Oliver returns home around 6 pm.

'How was your dentist appointment?' I ask as he walks into the kitchen, hoping my tone of voice is casual.

'Fine.'

'What did you have done?'

'The usual. Why?'

I can't do this. I can't do all this pretending. 'Okay, let's cut to the chase. Where were you, really?'

Oliver opens his mouth and closes it again. 'What's going on, Stephanie?' he asks, narrowing his eyes. He always uses my full name when he's annoyed with me.

'You didn't have a dentist's appointment at 3 pm, did you?'

'No. They got it wrong; it was at 4 pm. I met with a postgraduate student at 3 pm and then went on to the dentist. What's the problem?'

'What was the student's name?'

'Stephanie, you're worrying me.' He steps forwards and holds me by the shoulders, peering at me as if there's something seriously wrong with me.

I shake my head and wriggle free.

'It's all this bloody Alison stuff, isn't it? Do you want me to see if we can bring your doctor's appointment forwards?'

'No, it's just … it doesn't matter. I've had a massive headache all day today. Forget I said anything. Would you like a drink?'

He looks at me strangely, which is not surprising. 'Later, maybe. I'm going to take a shower.'

As I hear Oliver's footsteps recede upstairs, I sink into a chair. I made a right screw-up with that conversation. It's me who has been acting out of order, meeting up with an ex behind my husband's back and then following my husband like some insecure idiot wife. The last thing I want to do is destroy my marriage for no reason. I love Oliver, and although he doesn't say it often, I am confident he loves me back. He certainly adores the children. In fact, I can hear them now, racing around upstairs, squealing as Oliver throws them into the air.

But the meeting with Rahul has unsettled me. He's a much gentler, softer person than Oliver, and frankly, I felt more comfortable in his presence than I have around my own husband of late. Oliver may be attentive and caring, but it's stifling and it's out of character. I don't need to visit the doctor. There's absolutely nothing wrong with me other than I'm pregnant and I wish I knew what had happened to Alison. I need to think through the last few weeks rationally, as if I really were a lawyer. What are the factual things that are giving rise to my suspicions of my husband?

I list them in my head. How Oliver is adamant that I shouldn't talk to David Green; how he's changed the code on our safe; how he has been on lots of buying trips; how he had an affair with Alison yet only just told me; how he said he was going to the dentist, but I'm not sure if he really went; how he's very friendly with Nahla, the young, beautiful lecturer, or, at least, I assume he is very friendly with her. I try to be logical. None of those things should give me any reason to be suspicious of my husband. But I can't shift that unease in my sternum. I'm sure something is amiss.

19

I am getting seriously behind with my studies, and I'm disappointed with myself. There are various things that I'm struggling to understand, and I'm losing the impetus to carry on with such a challenging subject. On a whim, I call Nahla Madaki. I want to know more about her and try to uncover whether there is anything untoward about her relationship with Oliver. I assume she'll be teaching and her phone will go to voicemail, but it doesn't.

'Stephanie, how lovely to hear from you! I was only thinking yesterday that I must give you a call.'

'I was wondering if you'd be free for that coffee sometime.'

'Yes, certainly. Let me check my diary. It's probably a bit short notice, but I could do coffee tomorrow early afternoon or otherwise the week after next. I'm off on a trip to Florence next week.'

I'm relieved that Oliver isn't also going on that trip. 'Tomorrow is good for me,' I say. We arrange a time and a place.

I'm trying to recall when was the last time that

Oliver accompanied students abroad, when my phone rings. It's a withheld number, and once again I hesitate before answering.

'Stephanie, it's David Green. Please don't hang up on me.'

I sigh. I am totally conflicted.

'I wanted to apologise for when I came over to your house, but–'

'No,' I say, interrupting him. 'You were snooping around my house, and I don't want any more to do with your research.'

'You're right, I'm sorry. Please just hear me out. There is something really important that I need to tell you about. Can we meet somewhere this evening?'

'No, I'm sorry. That won't be possible.'

'I can't stress the urgency,' he says. 'I've found out something that I need to tell you, to show you, without anyone else knowing.'

My initial reaction is to say no, but I'm seriously worried that he might have found out about Oliver and Alison's affair, and surely it's better to know what we're up against? I'm silent for a long time.

'Can't you tell me on the phone?' I ask.

'No. I really need to see you in person,' he says. 'I'm in London today, tied up in meetings, but I'll be free around 6 pm.'

'It's really inconvenient.' It's Thursday, and Oliver has a staff meeting this evening, as he does every Thursday. Nevertheless, I'm sure Mum would step into babysit.

'Please,' he says. 'I wouldn't ask if it wasn't important.'

'Okay,' I say eventually. 'I've got something I need to tell you, too.' I'm going to show David those threatening letters, and then he'll understand why I can't be involved with his research anymore. 'But I want to meet at a totally neutral place, somewhere I wouldn't normally go.'

'Fair enough. There's a pub I know near Clapham Common. Do you regularly go there?'

'No,' I say.

'In which case I'll text you the name and address.'

I ring Mum and ask her to babysit. I have to lie to her, too, because there is no way she would let me meet David Green after having sight of those letters. I tell her I'm meeting up with an old uni friend who has returned from abroad, and I hate myself for telling such a fib. All this lying is going to have to stop.

David sends me a text message.

'See you at 6 pm at the Hen and Mare Pub, 23 Corner Street, Clapham. If you want to take the bus, the number 77 bus stops on the other side of the road. David.'

I am so careful when leaving the house. I wear a baseball cap pulled down low over my forehead and an ancient anorak that is much too big. I leave myself plenty of time and constantly look over my shoulder, trying to work out if anyone is following me. I take the bus. It's quicker, but also I feel safer. Waiting at the bus stop, I hang back until everyone else has climbed on board, and only then do I step forwards. No doubt I'm being ridiculous, but I need to be careful. If the person who wrote those notes was being serious, then I'm potentially putting myself in danger. And, of course, I'm also going against police advice. I take the stairs and sit on the top deck, right at the back, so I can see who is getting on board.

As I'm sitting there, I wonder what the police have discovered about the blood in the jam jar and the letters. I shudder. I make a mental note to ask Oliver if he's heard anything.

The traffic is surprisingly light; I arrive in good time. The Hen and Mare is an old-fashioned pub and certainly not one of those gentrified ones with home-baked meals and Farrow and Ball wainscoting. This place looks as if it hasn't had a paint job for thirty years, with the ceilings still brown from those long-gone days when people used to have a cigarette with their pint. In a way, I'm glad. There's no chance of running into anyone I know here, but it does make me wonder about David Green. I suppose in the course of his work, he has to do some unsavoury investigating.

I walk up to the bar. A couple of old, unshaven men look me up and down, but I don't care. The young man behind the bar asks me what I'd like, and I order a sparkling water. He squirts the nozzle of water on tap into a grubby glass, and I carry it to a table that has two wooden chairs, positioned in the window, where I have a clear view of the street. I feel ridiculous with my base-ball hat still on, but I'm feeling nervous. I'm doing exactly what those notes told me not to do. I remind myself that no one knows I'm here, and that's for the best.

A text message pings through. It's David.

'Sorry, Tube got stuck, and now I'm on the bus just coming up Lavender Hill. Should be with you soon. Are you okay to hang on?'

'Yes, no problem.'

'Grr. More traffic. Sorry about this.'

'Have you found out anything more about Alison?' I type.

'Have you ever heard of Amerling?'

I haven't got a clue what he's talking about. Has that got something to do with Alison?

'No. What's Amerling?'

'I'll tell you everything in a few moments. The bus is pulling into the bus stop now.'

I put the phone onto a cardboard beer mat on the sticky table and peer out of the window. I can see a red London bus pulling into a bus stop a bit further down the busy road on the other side. And then I see David Green. He is dressed more scruffily than when I've met him previously, in black trousers that seem too long and a black raincoat. He walks quickly towards the zebra crossing. He must see me in the pub window, because he raises a hand and smiles at me. He presses the button on the pedestrian crossing and jiggles his feet impatiently as he waits for the lights to change. He glances in both directions, back and forth quickly, and then decides to cross. I can't see if the lights have actually changed or not.

I hear the screech of tyres. A black four-wheel-drive vehicle appears, seemingly from nowhere, driving much too fast for a London street. Time slows down. I try to make sense of what I'm seeing just a few feet away from me. That black car, rather than swerving to avoid David, drives purposefully towards him. David is thrown up into the air like a rag doll, arms and legs waving, his messenger bag flying through the air and skidding onto the pavement, and David landing with a thud on the tarmac in the middle of the road. The hooting of a horn. More screeching brakes. A high-pitched scream. I am frozen, staring at the bedlam on the street, wondering whether it's for real or if this is another horrible nightmare. But no, it's David lying there motionless. A bus comes to a full stop, blocking the road.

A couple of people at the adjacent table in the pub stand up and shout to the bar staff. And then I'm spurred into motion. I run out of the pub, knocking over chairs in the process, racing onto the street, pushing people as I run onto the road. I'm sobbing as I lean over David, kneeling on the tarmac. There is blood on the road, and his eyes are shut. I wish I knew first aid, but I don't.

'Help!' I scream. A few people congregate around us, peering at David, who is motionless.

'Out of the way. I'm a doctor.'

Feet step backwards, but I stay there, staring at David's face, willing him to open his eyes. A young man wearing jeans and a hoodie kneels down next to me. Very gently, he places his fingers over David's wrist; then he leans back on his heels and says firmly, 'Everyone stand back. Right back on the pavement, please.' People do as he says and walk back onto the pavement. He turns to look at me. 'You too, please.'

I'm so relieved he's taking control that I do as he says, getting up and walking backwards, my eyes glued to David's motionless body. I stand there, shaking violently at the side of the road, my arms wrapped around myself.

'Are you alright, love?' An elderly woman pushing one of those old-fashioned shopping trolley bags looks at me with bloodshot eyes.

I can't formulate words and just shake my head.

And then I hear the sirens, and I'm so relieved. An ambulance screeches to a halt, and two police cars arrive from different directions. That's the advantage of living in London; you're never too far away from a hospital or the emergency services. The young doctor who is doing something to David stands up and talks animatedly to the paramedics. I walk forwards.

Two policemen jump out of their squad car. 'Please, ma'am, stand back,' one of them instructs me.

'I know him. He's my friend. He was here to meet me.' My voice is barely a whisper. 'Is he alive?'

'I don't know. We have to let the paramedics do their thing. Are you here alone?' He throws me a sympathetic glance.

I nod.

'And you saw what happened?'

'Yes. A black car drove straight at him, hit him and then sped away.'

'And what's your name?'

'Stephanie Siskin.'

'Okay, Stephanie. We'll need to take a statement from you. The gentleman who is hurt, what's his name?'

'David Green. I don't know much about him. He's a researcher. I've only got his mobile number.'

'Well, let's get Mr Green off to hospital, and then we'll take a statement from you.'

'I've left my handbag and coat in the pub.'

'Alright, why don't you go back inside, and I'll come and find you in a few moments.'

Somehow I manage to put one foot in front of the other and walk into the pub. There's old-fashioned music playing, 'Lovely Day' by Bill Withers, and it's just so inappropriate. I used to love that song. I have to hold onto the wall and the backs of chairs as I make my way to where I was sitting. I gasp as I realise that my handbag, mobile phone and coat are gone. It's been what, ten minutes, fifteen at the most? I stand there looking at the bare table and burst into tears. I know it's the shock, but really …

A woman comes bustling over to me. She's rotund with deep laughter lines around her eyes and is rubbing her hands on a white tea towel.

'Were you sitting at that table, dear?'

'Yes,' I sob.

'I've got your things. I saw you rush out, so I picked

up your belongings and put them behind the bar for safekeeping.'

'Oh, thank goodness,' I say, collapsing onto the chair, grateful that there are kind people in this world.

'What a horrible thing to have happened. I do hope that man is alright. You wait there, and I'll bring you over a nice cuppa with a couple of spoonfuls of sugar and a glass of brandy. You'll need it, what with the shock.'

'Thank you,' I murmur.

A minute later, she's back with a big mug of milky tea and a couple of chocolate biscuits and a round brandy glass filled halfway up with the amber liquid. She puts them down on the table, goes back to the bar and returns with my bag and coat.

'I slipped your phone into your bag.'

'You're so kind. How much do I owe you?'

'Nothing. It's on the house. You had a terrible shock seeing what happened. Did you know the man who got hit?'

'Yes, I was meant to be meeting him here.'

Her eyes widen. 'Is he going to be alright?'

'I don't know.'

We both watch as the paramedics lift David onto a stretcher. Is he still alive? Is it even possible to survive such a violent hit-and-run? In my mind's eye, I see his body flying up into the air and landing with a thud. I'll reckon I'll see that horrific image in slow motion for the rest of my life.

A few seconds later, the ambulance speeds away, its siren blaring, but the street is still humming with blue flashing lights and people standing around in little groups, still rubbernecking, even though the star of the show has left.

20

I take one sip of brandy and splutter. I hate the taste; it's too sweet and burns the back of my throat. Besides, I shouldn't be drinking because I'm pregnant. I've probably just witnessed death, and inside me there is life, yet it's too much to comprehend. I put the brandy glass down and pick up the mug of tea instead. Tea slops onto the table as I bring it to my lips because my hands won't stop shaking.

Perhaps five minutes later, the policeman comes into the pub and looks around, evidently searching for me. I raise my hand to attract his attention, and he walks over.

'Are you here alone?' He glances at his little notebook. 'Ms Siskin?'

'Yes.'

'It seems that you were one of the few witnesses.'

'How's that possible? This is a busy London street.'

'I'm afraid it's often the way. For now, it seems that it's only you and the bus driver who saw exactly what happened. Would you mind if I sit down so I can take a full statement? It would be extremely helpful.'

'Yes, of course.' I gesture to the empty seat where David should be sitting.

'Were you sitting here when the accident happened?'

I nod. 'David got off the bus, and he waved at me as he stood on the other side of the zebra crossing. He pressed the button and looked from right to left. I'm not sure if the lights had changed when he started walking across. And then this big black car just appeared. I might have imagined it, but it really looked like it steered into David. Then it accelerated away.' I shudder as I recall that moment.

'Did you see the driver?'

'No, I'm sorry. I was looking from the side, and I think it had darkened windows. I don't even know if it was a man or a woman driving, or if there was anyone else other than the driver in the car.'

'And the make of the car?'

'I'm not sure. It was big, so a four-wheel drive probably.'

'Did you glimpse any part of the number plate?'

'No, I'm sorry. I was just so shocked. I saw him being thrown into the air, and I just ran outside.' I shudder. 'You will be able to catch the driver, won't you? There are so many cameras around London.'

'We certainly hope so. Is David Green a friend or a business colleague?'

'Neither, really. He's a researcher for a true-crime television programme.'

The policeman raises an eyebrow. 'You say that the car appeared to aim directly for Mr Green. Does that mean you think this was a deliberate hit-and-run?'

I bury my face in my hands. Did I imagine it? Was the driver perhaps just swerving and he or she lost control of the vehicle?

'Ms Siskin?' he says softly.

'I don't know. Now I'm not sure. At the time, yes, that's what I thought, but I'm probably mistaken.' I wonder if I am. David Green might have made enemies over the years, sticking his nose into other people's business, digging up memories that people want to keep buried. He's much more likely to have enemies than the average person.

'And what was the purpose of your meeting?'

I nod. 'He wanted to talk to me about the disappearance of Alison Miller nearly a decade ago.'

The young policeman looks at me with surprise. 'And what was your involvement in that case?'

'I was her flatmate. David said he wanted to discuss some things with me.' I try to take another sip of tea, but I simply can't get the mug to my lips. It's as if my whole body is trembling violently. The policeman frowns with concern.

'Would you like the paramedics to check you over, Ms Siskin?'

'It's Stephanie. And no, no,' I say. 'I'm fine. I just want to go home.'

'Is there anyone who can collect you?'

'I can get an Uber.'

'I think it would be better if you had someone collect you. You've had a terrible shock.'

'My husband, then.' I'd prefer Mum, but she hasn't got a car, and besides, she's babysitting the kids. I just hope that Oliver has finished his meeting and answers his phone.

'Why don't you call your husband, and then I'll take down your personal details?'

I nod. My fingers slip as I try to call Oliver, but when I manage it, to my relief, he answers quickly.

'Steph, what's up?'

'How quickly can you get to Clapham?'

'Clapham? Why?'

'I'm in Clapham.'

'What on earth are you doing there?'

'I need you to come and get me, in the car, please. I'll explain when you're here.'

'Are you alright?'

'Yes. No. I'm okay, but please come and get me. I'm at the Hen and Mare Pub, it's at 23 Corner Street. How soon can you get here?'

'I'm not at home yet. It'll take a while to collect the car and get to you. What's happened, Steph?'

'I was a witness to a hit-and-run, and I'm in shock.'

'Oh, darling. I'll get in a cab and come straight to you.'

'Thanks, Oliver.' I slip the phone back into my bag and turn to the policeman. 'My husband is coming.'

The policeman takes down my name, address and phone numbers and tells me they might need to interview me again.

'Will you be alright waiting here?' he asks as he stands up. I nod.

'How can I find out how David is?' I ask.

'He's probably been taken to Chelsea and Westminster Hospital, so you'll be able to get an update from the hospital. If there are any changes, I or a colleague will be in touch. You take care, Stephanie.' He hands me his business card.

I know exactly what he means by 'if there are any changes'. If David doesn't make it, this will turn into a murder enquiry.

It takes Oliver forty minutes to arrive, by which time I'm much calmer. Back after Alison disappeared and when the nightmares started, Oliver took me to see a

doctor. I was referred for therapy – cognitive behavioural therapy, to be precise. It helped quite a bit, in the
daytime at least, if not at night. Now I try to recall some
of the techniques. I turn my back to the flashing lights in
the street and do deep breathing. I drink the cup of tea
and eat the stale biscuits and order another tea. The
street is still blocked off, with scene of crime officers
combing the street and speaking to possible witnesses.
As I'm sitting there, offering up silent prayers that
David will make it and not be severely injured, I realise
that I'm going to have to tell Oliver the truth, that I was
meeting David Green. I just hope my husband doesn't
blow a gasket.

I stand up as he enters the pub, looking around for
me, his face creased with concern.

'Here,' I say quietly.

'Darling!' He wraps me in his arms, and I feel inde-
scribable relief. 'Let's get you out of here.'

I wave goodbye to the landlady, who was so kind to
me. Oliver keeps his arm around my shoulders as he
escorts me out of the pub. I can't look at the road and
instead keep my eyes firmly on the shopfronts to our
right. Oliver leads me around the corner and into a
waiting taxi. When we're settled inside, he takes my
hand, then turns to me.

'What happened?'

I take a deep breath. 'Don't be angry, please. I was
meeting David Green. He had something urgent he
wanted to tell me.'

'For god's sake, Stephanie,' Oliver hisses.

'Hear me out, please. As David was crossing the
road, on the zebra crossing, a car roared towards him,
hit him, and I don't know if he's dead or alive. It was
awful, Oliver,' I say, my hand muffling my mouth.

'What a horrible accident to witness,' he says,

squeezing my hand. I don't voice my suspicions that it was no accident. 'Have the police arrested the driver?'

'I don't know.'

'I'm sorry that you saw this, but what the hell were you doing meeting him? I thought we'd agreed that you weren't going to have anything more to do with the man. I can't understand what's gotten into you of late. You're behaving so irrationally.'

I bite my lip as I think that it's not me who is behaving irrationally. Frankly, if anyone had been through what I have, they would think I was being totally sane. I stare out of the window as we drive slowly through London's streets, over the river Thames towards home. But I can't stop thinking. Who would want David dead? Is it anything to do with his investigations into Alison's disappearance, or am I catastrophising things? I try to play back what I saw in my head, but the more I think about it, the more horrifying it is. I want to tug the image and the noise out of my head and throw them away forever.

I don't sleep. I lie tossing and turning whilst Oliver stays motionless next to me. I think I'm scared of going to sleep. What if I dream of Alison *and* David? I can't cope with the awful realities and the terrors of my nightmares. By the time a pale grey light seeps around the edges of our sage green curtains, I am aching all over, as if I'm going down with the flu. I drift off to sleep for a couple of hours and then am brutally awakened by the alarm clock. Oliver gets out of bed and stretches.

'I didn't sleep,' I say, forcing my eyes open. 'I feel awful. Is there any possibility of you getting the kids up and off to school?'

'Yes, but I need to be able to trust you, Stephanie. I still can't get over the fact you met with David Green when I expressly told you not to. It's for your own bloody good.'

I turn my back to him and bury my face in my pillow. How ironic that he feels he can't trust me. That's exactly how I feel about him. And what does that say about the state of our marriage?

My darling little Bea brings me up a cup of tea and a piece of toast heavily coated in orange marmalade. I tell the kids that I'm not feeling well, reassure them that it's not catching and I'll be better very soon, and wish them a good day at school.

'Call me if you're really not well,' Oliver says. 'If your mum can't pick up the kids from school, I'll leave work early.'

'Thank you,' I say. 'And I'm sorry.'

He shrugs his shoulders. 'I meant to tell you that we're having a departmental drinks party the Thursday after next. You'd mentioned you'd like to come, so perhaps you can put it in the diary.'

'Yes, of course,' I say.

He throws me a brief smile. 'Keep the doors locked, Steph. See you later.'

I sleep for a couple of hours, but still feel lousy when I awake. I take two paracetamol and call Chelsea and Westminster Hospital. Frustratingly, other than confirming that David Green is indeed a patient, they won't give me any further information. I suppose the fact that he is a patient must be good news; at least it means he's alive. I call the friendly policeman who interviewed me yesterday, and he brings me up to date.

'David Green is alive, but I'm afraid he's in a drug-induced coma. I don't know his prognosis, but obviously we hope to interview him as soon as he's well enough. Have you remembered anything else?'

'No, I just wanted to find out how he is. Have you tracked down the driver of the car?'

'Unfortunately, not yet. My colleagues are studying the CCTV footage from nearby cameras and trying to put a picture together of what happened.'

I potter around the house for a while, but the exhaustion hits again, and I crawl back to bed. It's just as I'm drifting off to sleep that I remember the text message exchange that David and I had. How could I have forgotten? I grab my mobile phone and scroll back. He asked me, *Have you ever heard of Amerling?* I sit up in bed and do a Google search for Amerling on my phone.

The very first thing that comes up is information on an artist called Friedrich von Amerling. I frown. What has an Austrian painter who lived in the nineteenth century got to do with finding out what's happened to Alison? It doesn't make sense. I scroll through pages and pages of Google searches, but the most famous Amerling to have ever lived is that artist. I return to information on him. Born in Vienna, he was considered to be one of the most important portrait painters of the century. He worked and studied all over Europe and painted over one thousand portraits, predominantly of the aristocracy and wealthy middle classes of the Biedermeier period, a term used to describe the thriving artistic styles that flourished in the arts between 1815 and 1848 in Central Europe. All very interesting, but I can't begin to fathom how this relates to Alison or what David intended to tell me.

It isn't until I start browsing through Amerling's paintings, many of which have sold for tens of thousands of dollars, that I stumble across a portrait that looks incredibly familiar. I try to rack my brain to recall where I've seen it before. At William's auction house, perhaps, or in their grand home. And then I realise. It's much closer to home. It looks incredibly like that ethereal oil painting of a woman with dark ringlets that Oliver has in our safe. *Our safe!* I hurry downstairs to Oliver's study, where it is as neat as always. I open the door to the safe and put in the code, his grandmother's birthday. Nothing happens, so I try again.

I lean backwards against the desk. Oliver has changed the code once more and has failed to tell me. I now have no doubt in my mind. There are things in this safe that my husband doesn't want me to see or to know about. My husband is lying to me.

And then I wonder. Where was Oliver yesterday evening when David was hit? He tells me that he attends a departmental meeting every Thursday evening, but perhaps he doesn't. Perhaps he has a woman whom he meets every Thursday, Nahla perhaps, or even worse than that, maybe it was him in that big black car. I run my fingers through my hair. This is getting ridiculous. We own a small silver Prius, a sensible city car. And Oliver is a kind man; he would never knowingly hurt someone. But he is so against me talking to David, and that just doesn't sit right.

My phone beeps at me to remind me I'm due to meet Nahla for a coffee. I don't feel up to leaving the house, but I would like to talk to her. I call her.

'Nahla, I'm sorry to bail out on you, but I'm feeling really under the weather. Can we rearrange?'

'Of course. Oliver told me that you witnessed a horrific hit-and-run last night. That must have been terrible.'

I narrow my eyes. Is it normal for Oliver to share such information with a colleague?

'I hope I didn't interrupt things. What time did the departmental meeting finish last night?'

'Last night?' she queries.

'The departmental meeting,' I reiterate.

'It was cancelled last night.'

'Oh.' I hurry to end the call. 'Have a good trip to Florence. I'm looking forward to catching up when you're back.'

I close my eyes. If Oliver wasn't at his departmental meeting yesterday evening, where the hell was he?

21

Oliver wasn't where he said he was.

Oliver has locked me out of the safe again.

Oliver had an affair with Alison that he didn't tell me about.

Oliver doesn't want me talking to David Green.

Oliver might have a Von Amerling painting in his safe, and David wanted to talk to me about Amerling.

I feel like I'm going mad. I stumble up the stairs, muttering to myself like a crazy woman. *I don't trust my husband. My husband is lying.* What the hell am I going to do? I have no money, no qualifications. I'm pregnant and already have two children, with a third on the way. If I have to leave Oliver, what will happen? Will he try to get custody of the kids?

But I don't *want* to leave Oliver; I love him. Or at least I think I do. I'm shivering violently again, feeling intermittently freezing cold and burning hot. My teeth are clattering, and my leg feels as if it has a hot poker digging inside it. I tumble into bed and burst into tears. I feel so alone. So very confused. There is only one person whom I can turn to, and that's Mum.

When I've controlled my pathetic sobs, I call her.

'I'm not well, Mum. Could you pick up the kids?'

'I was planning to anyway. What's up with you?'

'I saw ...' And then I burst into tears, snivelling, incoherent, self-indulgent cries, knowing that Mum is the only person in the world who can metaphorically and physically pick me up and make me feel better. She's always brilliant when someone is ill; I often thought she would have made a wonderful nurse.

'I'm coming over,' she says. 'Stay in bed, try to sleep, and I'll let myself in.'

By the time Mum arrives, I am writhing in agony, moaning out loud, my body covered in a sheen of sweat, yet I am also freezing cold. She walks into our bedroom, takes one look at me and then rushes to the side of the bed, throwing her arms around me. Should I really still be so dependent on my mother aged thirty-two? Frankly, I don't care.

'You've got a fever, love,' she says, stroking my forehead. 'And the pain, is it the old injury?'

I nod, trying to stop myself from crying. She's seen me like this many times before. You would have thought that I might have developed better coping strategies, but the ferocity of the pain always takes me by surprise. It's as if we humans have no capacity to remember pain, both physical and emotional. I suppose it's our brains' coping mechanism, but for me, the violence and the agony seems to be getting worse every time rather than better.

'What painkillers have you taken?'

'Just paracetamol,' I pant. 'I can't take anything stronger. I'm pregnant, remember.'

'We need to call a doctor. You've obviously got a bug, and the old injury is playing up. Can't take any risks.'

I know what Mum is saying. Because I have metal in my leg, she's always been concerned that I might be more susceptible to sepsis. I'm not sure she's right, but I'm happy for her to take charge.

'Try to do some deep breathing whilst I make some phone calls. Is your doctor's number on your phone?'

'Yes.' I point to my mobile, which is on my bedside table. 'Code is Dad's birthday.'

Mum throws me a sad glance and takes the phone. I listen to her quick steps as she hurries downstairs. I try to breathe in slowly and out again, but when the pain is so fierce, it's almost impossible. It seems like ages before she returns upstairs, but it's probably only five minutes or so.

Mum walks into the room carrying a tray with a jug of water, a clean glass, a banana and a piece of buttered toast.

'Have you eaten anything?'

I shake my head.

'Right, let's get something down you. I've left a message at the doctor's surgery, and Oliver's on his way home.'

'Why did you disturb him?' I ask, my voice a bit screechy.

'Because he loves you, and he needs to look after you. I rang to tell him you weren't well, and it was he who said he'd come home. You need to let him look after you, sweetheart. He wants to.'

I let the tears flow into my pillow, because what Mum doesn't know is everything I've found out about my husband, all those secrets, and the big ones that I'm keeping from him.

'Oh, and you got a phone call from a gentleman called Rahul. He said he was a colleague of yours. Is that what students call each other these days? Anyway, I told him that you weren't well and you'll call him back when you're better.'

If I weren't in so much pain, I'd have to laugh. Mum is so unsuspecting.

The doctor listens to what Mum tells him and decides that I am worthy of a home visit. Another advantage of being in London. He is an older man, reassuring and no-nonsense. He's clearly read through my records, even though I've never met him before. He takes some blood, but reassures me that it's unlikely I have sepsis. Nevertheless, he'll rush the blood through for testing. I whisper to him that I'm pregnant, and when I say my husband doesn't know yet, he doesn't even raise an eyebrow. For that, I decide I like him.

Whatever the doctor gives me makes me feel like I've been cloaked in a chemical blanket. My limbs feel leaden, and the vice-like spasms in my leg ease. I feel my eyes close, and I welcome the prospect of sleep, even if I have to face the nightmares. It's just as I'm dozing off that I hear Oliver and Mum talking in the corridor just beyond the slightly ajar bedroom door.

'I'm worried, Helena. Stephanie was doing so well. No nightmares, infrequent bouts of pain, all until that bloody TV researcher tipped up. Ever since he's started digging around, he's opened up Steph's old wounds. I just want us to get back to how things were a couple of months ago. I'm desperate for her to get better and to heal from all the traumas that she's had to face in her past. I really love her, Helena.'

'I know you do, Oliver,' Mum says. Her voice sounds muffled, and I assume they're hugging each other. Oliver sounds utterly convincing. When I hear him talk about me like that, I begin to question my doubts.

I sleep most of the next couple of days. Either Mum

or Oliver is in the house all the time, and it's such a relief to know I'm safe and being looked after. I just wish I knew how David Green was.

'Who's Rahul?' Oliver asks as he brings me a tray with supper on it, prepared by Mum.

'An old friend from uni. Why?' I turn my face away from him. I'm glad I never told Oliver about Rahul.

'I'll bring it up in a moment.'

'Bring what up?' I frown and pull myself up in bed so that I can eat off the tray. My heart is pounding as I wonder what Rahul has done. Nothing stupid, I hope.

A couple of minutes later, Oliver reappears with a bouquet of flowers, its stems encased in plastic, an assortment of blooms in pale pinks and whites that contrast with the sprigs of eucalyptus. There's a small card wedged into the flower arrangement. I open it up.

Dear Stephanie,

I gather you haven't been well. Just wanted to wish you a speedy recovery.

Best wishes,

Rahul

There is nothing suggestive or inappropriate in the message, other than perhaps it's questionable to send flowers to someone else's wife. But then again, Rahul has been nothing other than kind to me. He's not pretending. At least, I don't think he is. I suppose he must have asked Mum for our address when she told him that I wasn't well.

'It's really kind of him,' I say.

'How did he know you weren't well?'

'He rang when I was in bed, and Mum answered.'

'I didn't realise you were still in touch with your old university friends,' Oliver says.

'I'm not, or at least I wasn't. David Green reached out to him, too. I've been back in touch with various people David has contacted.' That, of course, isn't strictly true, although visiting Josh in jail and reconnecting with Rahul means I'm not telling a complete fib.

Oliver takes the flowers away again, and I'm glad that he leaves them downstairs.

By the weekend, I am feeling considerably better. On Saturday morning, I get up before Oliver and make a big breakfast of eggs, bacon and waffles for us all. Both Bea and Sam have parties to attend this afternoon, and I plan on cornering Oliver for a heart-to-heart. I wish I didn't have to do this, to lie to him in the way I fear he might be lying to me, but if I don't know what he's hiding in our safe, it's going to eat me up. I need to think about my own health and that of the baby growing inside me. I don't get the chance until the afternoon when he's sitting on the sofa reading the *Guardian* and I've finished cleaning up from lunch.

'Can you show me your collection?' I ask.

'What?' He frowns.

'All the things that you've collected over the past couple of years, the jewellery, the paintings, the stuff you have in your safe. I feel like I'm missing out by not having shown any interest in your hobby.'

'You're not missing out.'

'I'd love to see them. Please.'

He puts the newspaper down with a sigh. 'What's this about really, Stephanie?'

I turn my back to him and pretend to shuffle through some papers to avoid giving anything away. 'Nothing. Just curiosity. I can go and look myself, but I'd much rather you showed me.' Of course, I can't look because I've already discovered I don't know the new safe code. 'We don't do much together these days unless it's related to the kids, and I just thought it might be fun for me to start sharing some of your interests. It's either that, or you can come with me to Pilates.'

'Not bloody likely.' He stands up and walks to his study with me a few steps behind. The tendons in his neck are tight, as if he's clenching his jaw. He stands in front of the safe cupboard, blocking my view, so I can't see the code he puts in, then he swings open the door and stands to one side, making an exaggerated gesture for me to have a look.

'Oh,' I say. The painting has gone, leaving just the smaller boxes containing his collection of rings and other artefacts. 'Where's that lovely portrait of a woman?'

'Portrait?' He frowns.

'You had a painting in the safe.'

'Oh, that one. William sold it for me.'

'That's a shame. I thought it was beautiful and was going to suggest we hang it in our bedroom. How much did it make?' I open some of the boxes containing signet rings because I'm sure if I turn to look at Oliver, he will be able to read my mind. There is a long pause, and for a moment, I wonder if he heard my question.

'Did it make a lot at auction, that painting?'

Oliver sighs loudly. 'It wasn't sold at auction. William sold it to a private buyer. And it was meant to be a surprise. I was going to use the money from the sale to take you on holiday to the Maldives, away from all the unpleasantness you've been going through. I thought you could do with a holiday.'

Really? I stand up and slowly turn around to look at him, blinking to stop the tears welling in my eyes. He is staring at me with an exasperated expression, much like how he used to look when Bea had her toddler tantrum fits. Have I totally misjudged my husband? Have I forgotten that he is, in fact, a good man? Perhaps it's just my past experiences that are feeding into my negative assumptions that if something bad has happened to you once, it's quite possible it will happen again.

'That was kind of you,' I say, although I still have my doubts. It's only when I step back and Oliver moves to lock the safe that I remember the main reason for looking inside it.

'Was that painting by Von Amerling?'

He scratches the back of his neck and frowns. 'Who?'

'I've been doing a bit of research on artists, and I thought that lovely oil painting of the woman with ringlets might have been by Friedrich Von Amerling.'

He shakes his head. 'I think your amateur art sleuthing is a bit off track. It was a late eighteenth-century oil painting of an English aristocrat, painted by an unknown artist. Even though we didn't know its provenance, it fetched a fair bit. Enough to take you, my beautiful wife, on an exotic holiday. Perhaps you *should* get involved in my collecting, as you clearly have good taste in art.'

'I'm only as good as my teacher,' I say, giving him a little punch on the arm. It seems like the tense atmosphere is diffused.

'I don't know about you, but I could do with a cup of coffee. Would you mind putting the kettle on whilst I lock up here?' he asks.

I have no choice. It's not as if I can rebut Oliver, who is one of the leading lights in art history in the UK. It's just such a disturbing coincidence that David asked me if I knew about Amerling, and that Oliver's painting was, to my relatively inexpert eye at least, so very much like his nineteenth-century portraits. Someone else might think it's just a coincidence; the trouble is, I don't believe in coincidences.

22

'If I sleep well tonight, I think I'll be up to taking the kids to school in the morning,' I say to Oliver as I switch off my bedside lamp.

He strokes my hair. 'I'm so glad you're feeling better. I've had a chat with your mum, and she's offered to come and stay here this coming weekend to look after the kids, as I thought you could do with a break and a change of scene. William and Naomi have invited us to stay at their house for the weekend. Their two won't be home from boarding school, so it's the chance for us to have a bit of adult-only downtime.'

'I don't know,' I say quickly. 'I'm asking too much of Mum, and I've missed being with the children over the past week.'

Oliver tenses, closes his book and places it on his bedside table. 'It'll do us both good to get away.' He switches off his bedside light and shuffles down into bed, putting his arms around me. I know what this signifies, and although I feel a bit better, making love is most definitely not on my agenda.

'Please,' I say softly, wriggling away from his exploring hands. 'I'm really not in the mood.'

He lets out a puff of air and rolls over onto his back. 'That's why we need to get away for a night or two. You're so uptight at the moment, Steph. We need some time to chill. It'll do our marriage good. Don't you agree?'

'Okay. We can go to their place for the weekend.'

I suppose he's right. It does feel like our marriage is fragile at the moment, and I know that's largely down to me and the dark places that my imagination has taken me. So much of what has happened is circumstantial, and it seems that I'm alone in having doubts. Josh probably did kill Alison. David being hit by a car was likely just an accident, being in the wrong place at the wrong time. And it's not like I got a good look at that portrait in the safe. My knowledge of art, whilst better than most people, is still limited and certainly rusty, and David is, as far as I know, still in a coma. So I can't ask him if he was referring to Amerling the painter or someone else with the same name. If we go to the De Villeneuves', I'll get the chance to have a quiet word with William, and I can ask him about the portrait that Oliver sold.

But there is one outstanding problem, and that's that Oliver will expect me to drink alcohol. We always drink too much at the De Villeneuves' house, indulging in their excessive hospitality, consuming fine wines and after-dinner liqueurs. I'm going to have to face up to reality and tell my husband that I'm pregnant. Having another baby may not be what I want, but I know Oliver will be thrilled, and I'm not being fair keeping it from him. Sometimes I think that my husband is, deep down, really insecure. It's as if he needs to prove his virility, and a big family is evidence of that. But now isn't the time for too much introspection. Now is the time for honesty.

'Oliver,' I say quietly. He doesn't move. His breathing is quiet and regular. 'Oliver,' I whisper again, a little louder. Still no reaction. I sigh and turn onto my side, facing away from my husband. It will have to be a conversation for tomorrow.

The forecast for the weekend is good, and despite my initial reluctance, I'm looking forward to spending it at the De Villeneuves'. The children seem excited about the prospect of having Grandma all to themselves, especially when she promises them an outing to Hamleys on Regent Street, with twenty pounds each to spend. I try not to be irked, because I know that Mum can't really afford it, but remind myself she is their only grandparent, and if she wants to indulge them, so be it.

Naomi has invited us for early afternoon on Saturday. There isn't a cloud in the sky, and when we pull up to their grand entrance drive, I lean back and realise how lucky we are to have friends who live in such a glorious place.

I still haven't told Oliver about the pregnancy. The last couple of days have been manic. He had the staff meeting and the drinks on Thursday evening, which, due to still being under the weather, I didn't attend. Yesterday evening, Oliver was working late in his study at home, getting everything done so that he could free up the weekend. I could tell him now, on our journey down from London, but for some reason it still doesn't feel right. I'm sure the time will come. Perhaps tonight, when he makes love to me in the De Villeneuves' sumptuous spare bedroom.

We park at the front of the grand house, and I get out of the car and stretch. The sun is hot on my face, and I inhale the glorious scent of early summer. Oliver takes out our small suitcase from the boot of the car, and we walk up the steps to the front door.

'Just in time,' William says as he flings the door open. He's dressed for golf, and I spot a flicker of dismay on Oliver's face. My husband doesn't like playing golf, probably because he's not very good at it, but he accompanies William from time to time, just to appease his friend, I assume.

William puts his arm around Oliver's shoulders. 'A quick round, my friend,' he says. 'Just a quickie.'

Naomi appears, wearing a long white kaftan over a bikini, with bronzed legs and manicured toes peeping out of high-heeled sandals.

'Welcome, darlings,' she says, giving us both kisses. She slips her arm through mine. 'I thought we could have a relaxing afternoon by the pool whilst the men go for their round of golf. We need to make the most of this unseasonal English sunshine. I'm sure a bottle of bubbles and soaking in the rays will make you feel much better.'

I smile weakly. I've never been that keen on sunbathing. I am very careful not to expose my scars to the sun, in case it makes them worse.

'Why don't you go and get changed whilst I get us some champagne glasses. I'll meet you outside.'

'Okay,' I say, noting that Oliver and William have already disappeared.

Having spent so much time in their house, I know my way around. The spare bedroom we sleep in is up the staircase and two doors down on the left. They have three spare rooms, but ours is the nicest, with views onto their sumptuous gardens and a pale grey marble en-suite, with fluffy white towels and The White Company toiletries in white-and-black packaging, just like in an upmarket hotel.

I pull on a swimming costume and put a bright yellow sundress on over the top. I find my sunglasses and then walk downstairs, through the living room and out through the open patio doors onto the veranda. Naomi is lying face down on a sun lounger with her bikini top unclipped. She turns her head towards me and smiles as I sit down on the lounger next to her.

'Do you want to do the honours? There's a bottle of champers in the cooling bucket.'

'Actually, I think I'll pass,' I say.

She frowns. 'Really?'

'Do you mind if I go for a walk?' I ask. I feel like stretching my legs, and it's the perfect opportunity to explore their extensive garden.

'Do whatever you like. I'm going to doze like a beached whale. That bloody personal trainer worked my butt off this morning, and I'm knackered.'

I smile. Naomi's butt is pert, and her hip bones jut out. If anything, she's too thin.

'We'll open the champers when you return,' Naomi says, with a yawn.

If I think back to all the occasions we've visited the De Villeneuves', we've always been kept busy, with dinner parties, drinks, outings to Chessington Theme Park with the kids, or to the local wineries when us adults have been alone. Yet they have everything they need right here. A beautiful turquoise swimming pool surrounded by limestone flagstones and the type of umbrellas and sun loungers found in luxury spa hotels. As I walk down several steps to the sprawling lawn, other than the tennis court hidden behind a yew hedge, I have no idea what lies beyond it. I take off my sandals and luxuriate in the sensation of my toes sinking into the soft grass. The air smells of freshly cut grass, along with the sweet scent of jasmine and lilac.

I walk towards a large flower bed at the bottom of the lawn, filled with vast shrubs and mature trees beyond. There is a discreet wrought-iron gate, which I open. In front of me is a pathway made from flat stones with moss growing around them. It meanders between mature oak trees and silver birches, and I feel as if I'm in a secret garden, leading to a fairy world where wondrous things will happen. It's no surprise that William employs three gardeners. This place is vast.

And then, to my surprise, the trees give way to a lake. I stand in wonder. No one has ever mentioned a lake on this property, but perhaps it's not something that would come up in conversation. It's not a big lake, but certainly larger than my definition of a pond. Tall reeds grow around the edge, as well as the gigantic leaves of gunnera bushes and irises in deep blues and yellows. In the centre of the lake there's a little island planted with a couple of trees that look like cherry. At the foot of the island is a birdhouse, probably for the resident ducks, and water lilies poke their heads up between large flat leaves. It really is delightful. I pad around the edge of the lake, standing for a while and watching the green and blue dragonflies swoop down onto the still surface of the water, listening to the chirruping birds and the gentle rustling of leaves in the breeze. I inhale the sweet-smelling air and raise my face to the sun. I'm so lucky to be here, so lucky to be married to my husband, even if he does have his faults. As I place my hands over my flat stomach, I apologise to my unborn child for having had negative thoughts towards him or her.

I carry on walking around the lake and see yet another path. This time, it leads to a large rockery, with tumbling giant rocks, crevasses filled with sprawling alpine plants. It's more ramshackle here, as if this might have been a formal garden once upon a time, with overgrown yew hedges and giant rhododendron bushes. I pass a statue of a woman carved from stone, slightly green in colour from moss and years of neglect. And then I emerge into another small section, and I stand totally still. There's something very familiar about this place, but I'm not sure why, as I have never been in this part of the De Villeneuves' garden before. I swivel around, feeling frustrated that I can't work out why there's this sense of familiarity. It's as if I had a memory that was sparked, but the connection wasn't properly fused, blocking the full recollection. It's frustrating. Perhaps Oliver brought me here early on in our relationship and I've just forgotten, but I don't think so.

The sun is surprisingly ferocious now, unseasonably so for an early summer's afternoon in southern England, so I slowly make my way back towards the house. Naomi has a parasol over her and is sitting up in her lounger, reading some trashy celebrity magazine. She peers at me over the top of her oversized sunglasses.

'You must be thirsty by now, darling,' she says. 'Do you want to do the honours?'

I open the bottle of champagne rather expertly. It's funny to think that I had never drunk champagne before meeting Oliver, let alone actually opened a bottle. Just goes to show how much my life has changed. I pour some into a champagne flute and hand the glass to Naomi. I pour myself a glass of water from a jug that was filled with ice cubes that have now melted.

I know what Naomi is going to ask me before the words tumble out of her mouth. I consider lying yet again, but I'm tired. I can't be bothered to keep up with the fibs. Besides, I need a confidante.

'You're not drinking?' she asks, her head tilted to one side. 'What's the real reason?'

I sigh and sit down on the edge of the lounger positioned next to Naomi.

'Meds or pregnancy?' Naomi probes. 'No, don't tell me.' She wrinkles her nose. 'You're pregnant, aren't you? You've got that look. I mentioned it to William a few days ago, and he was going to ask Oliver.'

I throw my hands up in defeat. 'You're right. I'm pregnant.'

'That's fantastic news!' Naomi exclaims. 'Absolutely the best news. We've got something wonderful to celebrate tonight!'

'Um, no. Not yet. I haven't reached twelve weeks, and no one knows.'

'We're hardly no one, are we?' Naomi says. 'We're your best friends.'

'But I haven't told Oliver,' I say meekly.

'You what?' Naomi puts her glass of champagne down on the ground. It wobbles, and she saves it from toppling over just in time.

'I haven't had the chance to tell him. With everything that's been going on, and I only just found out. I was planning on telling him tonight.'

'Well, don't worry, I'm not going to steal your thunder. But you really should tell Oliver as soon as possible. He'll be over the moon. We all know how much he loves children, and how he wanted a big family. It will be good for you, and you can both forget about that tart Alison.'

What? I don't think I say the word aloud, but perhaps I do. What the hell has my pregnancy got to do with Alison? And why has Naomi even mentioned her? And why on earth call her a tart? It sounded so personal, vindictive even.

This time, I do speak out loud. 'What do you mean? Did you know Alison?'

She waves her hands around. 'Good heavens, no. I just saw her around. Must have been on a social evening. Or perhaps I just recognised her photo from having seen it in the papers so often. Anyway, it's not important. Let's talk babies. What would you prefer, a girl or a boy?'

But I can't think about my pregnancy. All I can think about is, why the hell did Naomi make such a strange comment?

23

I really don't know what to say to Naomi, so I settle down on the sun lounger next to her, put my sunglasses on and pretend to drift off to sleep. I hear her get up and pad to the side of the pool, and then there's a splash as she dives in. I listen to her rhythmic strokes, but it isn't until she pulls herself out of the water that something clicks inside my brain.

When Alison's mother was showing me her photographs, there was that lovely picture of Alison looking so happy in a park. But perhaps it wasn't a park after all. Perhaps it was here, in the De Villeneuves' garden. I didn't see a statue of a man with outstretched arms when I walked around earlier, but it doesn't mean it's not here. Could I really be right? I sit up and stretch my arms upwards.

'Just popping in to go to the loo. Can I get you anything whilst I'm inside?' I ask Naomi.

She's rubbing herself dry with a towel and shivering slightly. 'I'm fine, thanks,' she says, sitting back down on her lounger and taking a swig of champagne.

Inside the house, I hurry upstairs to our room and find my phone. I really hope that the Millers' phone number isn't ex-directory. I search the online phone book, using their address, and bingo, there it is. I shut our bedroom door and then go into the bathroom, shutting that door, too, to avoid being overheard. My heart is thumping as I dial. It rings for a long time, and I worry that they're not at home, but eventually Mrs Miller answers.

'Hello, Mrs Miller. This is Stephanie Siskin, Alison's old friend. I'm afraid I don't have any new information, but I think I might have recognised where that lovely photo was taken of Alison next to a statue. Is there any possibility that you might be able to send me a copy of it?'

'I don't know, dear. I'd have to find somewhere that has one of those photocopying machines.'

'Do you have a mobile phone?'

'Yes, why?'

'Could you take a photograph of the photo with your mobile and send it to me?'

'I could take a photo, but I'd have to work out how to send it. I'm not very good with technology.'

'If you give me your mobile number, I'll send you instructions on how to do it.'

'I'll happily give it a go, but can't make any promises. I'm not good with things like that.'

'I'd really appreciate it, Mrs Miller. It could be a missing link.' I pause for a moment. 'I couldn't say much in front of David Green, but I miss Alison every single day.'

'I could tell you do, dear. I appreciate it. We don't get a chance to talk about her much these days. I was hoping that nice man Mr Green might come and see us again.'

I swallow. It's obvious that Mrs Miller has no idea about David Green's accident – but then again, why should she know? I decide not to say anything.

'I'll wait to hear from you,' I say. 'And thank you.'

I send Mrs Miller a text message with instructions on how to attach a photograph to her reply to me and hope that they're clear enough for her to understand.

By the time I go back downstairs, William and Oliver have returned. I walk into the kitchen, where I hear their voices, and see that Naomi has come inside and is rifling in the fridge.

'Hello, darling,' Oliver says. He looks very cheerful; I wonder if William let my husband win the round of golf. He places a quick kiss on my lips.

'Do you need any help with supper?' I ask Naomi.

'No, because I've got a local lady who's coming in to do it all for us. She'll prepare supper and clear away so we can relax and have a jolly time. And we've got lots to celebrate, haven't we, Steph?' She throws me a very unsubtle wink, which grates. I wish I hadn't told her that I was pregnant, because now she's forcing my hand. But then again, I wouldn't have gotten away with not drinking alcohol tonight without questions from Oliver and Naomi. It's time I tell him anyway, and I can't work out why I've been so reluctant. Because it makes it real, I suppose. And because it's going to dash my dreams.

'I'm going to have a shower,' Oliver says.

'I'll join you,' I say.

'Ooo ah!' William jostles Oliver. 'Lucky you!' He laughs.

'Not like that,' I say, rolling my eyes.

Back in our bedroom, Oliver sits on the edge of the bed to remove his shoes. I stand in front of him with my back to the window. 'I've got something to tell you,' I say, wringing my hands.

He glances up at me and lifts an eyebrow.

'I'm pregnant.'

He is stock-still for a moment, and I wonder if I got him all wrong. Maybe he is shocked and will want me to get rid of the baby. Maybe he thought that two children completed our family. We stare at each other for a long moment, and then his face cracks into a smile. He jumps up, flings his arms around me, lifts me into the air and throws me onto the bed. He leans on his elbows over me, and those beautiful blue eyes lock onto mine. Sometimes I wish Oliver weren't quite so good-looking.

'It's unexpected,' he says, gently grazing my lips with his. 'But it's wonderful news, nevertheless.'

'What about money? How will we cope with a third child? The house is too small.'

'Stop looking at the negatives,' he says. 'I always wanted a big family, and my dreams are coming true. We'll cope.' He kisses me deeply and starts to remove my clothes.

'Not now, Oliver,' I say. 'I'm not in the mood.'

'You're my wife,' he says huskily. 'And the mother to my three children.'

My feeble attempts to remove his hands don't stop him. I lie there, furious with myself. Furious that I've let him push me into doing things I don't want to do yet again. It is so damned confusing. I love Oliver, but more and more frequently, I feel that I can't be myself around him. That my true self is dissolving into the version of me that Oliver has invented, and I don't like that person.

I am subdued at dinner. We sit in their sumptuous dining room with dark red papered walls, at a long table made with inlaid wood by David Linley, the Queen's nephew, which according to Oliver is worth upwards of fifty grand, and matching dining chairs that quite possibly push the value up by another thirty thousand. I suppose the pictures on the walls are valued at ten times that, and then there's the silver cutlery and the beautiful Czech cut-glass goblets and the silver serving platters. Yet William and Naomi seem so comfortable around all of this wealth, as if it's no different from the Ikea crockery that we use at home. I'm not sure I'll ever get used to it.

We sit at the far end of the long dining table, furthest from the door to the kitchen. The lights are low, and flames flicker from the white candles in the ornate silver candelabras. William brings out a bottle of champagne, and the three of them toast our expanding family.

By the time we're eating the salmon pâté topped with fresh asparagus and accompanied by Melba toast, the three of them are onto white wine. And then along comes the red wine to accompany the beef Wellington. It's a convivial evening, lubricated by the fine wines, and none of them seem to notice that I'm not very engaged in their conversation. After the main course, I slip away upstairs on the pretext of needing the toilet, but I want to check if Mrs Miller has sent through that photograph.

I'm disappointed that I've received no messages. I make a quick call to Mum so I can say goodnight to the children. They both sound content and happy, having had a wonderful afternoon wandering around Hamleys, followed by a trip on a boat up the river.

'You sound tired,' Mum says.

'I'm still a bit under the weather,' I say, but physically, I don't feel too bad. It's the thoughts swirling in my head that are draining.

By the time we've finished the meal, all three of

them are sozzled. Naomi can barely stand upright, and the slightest little thing sends her into paroxysms of hysterical laughter. Even though the things she thinks are funny really aren't, her ebullient mood is contagious. I have to support her when we leave the dining room and walk into their living room, as I'm sure she'll tumble over her Louboutins. William turns on their sound system, because despite the antique furniture and the fine oil paintings, they also have all the latest mod cons and must-have technology, with speakers set into the walls and ceilings, and quite bizarrely, a full set of disco lights that are totally out of keeping with the decor.

William fiddles with something on his phone, and the music starts blaring, seemingly from nowhere. Then the lights dip and begin flashing, and this fancy living room is turned into a seedy disco.

'Is this new?' I have to shout at Naomi to make myself heard over the thumping, deafening dance music.

'Yes. William's latest gadgets. Nightclub in our own house.'

William starts shifting some of the chairs to the side of the room to create a modest area in front of the fireplace to be used as a dance floor. He puts his arm around Naomi's waist, and they start dancing together, if you can call William's over-exaggerated moves dancing. They look quite ridiculous, and even I can't stop laughing. When Oliver pulls me to my feet and starts gyrating his hips at me, I realise I don't need alcohol to have fun.

Frustratingly, I don't get the opportunity to talk to William alone. I had wanted to ask him about the Von Amerling and to find out more about the painting that Oliver sold. It'll have to wait until tomorrow; hopefully

I can engineer things so we get a few minutes to ourselves.

I leave them to it shortly after midnight and wander upstairs to bed. There is still no message from Mrs Miller on my phone, so I take a quick shower and sink gratefully onto the soft mattress of the super king bed, luxuriating in the soft, smooth linen sheets. Who needs a hotel when they can stay in the house of friends like this? I drift off to sleep quickly and have no idea what time Oliver comes to bed.

When I wake, the birds are singing, and sunlight is pouring in through a gap in the curtains. Oliver is still fast asleep, snoring loudly, his arms flung above his head. I can't stop thinking about the photo of Alison. If it was taken in the garden here, the implications are too awful to contemplate. I try to push the thought away. I'm probably mistaken anyway. I slip out of bed, take a shower and get ready for the day. There is still nothing from Mrs Miller. I fear I might have to wait until next week and make my way to Croydon to look at the photo again in person.

Everything in the kitchen has been neatly tidied away from last night, so I rummage through the cupboards to find some breakfast things and put them out on the table. I sit for a while, drinking a cup of tea. I wonder how David Green is. I could try calling the hospital again, but I expect it'll be like last time and, as I'm not family, they'll refuse to give me any information.

William and Naomi emerge together, and by the time Oliver surfaces, William is frying us up breakfast. I can't stomach a full English, but the other three look much worse for wear and definitely need it. Just before 10 am my mobile phone pings. I pick it up and see that I've received a text message with an attachment from Mrs Miller. My heart pounds.

'Who's sent you a message?' Oliver asks, taking a big mouthful of crispy bacon.

'Just Mum. The kids are fine. I think I'll just take a walk through the garden,' I say. 'I've been up a little longer than you sleepyheads and could do with a stretch.'

'Of course. Enjoy.' Naomi smiles at me.

'I thought Oliver and I could have a knock up on the tennis court this morning to try to dispel our hangovers,' William says. Oliver groans.

'I've planned for a light lunch, and we can have our main meal for supper,' Naomi says.

'Oh, I didn't realise we were staying tonight, too.' I frown at Oliver.

'All sorted with your mother,' he says. 'It's William and Naomi's wedding anniversary today, so it's another day of celebration.'

I feel totally wrong-footed. I'm not sure why Oliver didn't tell me this, and feel bad that we haven't bought them a gift to mark the occasion.

'Don't worry, darling,' Naomi says, noting my look of dismay. 'It's sixteen years, not a special one. Go and have a walk, and I might take another quick nap. I'm feeling rather worse for wear after last night.'

I don't open the message from Mrs Miller until I'm far down the garden and out of view from the house. I lean against a solid old oak tree. The photo opens up, and I swallow hard as I see the picture of Alison again, looking so happy and full of life. I zoom in. It does look very much like this garden, but it's difficult to be sure. The plants will have grown and changed over the years. What I need to do is find that statue. If that is still here, then I'll know for sure.

I follow my steps from yesterday, walking beyond

the lake and into the secluded area with the large rhododendron bushes. Everything is quite overgrown here, so
I push shrubs to one side to see if I can spot anything
beyond them. There is a glorious sweet scent that pulls
me forwards, and I spot a viburnum laden with heavy
white blooms. I stroll around the area, sweeping back
branches and bending down low to see if I can spot any
stones or statues in amongst the tree trunks, but I see
nothing.

I've almost given up when I see the glinting of something metal. I squeeze through a couple of bushes that
scratch my arms, and see that there's a wire fence. I
wonder if this is the edge of William and Naomi's property. I follow the fence for a few feet, and then it stops.
There's a rusty old gate with no padlock. It squeaks as I
push it open. I find myself in another small enclosed
area with long grass poking up between paving stones
and yet more rhododendron bushes. I walk just a couple
of feet further, and then I spot it. It's a stone statue of a
man holding an outstretched sword.

I gasp. I click on my phone and bring up the photo.
This part of the garden was neat and manicured ten
years ago, but there is absolutely no doubt in my mind
that Alison was standing right here, next to that statue,
with the sun glinting down on her hair and the trees
behind her looking identical, still interlocking in the
way that beech tree trunks grow and weave together.

I am utterly positive that Alison was here at William
and Naomi's house, so why have they denied knowing
her? Could it be possible that Oliver brought her here
without the De Villeneuves' knowledge? But that hardly
fits with Oliver's protestations that their relationship
was a quick and meaningless fling. You don't bring a
one-night stand to the luxurious home of your best

friends. My only conclusion can be that Naomi and William have been lying in order to protect Oliver. And that Oliver, my husband, was a lot more involved with Alison than he admitted to being. Why has he played down their relationship? Is it just to spare my feelings, or has he got something much more damning to hide?

24

The weather turns by lunchtime. Naomi still hasn't resurfaced, and the men are holed up in William's study, talking about art or whatever else they chat about. I find a big puzzle in the living room. The box displays a lovely Venetian scene taken by the celebrated photographer Juliette Scott. I make a start on it, sitting cross-legged on the plush cream rug, and laying out all the pieces on the six-foot-long glass coffee table. But after an hour or so, I'm frustrated. I can't think straight; I'm not doing the jigsaw justice.

I walk upstairs back to our bedroom. I've brought my laptop with me, in the vain hope that I might have time to do a bit of studying, although there's little point in thinking about that now. Oliver and I haven't had the discussion about my legal training, but I don't suppose for one moment that it'll go my way. Nevertheless, I open up the laptop and place it on the dressing table.

First of all, I send David Green an email. I have no idea if he's still in a coma or whether he or anyone will else will read the email, but I need to send my best wishes and hope that he makes a full recovery. Then I decide to do a bit more sleuthing on Von Amerling. I trawl through lots of websites. Unfortunately, most of the art sites require buying subscriptions or paying for online searches, which I don't want to do, so I realise my sleuthing will be limited. I find a copy of the painting of the woman with brown ringlets, the one that I'm sure Oliver had, and I expand it to fill my screen. I stare at it for several long moments, willing that young aristocrat, dead for centuries, to yield some answers.

Then I hear the creaking of floorboards behind me. I jump and look over my shoulder. Naomi is walking towards me. I slam the lid down of the laptop, but I can't tell whether she has already seen what I was looking at. Her face is expressionless, and my heart is thumping.

'What are you up to?' she asks, wrapping a long, pale grey cardigan around herself.

'Just catching up on a few bits and bobs. Did you have a good sleep?'

'Yes, and a long soak in the bath. I was wondering if you'd like to come down for a cup of tea?'

The next few hours are convivial enough, but there is none of that relaxed banter of last night, probably because the other three are still hung-over and only drink in moderation. Dinner is soup followed by salmon, and most of the conversation revolves around the children and schools before veering off to discussions about an upcoming auction at Sotheby's. I bite my tongue as I listen to Oliver talking about bidding on a couple of men's rings. Surely he needs to stop spending so much on his collections now we've got a third child on the way. We're going to have to have that dreaded discussion about money sometime soon.

After supper, William suggests that we watch a film in their newly constructed cinema room in the basement. They have kitted it out with eight large, fully extendable padded chairs that are so comfortable, I find myself nodding off to sleep. Oliver has to wake me when the film is over. As we all have to get up in good time in the morning, we're in bed by 11 pm. Oliver wraps his arms around me and strokes my stomach as we fall asleep, and for those few minutes, I feel safe and secure.

But something awakens me. I turn to press the light on my alarm clock and am surprised that it's only 1 am. I feel parched. Silently, I slip out of bed, and it's only when I jab my toe on the edge of the suitcase and turn on the light of my alarm clock that I realise Oliver isn't in bed. I open the bathroom door, but he's not inside. That's strange.

I turn on a bedside lamp and reach for my clothes. I didn't bring a dressing gown with me, so I slip my jeans on underneath my nightdress and shrug a sweater on over the top. Our bedroom door isn't properly shut, so I assume he's downstairs talking to William about goodness knows what in the middle of the night. I'll just slip down to the kitchen and grab a glass of water.

The lights are off in the upstairs corridor, but are still switched on in the hallway, with those trendy in-built spotlights at the tread level on the staircase. Downstairs, the floor is cold under my feet, and I wish I'd put on a pair of socks. I can hear the faint murmur of voices coming from the kitchen.

The kitchen door is almost closed, with just a sliver of light seeping through to the hallway. Before I push the door open, something stops me. I stand with my back against the wall just to the side of the door.

'She must know about it,' Naomi says.

'What did you see *exactly*?' William says.

'She was looking at a portrait by Von Amerling on

her laptop, the woman with the dark ringlets,' Naomi says. 'I don't know if it was on a stolen art website, but she's probably clocked it. What do you think, Oliver? You know your wife the best.'

He groans. 'She saw the Von Amerling in my safe, but it's unlikely she knew what it was. The thing is, she was asking about it again just this week. So she might have identified it, but the chance she understands its provenance is close to zero. Nevertheless, it freaked me out.'

My heart is thudding so loudly in my ears it sounds like thunder.

'Bloody hell, Oliver. You really like nosey women. You haven't fucking learned, have you?' William says.

'Very funny,' Oliver replies. There's a tone to his voice that I've never heard before, and it makes my blood run cold.

'So what are we going to do?' Naomi asks.

I shut my eyes. I wish I could shut my ears too, because I don't want to hear any of this, but I can't tear myself away.

There's a scraping of chair legs on the stone floor; I take a deep breath. 'I don't want any violence,' Oliver says.

I bite down onto my lower lip. What *is* he saying?

'The thing is,' William says with a sigh, 'it's your fault, Naomi. What the hell were you thinking, sending those bloody notes? And then sending a jam jar full of fake blood.'

'For god's sake, William. Stop stressing,' Naomi says.

'It's because of you that we're in this situation,' William says. 'You went much too far. You just don't understand psychology, do you? The more you laid it on thick, the more Stephanie probed.'

'That's not fair! All I was trying to do was get that

researcher off our backs. It's not my fault! It's Oliver's fault for being careless and marrying that idiot in the first place. You should have got a surrogate to give you a family, but no. You are so desperate to be conventional, aren't you? Thought you could get yourself a young, compliant, fertile little wifey who would do whatever you told her. Didn't exactly work out that way, did it?'

I wait for Oliver to object, but to my utter dismay, he doesn't say a word.

Anger rises through me, and I push open the kitchen door. I stand in the doorway and stare at them, my eyes moving from one shocked face to the other.

'I heard what you were saying.' I am surprised how strong and steady my voice sounds.

William and Oliver look at each other, their faces white. Naomi stands up.

'You'd better sit down,' she says, pulling out a chair for me at the end of the table. Those few steps seem to last for ever as I walk towards it. I know that what I am about to hear will change my life for ever, and not in a good way. I sit down. William is on my right, Oliver on my left. Naomi remains standing up, her arms crossed.

'Why did you marry me, really?' I ask Oliver. My whole body is trembling as I wait to find out if the past decade has been one long sham.

'Because I love you. Because when you found out you were pregnant, it was the best day of my life.'

'So why didn't you refute what Naomi was saying when she said you only married me because I was fertile and compliant?'

'Because William and Naomi both know that it's not true. Do you really think I could have pretended for all of these years? That's absurd, Steph. Whatever else has happened, you've got to know that my feelings for you are, and have always been, genuine.'

'And what else has happened?' I ask. 'Why is it that you are all so desperate for David Green to stop digging?'

For the first time, I see fear in Oliver's eyes as he looks at William, who in turn looks at Naomi. She has edged towards the door and is leaning against the stainless-steel kitchen counter.

'Steph needs to know,' Oliver says.

William nods.

'No,' Naomi says.

'Why did you send me those letters, Naomi? And the blood? Why did you want to scare me?' My voice sounds so much stronger than I feel.

'Because you were letting David bloody Green get too close to the truth,' William says, answering for her.

'What truth?' I exclaim.

'No! You can't tell her!' Naomi shouts.

'What's the alternative?' Oliver asks. 'She's my wife, and she deserves to know.'

'We can't trust her. She'll be like Alison.'

'If you don't tell me, I'm going to call the police straight away,' I say, moving as if to get up from the chair.

'Sit down,' Naomi says.

I lower myself back into the seat.

There's a beat of silence.

'We've been running a black-market scam for years,' William says, his voice a whisper.

'Shut up!' Naomi exclaims.

William ignores her. 'If David Green finds out, we're finished. We'll all be thrown into jail, and Phoebe, Hugo, Bea and Sam will be parentless.'

'They have me,' I say.

'If you breathe a word, we'll throw you to the wolves,' Naomi says. 'Or worse. Much worse.'

I look at Oliver, but he won't meet my eyes.

'What scam?'

William sighs. 'If someone brings me a painting or a piece of jewellery of real worth, I provide a valuation at much less than its true value. I tell the vendors that it's worth maybe ten or fifteen per cent of its real value and offer to sell it to someone in my network of private dealers quickly and for cash. Nine times out of ten, they agree to that. I have a network of collectors from all over the world. They reward me by letting me sell artwork that must never get onto the open market, and I get a very high percentage for the privilege.'

I take a moment to absorb what William is telling me.

'You mean you're the conduit for stolen artwork, like stolen Nazi art?'

William nods. 'I have private collectors of every nationality. People who are less questioning about the provenance of pieces. Connoisseurs who collect for the sake of collecting.'

'All black market?' I ask.

'Yes.'

'And the auction house?'

'It hasn't made a profit in years. Never, actually. It's just the respectable front, allowing me to run this extremely lucrative business on the side.'

'And what about you, Oliver? Where do you come into this?'

My husband can't meet my eyes, so once again, William speaks for him.

'Oliver helps me with the research. In return for a share in the business, he is able to collect on the side. I couldn't have done this without Oliver. I'm not nearly as clever as he is. Oliver makes sure that all the artwork is stored safely, and that it's refurbished through our reliable network of hush-hush restorers. It's useful to have an academic with an excellent eye on board to help create provenance and pick up on any flaws.'

I shake my head as I try to absorb the scale of the scam. 'Where do you keep all of this stuff?'

'It's better I don't tell you,' William says.

'Tell me,' I say.

William opens and closes his mouth.

'I'm sorry, Steph,' Oliver mutters, his head hanging. 'But it's given us a way of life we'd never be able to have without. Financial security for you and the children for the rest of your lives.'

'And Alison. What has this got to do with Alison?'

'Nothing,' William says.

'I don't believe you,' I retort. It's only now that I realise Naomi has slipped out of the room. 'I know Alison was here. I've seen a photo of her in your garden. Did Alison find out what you were up to?'

It's all so clear to me now. Alison had an affair with Oliver, and he brought her here. I suppose they weren't as careful back in those days, and Alison discovered their highly lucrative scam. Righteous Alison wouldn't have hesitated to report their fraudulent dealings to the authorities, and the only way they could have silenced her was to kill her. My chest contracts, and I find it hard to breathe.

'We didn't kill Alison,' Oliver says, as if reading my mind. 'You know that I couldn't kill a spider, let alone another human being. Surely you know me better than that!' Oliver reaches towards me and tries to take my hand. I move away from him.

'Oliver is right,' William says. 'We don't know what happened to Alison.'

'I don't believe you.' I stand up quickly. The chair topples to the floor.

'Don't move!'

I swivel my head to face the door. Naomi is standing in the doorway, holding a shotgun and pointing it directly at me.

William and Oliver jump up from their chairs.

'Don't move!'

'What the fuck are you doing?' William's voice sounds totally panicked.

'Clearing up your mess, exactly as I did last time.'

'What do you mean?' William asks.

'You're both as pathetic as each other. Someone had to sort things, and it was bloody obvious that neither of you two had the balls to do it. I got rid of Alison, exactly the same way as I'm going to get rid of Stephanie.'

I'm not sure what shocks me more. The fact that Naomi is standing there coolly pointing a gun at me, or that William and Oliver are frozen in shock, clearly as horrified that Naomi is admitting to killing Alison as I am.

'Put the gun down,' William says, taking cautious steps towards Naomi.

Oliver steps in front of me.

'Stand back, Oliver. Let me sort your mess.' Naomi takes several steps into the room, her eyes fixed on me and Oliver.

And then William is charging towards her. They are wrestling each other in front of the bank of ovens, and I see my opportunity to escape. I dart past them, out of the kitchen, and run along the corridor towards the back door that leads out to the rear of the house and the garden. My fingers slip as I turn the key in the door, and I manage to unlock it and wrench the door open. I take a step out into the darkness. Then there's the sound of a shot. It's so loud. Reverberating. Terrifying.

Oliver. Did she shoot Oliver?

I haven't got time to think about it.

I run.

25

Motion-detector lights flood the back of the house, making it easy for me to race across the terrace and down the patio steps into the garden. The grounds are so big, with all those hidden nooks and crannies and overgrown shrubbery; my best bet, surely, is to run to the edge of the property, near where I found the statue, and then hide. When everyone has stopped looking for me, then I'll make my way through the fence to freedom. My heart is pounding and my breathing heavy as I run. The only light now is from the moon, and I stumble, but quickly pick myself up. I run across the lawn and then into the informal part of their grounds, my bare feet getting torn to shreds from brambles and stones, but I don't care. I need to keep going. I stumble again, my eyes finding it hard to adjust to the low light.

I can hear running footsteps behind me.

'Wait, Steph! You need to wait for me!' Oliver shouts.

I'm relieved Naomi hasn't shot him, but of course, I'm not going to wait for my husband, who has used me and lied to me for years. I feel sickened. I can't think about him now. I just need to get away.

'Steph, I need to explain!' He is panting, and it sounds as if he's right behind me. I'm nearly at the lake, and all I can think about is, *Was Oliver complicit in killing Alison? And am I next?* The utter terror distracts me for a moment, and I glance back over my shoulder. Then I trip, stumbling forwards. I feel strong hands grasping my shoulders from behind, stopping me from falling.

'We need to get out of here now!' Oliver says in a low whisper. 'Naomi is dangerous.'

'You knew she killed Alison, didn't you?' I ask, shrinking away from my husband, his breath warm on my cheeks.

'I didn't. I promise.'

'I don't believe you!' I try to wriggle free from his grasp, but he's clutching me too tightly. 'Let me go, Oliver.'

'William and I didn't have anything to do with it. She'll hunt us down, you and me. We need to run. She shot William. She shot her own husband! I've called the police, but I've no idea when they'll get here.'

'Stop with all the bullshit!'

Oliver loosens his grip – just a fraction, but I'm ready. I bolt, running around the edge of the lake. I've got to get away.

'Stop!' The voice is Naomi's, and the tone is unlike anything I've ever heard before. I look over my shoulder and freeze. Naomi is pointing the shotgun straight at me.

'Put it away, Naomi,' Oliver says. I can hear his voice close to me, but I daren't turn my head to see exactly where he is.

'Stand back, Oliver.'

'No, Naomi.'

Oliver darts towards me.

BANG!

The noise is so loud and so brutal, it feels as if my ears have exploded. The sound reverberates through the silent night. My ears burn with pain, and the world sounds muffled. I can't turn around to look, so I run, weaving from left to right, getting torn by branches, seeing only Bea and Sam in my mind's eye, knowing that I have to escape for them.

The lake appears up ahead of me. Without thinking, I plunge straight into it, my feet sinking into mud, reeds scraping my face and my arms. All I can think of is, *I can swim. If I stay under the water, I'll survive.* But it's so freezing cold, and my limbs are getting tangled in weeds and water lilies, and I'm being pulled downwards into the bitter, suffocating blackness.

WHEN I WAKE UP, I am utterly confused. The light is bright, and the ceiling is white. There are beeping noises, and everything hurts, from the top of my head to my toes.

'Hello, Stephanie. You're in hospital, and you're safe now.'

I turn my head to look where the female voice is coming from. The nurse is young, with red spiky hair and green eyes behind a pair of oversized spectacles.

'How are you feeling?'

'Rough,' I say. My voice sounds strange.

'Let me get Doc. He'll want to check you over.'

I close my eyes again and try to remember. Why am I here? And then it all comes flooding back. I feel warm tears dripping down my cheeks. The last thing I remember was swimming in that inky water of the De Villeneuves' lake. And Naomi holding a gun. Firing the gun. Once in the house, and again by the lake.

'Hello, Stephanie. I'm Dr Philip Kiltane. I'd like to do a few checks on you, please.'

He takes my blood pressure and listens to my chest and shines a bright light into my eyes; then he picks up a board from the bottom of the bed and writes something on a piece of paper. When he slips it back into the pocket at the foot of the bed, he smiles at me.

'The good news is your baby is fine.'

I open and close my mouth. I'm not sure how to reply. I had forgotten I was pregnant.

'Oliver?' I ask.

'Your mum is here. She's been waiting for hours, and there's a policewoman outside who would like to have a word with you first. Do you think you're up for that? They really need to speak to you to find out what happened.'

'Okay,' I say softly, but I turn my head away and squeeze shut my eyes.

'Hello, Stephanie, I'm DC Zara Lee. I need to ask you some questions.'

I look at the policewoman. She's wearing grey trousers and a white blouse. Her hair is in a short bob, and it makes her look younger than I suspect she is. She pulls up a blue plastic chair and sits down.

'Where's Oliver?' I ask.

She glances away. 'I'm very sorry to have to tell you that Oliver didn't make it. By the time the police arrived, he was already dead. William De Villeneuve was dead, too. They had both been shot at close range.'

'And Naomi?'

'She is currently in custody. She was found with the gun and her arms around her deceased husband. She has admitted to killing both men, although we believe the killing of her husband was accidental. I know it must be a terrible shock, but would you be able to talk us through what happened?'

I suppose in my heart of hearts I knew that Oliver hadn't made it. Tears drip down my cheeks.

'Has Naomi admitted to killing Alison?' I ask, tears soaking my pillow.

'Who is Alison?'

'She was my flatmate. She disappeared ten years ago, and her boyfriend Josh was accused of her murder. Her body was never found. I think Josh was wrongly accused.'

DC Lee tries to stifle her surprise. From the look on her face, I assume she recalls the case, but hasn't put two and two together.

'You believe that Naomi was involved in Alison Miller's disappearance?'

I nod, but it hurts my head. The searing headache reminds me of David Green.

'You need to talk to Naomi. She's behind everything,' I say, sobbing.

'Naomi is refusing to speak. She hasn't said a word since her arrest.'

'How did you find me?' I say. 'How did you get me out of the lake in time?'

'Your husband made a call to the emergency services and said that you were both in danger. My colleagues found you in the lake. Do you remember any of that?'

I shake my head. I don't want to remember. So Oliver was telling the truth. He did call the police. 'Can I see Mum now? And Bea and Sam. I need my children.' The sobs are violent, and the nurse puts her head around the door.

'That's enough for today,' she says to DC Lee, who nods and stands up.

'We'll keep you posted, Stephanie, and we will take a formal statement from you when you're feeling stronger. I'll also get the Alison Miller case re-examined. You get better quickly. You've had a terrible shock, and I'm very sorry for your loss.' She throws me a sad smile before she leaves.

They keep me in hospital for several days. The first couple of days I'm numb. I guess they give me some tranquilisers or something to dull the shock and the pain, because all I do is sleep, wake up, shuffle to the toilet, sob and return back to sleep. They tell me that I had hypothermia and a burst eardrum, and they were worried about the baby. My feet were cut to threads, so it's been painful walking on them. It's only today that I've been able to hobble without crutches.

My feet may be healing, but I don't think my heart ever will. All that time, Oliver lied to me.

Mum brought Bea and Sam to see me yesterday for the first time. She's told them that their daddy has gone to heaven as a result of an accident, but their mummy will be home very soon. It's a terrible thought, but I wonder if Naomi has done us a favour. I wonder what would be worse for my children. Knowing their father is in prison, having been embroiled in a massive art scam, spending their childhoods being labelled as the offspring of a criminal? Or grieving his death in ignorance?

I've got my own room here in the hospital. I'm not sure why, perhaps something to do with me being part of a high-profile murder investigation. It's a small consolation. I have chosen not to watch the news or read the papers, because I don't want to know what the world is speculating. Instead, I doze and try to remember happier times.

There's a knock on my door, and it's opened a few inches.

'Can I come in?' David Green asks.

I am relieved that David is out of his coma, but I'm conflicted about him. He started this whole thing off. David's face is still black and blue, and his hair has been shaven off at one side, revealing a row of stitches. His left leg is in plaster, and he walks on crutches.

'How are you?' he asks.

I shrug. 'And you?'

'Still a patient here. I suppose I'm lucky to be alive. As, by the sounds of things, you are, too.'

He slumps down on a plastic chair. 'Can we talk?'

I nod.

'It was a woman driving the car that hit me.'

I nod again. It doesn't surprise me.

'Her eyes were fixed on my face, and she steered the car straight at me. I honestly don't know how I survived.'

'I saw it happen, but from where I was sitting, I couldn't see who was driving.'

'They've identified the car now. It was a black Range Rover Evoque, hired at Heathrow Airport. The police showed me a photograph of Naomi De Villeneuve, and I've confirmed that she was the driver. You don't look surprised,' he says.

'I'm not.'

'I've got an admission to make,' David says, glancing towards the small window that looks out onto a central internal courtyard. 'Firstly, I'm really sorry for lying to you, but I had no choice. I'm not a TV researcher, and there's no crime documentary being made about your friend Alison.'

Surely this man hasn't put us through all of this for nothing. I think how much better our lives would be if all of this had been kept a secret from me. The children would have a father; I would have a husband.

But then I catch myself. My whole life would have been a lie. That's no way to live.

'I'm a hunter of stolen Nazi art. In particular, I'm trying to find a painting of my great-great-grandmother by an artist called Friedrich Von Amerling. I had hoped it would have turned up at William's auction house or in his warehouse, but it hasn't.'

'Was it a painting of a girl with dark ringlets?' I ask.

'Yes.'

'It was in our safe at home. It's gone now. Is that why you wanted to talk to me?'

'I didn't know that Oliver had it, but I worked out all the details of the fraud a day before the hit-and-run. And you? How long have you known?'

I turn to look at him. 'A few minutes before Naomi killed Oliver and William. I overheard them talking.'

'I suspected that William wasn't the respectable auctioneer he claimed to be. Then my investigations led me to his best friend Oliver Siskin, a leading professor of history of art at the university. I did some digging into Oliver's background and discovered your connection to Alison Miller. By posing as a TV researcher into Alison's murder, I could probe and ask questions about the art without raising suspicion.'

'You used us,' I whisper.

'I'm sorry, Stephanie. The reason for wanting to meet up with you on the evening that I got hit by the car was to give you a warning that I was about to blow the whistle on Oliver and William. I like you, and I think you're the innocent party in all of this. I wanted to prepare you for it. The police are pretty sure that Naomi hired the car and followed me with the express purpose of killing me. She couldn't risk their secrets being exposed.'

'But how did Naomi find you?'

'I expect through you. Did she ever have access to your mobile phone?'

'Yes,' I say, closing my eyes. Naomi and I were in and out of each other's houses. That afternoon she came over, when she found David in our house, she could easily have accessed my phone when I was out of the room.

'She probably put some tracking software on it so she could read your texts. Stupidly, I sent you a message confirming where and when we were going to meet. I made it easy for her.'

'You weren't to know,' I say. 'The police say Naomi isn't talking, so they can't confirm that she killed Alison.'

David sighs. 'We'll have to leave the murder investigations to the police. You need to know that I've made a full statement about the art fraud, and they're investigating right now. I haven't mentioned Oliver's name. There seems no point now he's dead. I'm very sorry that you have been caught up in this, Stephanie. And I'm so sorry for your loss.'

'Oliver said he sold the Von Amerling, or at least William sold it on his behalf. I just hope you'll be able to track the Von Amerling down.'

With nothing further to say to each other, David stands up, nods at me and hobbles out of the room. I think about the misery that has followed that painting, all in the name of greed. I wonder what will happen to poor Phoebe and Hugo, the De Villeneuves' children, and feel desperately sorry for them.

DC Zara Lee visits me again as I'm waiting for my

hospital discharge papers.

'I'm glad to see you looking so much better,' she says, smiling. 'Are you up to giving us a formal statement?'

I nod.

She asks me exactly what happened at the De Villeneuve place, and I talk her through as much as I can remember. It's not an easy conversation because I'm grieving, not only the loss of my husband, but the loss of everything I thought I knew. I am a pregnant widow at thirty-two, and quite probably, my marriage has been a sham. I can't stop hearing those awful words that Naomi said about me, that Oliver only married me because I would be compliant and non-questioning. And that deafening silence that followed when Oliver failed to contradict her. He told me that he loved me, but I won't ever know the truth.

And then I remember how he tried to protect me from Naomi. No. He *did* protect me. He gave his life for me. I start crying, and DC Lee hands me a paper tissue. When I've calmed down, I wipe my eyes, apologise and give her a watery smile.

'I think you're being incredibly brave,' she says. 'Considering everything you've been through.'

'Has Naomi said anything yet?' I ask.

'No. Not a word. Nevertheless, we're treating Alison Miller's disappearance and presumed murder as linked to this case. Based on the information David Green has given us and your evidence, we think that Naomi and/or William killed Alison because Alison accidentally stumbled upon their treasure trove of stolen art when she went to stay. We have a warrant to do a full search of their premises, so hopefully, we'll have some more information for you soon.'

I sigh. I hope it was Naomi and William only,

because the thought of my husband being involved in Alison's murder is too abhorrent to contemplate.

26

I t feels so strange being at home without Oliver. As I wander aimlessly around the house, I look at everything differently. All of those paintings on the walls, those clocks on the mantelpiece, the rings in his safe … are they really his, or have their original owners been fleeced? Was my husband just like his greedy friends, desperate to acquire things at any cost, whatever the deceit involved? Was I just another acquisition for him, a pretty thing to look at, designed to fulfil a certain purpose: Namely, to give him the family he desperately desired? Sometimes I wonder whether I am grieving a person or a mirage. I think of William's parents and struggle to comprehend how such good people could have a child capable of such deceit. Should I follow the lead of William's parents and reunite all of Oliver's collection to the people he and the De Villeneuves scammed? I'm not sure. I have no money and no means of supporting myself and the children until I finish my qualifications. The rainy days that Oliver said he was collecting for have arrived. Perhaps it's better if I sell some of the pieces so I can provide for my family. Assuming I can sell them, because I'm sure the provenance is fake. But for now, it's an academic question, because I haven't yet called up a locksmith to break into Oliver's safe, so I don't know what's stored inside.

The children are amazing, although I'm not sure they've fully comprehended that Daddy is never coming back. For now, Mum has moved in with us, and she is a godsend.

Rahul telephones me three days after I return from hospital. He has been abroad this past fortnight and has only just heard what happened. He's asked if he can come and see me. I've said no, not for now. If I see him again, I want to be ready and not push him away. Whether or not that will happen one day, I have no idea.

DC Zara Lee knocks on my front door on the fourth day I'm home. She's standing there with a colleague, and from the serious expression on her face, I know straight away that it's bad news. *More* bad news. I usher them through into the living room, and we all sit there, perched on the edges of the chairs.

'I need to tell you that we have found human remains on the De Villeneuves' property. It will probably be reported on the news tonight.'

I gasp, although I'm not sure why. I had expected this. 'Alison?' I ask.

Zara Lee nods. 'Obviously, we need forensics to confirm it, but from our initial findings, we think the remains are those of Alison Miller.'

'Where?' I whisper.

'She was found on a small island in the centre of the lake. Alison's mother identified the earrings found with her body, and we expect forensics to confirm through DNA that it is her remains.'

'Were they small opals?' I ask.

'Yes.'

'What about Alison's blood found in Josh's flat?'

'Naomi has admitted the murder. She turned up at your and Alison's flat to talk to Alison. She then invited her to her house for supper. As it was getting late, she suggested that Alison stay the night. She killed her at their home and then took some of her blood before burying her on their little island in the lake. She used Alison's key to Josh's flat to get in there when the boys were out, sloshing the blood around before cleaning it up with bleach. Of course, luminol shows where it was cleaned. Needless to say, further investigations will need to be made to verify her confession, but it seems very likely that Josh has been wrongly imprisoned and will be released.'

'Poor Josh,' I say. 'And poor Alison.'

I don't know how I get through the next few weeks, but somehow I do. Mum comes with me to the scan for my baby. When I see that little heartbeat, and when the sonographer asks me if I want to know the sex of the child, I say yes. I don't want any more surprises.

'You're having a little girl,' she says, and I burst into tears. Despite everything that has happened, despite initially not wanting this baby, now I do. Desperately. I will love this child in the way that I love Bea and Sam, and I will see all of Oliver's good qualities in her.

There is one thing that David Green was right about. The nightmares have gone. I suppose that my subconscious mind can relax now, because there is no mystery to be solved.

And then there are my exams. One way or another, I am going to get my law qualifications. I need to work now, not just for my self-esteem and because it's always been my dream, but for my family's welfare. I need to put food on the table. That decision feels good. I no longer have to answer to anyone; I'm in control of my own destiny. Perhaps Oliver's death has made me grow up, turning me into an adult aged thirty-two.

27

A YEAR LATER

I t's Saturday morning, and I'm upstairs in Bea's room, helping her with a school project. Rahul is in the kitchen, making lunch. He shouts from downstairs, 'Steph, do you want chicken or lamb?'

'What would you prefer?' I ask my daughter.

'Lamb. And can we have roast potatoes? I love Rahul's potatoes.'

'Bea says lamb and roast potatoes, please.'

'Tell Bea that her wish is my command!'

Bea and I smile at each other. Rahul is such a good cook, and I think the kids are delighted that I have been relieved of the majority of the kitchen duties whenever he's here.

We are moving to Leicestershire next week. Initially I thought it might be a wrench, leaving London behind along with everything and everyone we know. But now I don't think it will be. We've found a cottage that the children love on the edge of Market Harborough. It has a big garden, and we're going to get a Labrador puppy. We've completed on the sale of this house in Parsons Green, and it's raised a lot more money than I had antic-

ipated, enough for me to buy the lovely cottage and to
have sufficient cash in the bank to tide us over for a
couple of years until I'm qualified as a solicitor and able
to earn a decent living. Rahul is selling his flat and
moving in with us.

Some people may say that it's too soon, that I've
tried to find the first substitute for Oliver that I could,
but those people don't know about our past. Rahul
wasn't going to give up on me, and in the end, I agreed
to go on a date with him. There I was, eight months
pregnant with another man's child, sitting opposite him
at a little Italian restaurant in South Kensington. I was
on my way back from the ladies' when I overheard the
waiter asking Rahul if his wife needed some extra cush-
ions. Rahul didn't flinch; he just smiled politely and said
thank you. Rahul wasn't pushy; he was just supportive.
We had long, intimate conversations where we sat side
by side on the sofa, holding hands and sharing our
innermost thoughts. He let me talk about Oliver and put
his arms around me as I slowly came to accept that I will
never fully understand what happened.

Rahul was with me the evening that my waters
broke. I told him to go home, to call Mum, and I'd be in
touch in a week or so, but he refused to leave me.

He said that if I'd let him, he would bring up my
three as his own. He insisted on coming to the hospital
with me, holding my hand, rubbing my back, telling me
how beautiful and brave I was. And when Lottie was
born, the midwife handed her to Rahul, telling him he
had a gorgeous little girl. Neither of us corrected the
midwife; we just stared at my baby in wonder. Then
Rahul turned to me, kissed me on the lips and asked me
to marry him. Baby Lottie reached up, and her tiny
fingers grasped Rahul's index finger. I laughed and said
it's a bit soon, ask me again in a year. Next time he asks,

I'll say yes. I called my third child Charlotte in honour of Oliver's grandmother, whom I never met. But to us, she'll be Lottie.

And here we are, months later, ready to start our new life. I can't pretend that Bea and Sam are happy about living with Rahul, but so long as we're in London, he only visits at the weekends. Bea in particular has found it hard, and that's totally understandable, but I'm hoping it will be easier when we're all living in our new house in a new place without any memories.

Although life might be harder for me living in a village, having to integrate into the small community as a single mother, being forced to drive much more than I'm comfortable with and looking for a job as a solicitor in a provincial firm rather than a high-paying London one, I know in my heart of hearts that we have found our forever home. Mum is in the final stages of selling her flat, and she's moving up to Leicestershire too, and Rahul is fine with that because he understands the true meaning of family.

I think about Josh, who was pardoned and freed very quickly. So much of his life has been lost to injustice. But I think of Naomi more. She has been convicted of the murder of Alison and Oliver, and the manslaughter of William. She has also been convicted of the attempted murder of David and numerous theft and frauds relating to the artworks in their home and those found in William's warehouse. Her defence team tried to say that the fraud was all done by William, but the jury disagreed. She'll spend the rest of her life in prison. What a shock it must be, considering the life of luxury she used to live.

The real losers are Phoebe and Hugo, who are being brought up by Naomi's sister. Or perhaps that's what will save them. Naomi's sister seems a thoroughly decent, hard-working woman. I've no doubt that they will grow up with much better values than they would have done if Naomi and William had continued to parent them.

Then there's David Green, who started peeling back the layers of untruths. With hindsight, I'm relieved he wasn't really a TV researcher. It would have been terrible being part of a film speculating about Alison. Her parents were able to lay their daughter to rest properly, but sadly, Mr Miller passed away just a fortnight later. I think Naomi should be accused of sending him to an early grave, too. Anyway, David gets in touch from time to time. He's still searching doggedly for the Von Amerling, and I'm confident he'll find it one day.

AFTER A DELICIOUS LUNCH, I go upstairs to check on Lottie, who is having a lunchtime nap whilst Rahul puts on the dishwasher and cleans up the pots and pans. Most of our belongings are packed up into brown cardboard boxes, ready for the removal lorries that are arriving on Tuesday. The only room I haven't yet tackled is the loft, because everything is already in boxes. It's Rahul who suggested I go through them this weekend and chuck out what I don't need. Some of the boxes contain Oliver's stuff from his childhood, photographs of his parents and old, manky teddy bears that I'm keeping for the kids, so they have some mementos from their birth father. I've tried to avoid looking at them.

I pull the ladder down and climb up into the attic. There are exposed rafters, and I have to crouch in order to reach into the far corners. I am shoving some of the boxes around when something tumbles on me that has been wedged in the rafters. It's wrapped in what looks like an old packing blanket. I unwrap it and almost drop it as I realise what I'm holding.

I recognise this picture of the beautiful aristocratic woman with dark ringlets. This doesn't make sense.

'Hey, Steph. Are you okay up there?' Rahul shouts from the landing.

I can't answer.

A moment later, he is climbing up the ladder, and all I can do is watch as he appears. 'What's that?' he asks.

'A painting by Von Amerling. The painting that David Green has been searching for. Oliver told me he sold it.'

I sink to the floor, and Rahul comes and sits next to me. So far, the police haven't found any evidence that Oliver was involved in the art fraud. David kept his word and didn't mention Oliver, and to my surprise and gratitude, Naomi didn't mention his name at the trial. Perhaps it was her way of apologising to me for killing my husband. For that I'm grateful. The children can grow up remembering their father as a distinguished professor and not a fraudulent criminal.

But I know the truth. I know that my husband was a criminal who used his brilliant brain not only to educate the young but to line his own pockets. And I am holding the proof of that in my hands. If I give the painting back to David Green, he will know for sure that Oliver was as guilty as William and Naomi, although I suppose he knows anyway.

'What are you going to do?' Rahul asks, rubbing my back.

'The right thing,' I say.

I climb down the ladder and walk into my bedroom. I pick up my phone and call David Green.

. . .

DAVID RINGS the doorbell at 11 am on Monday morning. It's the first week of the summer holidays, and Mum has taken the children out for the day. She thinks I've asked her to have them because I need them out of my hair in order to pack up the house.

'I've parked the van a bit further down the road, and I've only put an hour on the metre. Is that sufficient?'

'Yes. And thank you for driving here and for renting a van.'

'How are you?' David asks as we sit down in living room on the same chairs that we sat in when he first came to our house.

'I've got away lightly, all things considered. The boxes are because we're moving to Leicestershire. And you, how are you?'

'The injuries have healed, and against all odds, I don't appear to have any lasting issues.' We're both silent for a moment. I can see he's burning with curiosity as to why I insisted he visit me in a van.

'I have some things I want you to have,' I say, standing up. 'I've put them out on the kitchen table.'

He follows me next door.

I hand him the painting that's still wrapped in the small blanket. I watch as David uncovers it, and as he stares at it, tears well up in his eyes.

'Where did you find it?'

'Hidden behind a rafter in our attic. I just wish I'd looked sooner.'

'Will you sell it to me?'

I stare at him and frown. 'Absolutely not. I'm giving it to you. It's yours. Oliver should never have had it in the first place. It belongs to your family in the same way as all of these items belong to other families. You were right about Oliver. He was as involved in the fraud as William and Naomi.'

'Yet the police don't seem to realise that.'

'No.' I pause. 'Will you tell them?'

David shakes his head. 'As I said before, Oliver's dead, so what's the point? All it will do is bring you and your children unwanted misery and attention.'

I let out a sigh. 'I've put together all of the rings and paintings and collectibles that I think Oliver obtained fraudulently.' I point to the pile on the table and the ten large boxes piled up next to it. 'I don't want to be the recipient of stolen art. It's all here, and I want you to take it away. I have no doubt that all of those portraits we had hanging on our walls were portraits of people like your great-great-grandmother, portraits that were looted Nazi art. I want them to be given back to their descendants. Can you help me track those people down to make sure they're returned to their rightful owners?'

David looks at the massive pile of antiquities and the boxes. 'Don't you need the money?'

'It's not mine to have. I've sold this house, and we've made plenty from that. All of this stuff needs to be returned. I wouldn't know where to begin, but I think you would.'

'You're right.' He smiles at me. 'There is nothing that would give me greater pleasure. But first, I want you to take photographs of everything I'm taking.'

After we've catalogued the items, I help David carry the boxes to his rented van, and he carefully places everything inside.

'Are you absolutely sure about this?' he asks.

'I have never been surer about anything.'

'In which case, I will let you know each time I repatriate an item to its rightful owner.'

'Where will you say it's come from?' I ask, thinking how the provenance might lead back to Oliver's ill-gotten gains.

'William and Naomi De Villeneuve's stolen stash. There's no need for Oliver Siskin's name ever to be mentioned. If anyone asks, I will use your maiden name and say that I have been working alongside my colleague Stephanie Lucas.'

I smile as I give David our new address and phone number and watch as he drives the van away as cautiously as a learner driver.

EPILOGUE

It's a week later, and we're semi-installed in our new house, surrounded by boxes. I haven't got as much unpacking done as I'd hoped, as I'm spending too much time in the garden with the children, listening to the birds singing and fixing the fencing in anticipation of the arrival next week of our new puppy.

Rahul is inside, painting Bea's bedroom walls in a particularly unpleasant lurid pink that she absolutely loves.

'There's post for you,' he shouts out of the bedroom window. He has a smudge of pink paint on his nose, quite possibly put there on purpose to make the kids howl with laughter.

I walk inside and pick up an envelope addressed to me in handwriting that I don't recognise.

Dear Ms Lucas,

I've been given your address by David Green. I under-stand that you were in possession of an amethyst signet ring, and through Mr Green and your philanthropic gestures, this ring has been returned to my family. The ring belonged to my great-grandfather. My family comes from Prague, now in the

Czech Republic. Although my grandparents were able to escape to England in 1940, my great-grandparents were not so lucky. They were sent to the concentration camp in Lodz, and in 1942 were killed in the extermination camp at Chelmno. I cannot fully express my gratitude for you returning this ring to us. Thank you so much for your kindness.

Yours sincerely,
Anna Kohn

A LETTER FROM MIRANDA

Thank you very much for reading What She Knew.

About a year ago, our family was contacted by a charming couple who are spending their retirement scouring auctions and repatriating items to their rightful owners. They had found an original sketch that had been commissioned by my grandfather in the 1920s. Just a few months later, we discovered that a portrait of my maternal great grandmother was being stored in the vaults of a European museum. My great grandmother perished in concentration camp, and our family had no idea that this painting existed. Neither of these items have much monetary value but their sentimental value is incalculable. Both things got me thinking about the financial and emotional value of antiquities, and so this book was born!

Fortunately, I have relatives who work in the art and auction worlds. My thanks to Alistair, Juliette, Samantha and Poppy. Your love and support mean so much to me and any mistakes are mine alone.

Writing can be a lonely job but I always feel supported thanks to the fabulous crew at Inkubtaor Books. I am so grateful to Brian Lynch, Garret Ryan, Jan Smith, Jodi, Claire and everyone else who makes up the dream team.

I would also like to thank the book blogging community who so generously review my books and share their thoughts with readers.

Lastly but most importantly, thank *you* for reading my books. I love to chat with readers via BookBub, Goodreads or Instagram. Without you and the reviews left on Amazon and Goodreads, I wouldn't be living my dream life as a full-time author. Reviews help other people discover my novels, so if you could spend a moment writing an honest review, no matter how short it is, I would be massively grateful.

My warmest wishes,

Miranda

ALSO BY MIRANDA RIJKS

THE VISITORS

(A Psychological Thriller)

I WANT YOU GONE

(A Psychological Thriller)

DESERVE TO DIE

(A Psychological Thriller)

YOU ARE MINE

(A Psychological Thriller)

ROSES ARE RED

(A Psychological Thriller)

THE ARRANGEMENT

(A Psychological Thriller)

THE INFLUENCER

(A Psychological Thriller)

WHAT SHE KNEW

(A Psychological Thriller)

THE ONLY CHILD

(A Psychological Thriller)

THE NEW NEIGHBOUR

(A Psychological Thriller)

FATAL FORTUNE

(Book 1 in the Dr Pippa Durrant Mystery Series)

FATAL FLOWERS

Published by Inkubator Books
www.inkubatorbooks.com

Printed in Great Britain
by Amazon

78577962R00164